Weaving the Strands

BARBARA HINSKE

Also by BARBARA HINSKE:
Coming to Rosemont, the first novel in the Rosemont series
Uncovering Secrets, the third novel in the Rosemont series
Drawing Close, the fourth novel in the Rosemont series
Bringing Them Home, the fifth novel in the Rosemont series
Shelving Doubts, the sixth novel in the Rosemont series
The Night Train
And Now on The Hallmark Channel…
The Christmas Club
Available at Amazon in print, audio, and for Kindle.

UPCOMING IN 2020
Guiding Emily, the first novel in a new series by Barbara Hinske
The seventh novel in the Rosemont series

I'd love to hear from you! Connect with me online:
Visit **BarbaraHinske.com** and sign up for my newsletter to receive your Free
Gift, plus Inside Scoops, Amazing Offers, Bedtime Stories & Inspirations from
Home.
Facebook.com/BHinske
Twitter.com/BarbaraHinske
Instagram/barbarahinskeauthor
Search for **Barbara Hinske on YouTube** for tours inside my own historic home
plus tips and tricks for busy women!
Find photos of fictional Rosemont, Westbury, and things related to the Rosemont
series at **Pinterest.com/BarbaraHinske**.
bhinske@gmail.com

Library of Congress Control Number: 2014907364
ISBN: 9781499182125

Casa del Northern Publishing
Phoenix, Arizona

Dedication

To every reader of **Coming to Rosemont** who reviewed my book or reached out to me to offer support and encouragement. Your enthusiasm for **Rosemont** poured jet fuel on my dreams, and I am profoundly grateful.

Chapter 1

The Honorable Margaret Martin peered uneasily out the cruiser window at the sea of angry faces as Chief Andy Thomas wove his way to the rear entrance of Haynes Gymnasium. A uniformed officer sprang to open her door. He shielded her from the jeering crowd and quickly escorted her inside.

"I would never have expected such an uprising in Westbury," she said, turning to the officer.

"People hate pay cuts," he replied curtly as he opened the door and stepped back outside.

Maggie sighed and made her way to the enclosure at the back of the gymnasium where she and the town council were gathering before the council meeting, scheduled to start in forty-five minutes.

"I'm sorry I'm late," she said as she joined them. "I was on my way when Chief Thomas intercepted me. He wanted to bring me in himself."

"That was my call," Special Counsel Alex Scanlon said. "I was afraid there might be trouble tonight. As mayor of Westbury, you're the focal point of all this animosity."

"I've lived here all my life and I've never seen anything like this," Councilman Frank Haynes interjected. "Maybe it wasn't such a good idea to move the council meeting to the largest venue in town."

"You may be right, Frank, but we're here now," Maggie replied. "And the people need to know what we've decided."

"Voting to cut employee pay and revoke the cost-of-living increases on town pension payments is idiotic," Chuck Delgado snapped. "I shouldn't have gone along with it. None of us will get re-elected."

Maggie wheeled on him. "We've been over this a million times. Until Alex and Chief Thomas finish their investigation into the fraud and embezzlement perpetrated on the town and the pension fund, we have to drastically cut expenses." She scrutinized each member of the assembled council. "You all agreed."

"Where's Councilwoman Holmes?" Russell Isaac asked. "She should be here by now. We said we'd do this together."

Maggie inhaled sharply. "Tonya called thirty minutes ago. Her son broke his arm at football practice and she's at the emergency room. She can't make it tonight."

"That's bullshit," Delgado exploded. "Now she can wash her hands of this entire fiasco."

"Calm down, Chuck," Haynes said. "She can't leave her kid alone at the hospital."

"Thank you, Frank," Maggie said. "Tonya's given me her proxy to vote for the measure."

"That's not the same thing as voting in person in front of this crowd," Isaac observed. He turned to Scanlon. "You could diffuse the situation. Just announce that you've finished your investigation and William Wheeler is the only person implicated. That you've got your man and you'll get a conviction. Soon."

"I can't do that," Alex answered sharply. "Our ex-mayor may not be the only one involved."

"Go to hell, Scanlon," Delgado spat.

"That's enough," Maggie broke in as Chief Thomas approached.

"It's time," he said. "Every seat's taken and more than three hundred people are waiting outside. I've got all available officers, plus some off-duty ones, in place. I'll remain on stage with you. If I think we need to end the meeting for safety reasons, you'll have to abide by my decision. It's my call."

Maggie nodded. How in the world had she gotten herself into this predicament? Less than three years ago she had been the wife of a college president, and a successful forensic accountant with a growing consulting practice. Now she was a widow and mayor of Westbury—as a write-in candidate no less—about to face a town's wrath over a problem she had no part in making. She shook her head and straightened her shoulders.

"I'll explain the budget we discussed," she announced with more confidence than she felt. "Then we'll all vote for it as planned."

R

Catcalls and comments from the floor derailed Maggie's presentation almost immediately. At one point, she felt certain Chief Thomas would step in to close the meeting. She finally finished and called for a motion to adopt the budget that would decrease the salary of every member of the audience as well as her own, a fact she had reiterated to the crowd. Haynes made the motion, which Isaac seconded. Maggie leaned into the microphone and voted yes. The crowd's boos and jeers drowned out her pronouncement of Councilwoman Holmes' proxy vote.

"Councilman Isaac?" she queried.

"I vote *no*."

Maggie spun toward him. He dropped his gaze to avoid eye contact.

"Councilman Haynes," she continued.

"I vote no."

Maggie stiffened. So this is what it felt like to be stranded on the bridge while the rats deserted a sinking ship.

"Councilman Delgado."

"I stand with my esteemed colleagues in support of our faithful town workers," he pontificated. "I vote no."

Pandemonium broke out in the auditorium as the crowd leapt to their feet and surged toward the stage. Maggie felt an arm around her shoulders pulling her firmly toward the rear exit. "You can deal with them later," Chief Thomas said. "Right now, I need to get you out of here."

Maggie complied in a daze. "I was set up, wasn't I?"

"It appears so, ma'am," the chief answered, sliding her into his cruiser with the practiced motion he employed for suspects heading to jail.

Chapter 2

Maggie followed the hostess to a table by the window overlooking the Shawnee River. She scanned the treetops just beginning to don the golden cloak of autumn, then checked her watch. Traffic had been light and she was twenty-five minutes early for her scheduled lunch with that preeminent expert on municipal finance, Professor Lyndon Upton. Maggie remembered his habit—annoying, really—of being early for every appointment. She didn't want to get off on the wrong foot by making him wait for her.

She settled back into her chair. Westbury was beginning to feel like home, and she loved living in Rosemont, the manor house she had inherited from her late husband Paul. Her decision to uproot her life and move instead of just selling the place as originally planned had been uncharacteristically impetuous, but she knew it was right at the time. Despite the town's unrest and the council's recent betrayal, most days she still felt that way. But she certainly wasn't living the quiet, solitary existence she had envisioned upon her arrival. Ever since she had assumed the position of mayor six months ago, she'd lived at a blistering pace, in the process breaking every promise to visit her family in California and to spend time with the new man in her life, Dr. John Allen.

Maggie shifted restlessly in her chair and retrieved the morning paper from the oversized satchel that served as her purse. There was no point in beating herself up over things she couldn't change. Her family and John would have to understand that her obligations and responsibilities to the town came first.

She turned her attention to yet another article detailing the deplorable state of Westbury's financial condition. The less than completely objective piece also decried the lack of progress in prosecuting former mayor William Wheeler for the fraud and embezzlement that had brought the town to the brink of bankruptcy. She hated to admit it, but the paper was right. The fraud investigation was stalled and, as she had discovered at the recent town council meeting, the council refused to take the necessary steps to restore the town's ailing finances.

In spite of herself, Maggie turned to the editorial page where she was routinely the subject of criticism. Today was no exception. The editor's column was titled "Martin's Election a Failed Experiment in

Democracy," and all six of the published letters to the editor featured scathing indictments of her leadership. Her lack of experience in politics and her unfamiliarity with the town and its people were a constant refrain. *Why had they elected a write-in candidate with no prior experience in public office, especially since she had moved to Westbury only a few months before the election?* they queried.

Maggie agreed with much of that. The politics of this job were far beyond what she had ever anticipated. She didn't know whom she could call on for assistance. Worse, with the exception of Tonya Holmes she didn't trust any of the other councilmembers. For all she knew, some or all of them were involved in the corruption that had toppled Wheeler.

She fished an antacid from the roll that now lived in the outside pocket of her satchel, then took a drink of water and tossed the paper onto the floor by her chair. Whether or not she was qualified to clean up the mess that now defined the Town of Westbury, she was responsible for doing just that. Knowing she needed reinforcements, she had contacted her old colleague Professor Upton. If she were lucky, she'd enlist his aid over a nice lunch.

R

Maggie smiled hopefully across the table at the professor. "It's kind of you to join me for lunch on your way back to Chicago. I know this takes you out of your way. I wasn't sure you'd remember me."

"My pleasure, Maggie. Or should I call you Mayor Martin? Of course I remember you. We worked on that big fraud case some time ago. Our testimony put the defendant away for years, as I remember. Besides, your being the first write-in mayor in your state made news in Chicago. So I was more than a little intrigued when I received your call."

"Have you heard anything about the arrest of our former mayor on fraud and embezzlement charges and the mess that the town's finances are in?"

"A little bit, yes."

"Well, that's why I've invited you to join me today. And I've asked Special Counsel Alex Scanlon to be here as well. He should be along any minute. We need your help."

Professor Upton raised an eyebrow. "I don't recall any of the specifics. Can you fill me in?"

"Sure. *Reader's Digest* version—Mayor William Wheeler was indicted on charges of fraud and embezzlement. He orchestrated risky high-interest loans from the pension fund secured by shopping centers around town. When the Recession hit, most of the borrowers couldn't—and possibly had never intended to—make their payments.

9

The pension fund foreclosed and sold the shopping centers for pennies on the dollar to offshore entities controlled by Mayor Wheeler. In effect, the pension fund lost a lot of money on these loans and Wheeler's entities got to buy the shopping centers at an absurdly undervalued rate. To make matters worse, most of the shopping centers were owned by other offshore entities that he controlled. Those entities had taken out loans against the shopping centers for way more than the properties were worth, made only one or two mortgage payments, and then pocketed the remaining loan when the shopping centers went into default."

"Classic equity skimming," the professor remarked. "With multiple offshore entities involved, this was a very sophisticated scheme. Anyone else implicated? In my experience, carrying off this type of fraud takes more than one person."

"That's what we suspect, too. Wheeler was the only one indicted. I was part of the citizen's group that investigated after the town workers were told that the pension fund might not be able to make its payments."

"Who else do you think is involved?"

"Honestly, all of the council with the exception of Councilwoman Tonya Holmes. She was the first one to uncover the problem. She formed the citizen's committee to investigate and obtained records as well as bank statements clandestinely from the town clerk, which the committee used to put the pieces of the scheme together. The pension fund also made loans on a bunch of vacation condominiums in Florida that Wheeler used to visit. Most of those have been foreclosed upon as well. We took our information to the police and Wheeler's indictment followed shortly thereafter. I'd bet my bottom dollar that Councilmen Chuck Delgado and Russell Isaac are in this thing up to their eyeballs. Delgado's brother, Ron, is the pension fund advisor, and he has to be involved, too. The only one I'm not sure about is Councilman Frank Haynes." Upton looked like he was about to speak, but stopped himself and motioned her to continue. "He's an extremely successful restaurant franchisee. Supports all the local sports teams, and founded and funds the no-kill animal shelter."

"If he's a legitimate businessman with philanthropic ties to the community, it'd be odd for him to get mixed up in this type of criminal activity," Upton replied slowly. "Why do you suspect him? Is he tied in with the others?"

"No, not that we know of. Other than being on the council with Delgado and Isaac." Maggie sighed. "Frank Haynes is a snake in the grass, for sure. I always get the impression that he's coiled and ready to strike. And that he doesn't do anything that isn't in his own self-interest, despite all of his charitable causes."

"That describes a lot of people. Doesn't make them criminals."

Maggie smiled. "True. He also backed Isaac in the special election last spring after Mayor Wheeler stepped down when he was indicted."

"That was the election you won?" Upton asked. "How did you decide to run as a write-in candidate?"

"That's the amazing thing—I never decided to run. I was a last-minute write-in candidate, and I didn't even know it."

Professor Upton leaned forward in his chair. "You've got to be kidding me. You didn't know you were a candidate?"

Maggie nodded.

"I really need to hear about this!" Upton held her gaze.

"The committee agreed that we would all support Alex Scanlon to oppose Isaac. Alex had run for mayor in the prior election against Wheeler. He was interested in the position, and more than capable and qualified."

Upton nodded.

"Alex ran a terrific campaign and was ahead in the polls the week before the election. We had one debate, held on the Thursday night before the election. Alex was brilliant, and it was clear he had the support of the voters. On the way home, he and his partner were in an auto accident. Alex was seriously injured, with multiple broken bones that required several surgeries and extensive physical therapy. On Election Day we knew Alex wasn't capable of stepping into the mess in the mayor's office. I figured that the election would go to Isaac. I was so busy going back and forth to the hospital, tending to both Alex and Marc that I frankly didn't care. As it turns out, the committee mounted a grassroots effort to get me elected mayor as a write-in candidate. I was Alex's campaign manager and did almost as much speaking around town as he did, so I guess people knew me."

"Incredible." He took a sip of water and slowly shook his head. "A lot's happened to you in the last few years."

Maggie laughed. "That's for sure."

Professor Upton leaned back in his chair. "So, how are you finding public office?"

Maggie hesitated and turned to gaze out the window, considering her response. She desperately needed to confide in someone. "Truthfully, I'm feeling lost. I'm in over my head. Not only am I new to this town, I'm new to politics. As a forensic accountant, I understand the financial problems facing the town, but crafting workable solutions and getting the council to act on them is another matter. I came into office on a wave of public support, but that's dwindling fast. My approval rating is dropping like a rock. I don't care if I get re-elected; I just want to help the people of this town. I really care about them. They're warm and genuine. I don't want to fail them."

"Is this Alex Scanlon helping you?"

"Yes and no. He's a former prosecutor, and I appointed him as Westbury's special counsel to assist in Wheeler's prosecution. He's bogged down in all of that and, frankly, hasn't fully recovered from the accident. Although he wouldn't admit it, I think he resents that I ended up with the mayor's seat; even though, at this point in time, I'd gladly give it to him." She turned to face Upton. "I'm at my wit's end, Professor. That's why I called you. Of all the people I've met in my career, you're the only one with the expertise to bail us out."

Professor Upton looked like he was about to object when Maggie waved to a well-dressed man in his late thirties, standing at the hostess stand, scanning the tables in the restaurant. Alex spotted Maggie and nodded.

"Sorry I'm late," he apologized as Professor Upton stood and Maggie made the introductions. "I headed to Stuart's on autopilot and was parking my car when I realized I was at the wrong place."

"I wanted this meeting to be out of the limelight," Maggie replied. "Professor Upton and I became acquainted when we worked together years ago. He's currently a professor of municipal finance in Chicago."

As Alex sat, Maggie signaled the server to bring over an extra glass of water and some menus.

"I understand that the fraud investigation is ongoing," she said to Alex once the server had left. "But in the meantime, we need to get our town's finances straightened out and the pension fund on firm footing. That's why I've brought in Professor Upton."

"I believe that we're putting together a very solid case against ex-Mayor Wheeler," Alex declared. "I'm convinced he didn't act alone. Frankly, he isn't smart enough. We just haven't developed evidence against anyone else yet."

"I understand that, Alex. As I said, I need assistance with the day-to-day handling of the town's finances."

"Maggie, I've got my hands full with the investigation."

"I'm not asking you to jump in. Just supply the professor with what you know."

Professor Upton broke in, "Don't you have a treasurer and an accounting department? Don't you have an auditor? The finances for a town this size shouldn't be too difficult."

"That's part of the problem," Maggie said. "We're still not sure how widespread the corruption is and who's part of it. And we keep uncovering new issues. Just this morning I learned that a senior center known as Fairview Terraces may be in jeopardy because the town defaulted on the ground lease of the property we sublease to them. If that property gets foreclosed upon, more than three hundred senior citizens who've paid their rent on time and who've developed a community there will be thrown out on their ears. We can't allow that."

Maggie leveled her gaze at Professor Upton. "I do know one thing. I'm not going to let that happen."

"First I've heard of this," Alex snapped.

"It just came up." Maggie sighed. "Bottom line, Professor, things are getting worse, and the only people I can trust within town government, not counting myself, are Alex and Councilwoman Holmes. We don't have the necessary expertise. We need your help."

"It surely isn't as bad as all that is it?" the professor replied.

"Maggie isn't exaggerating anything, sir," Alex took over. "I've been so focused on getting the bad guys that I've turned a blind eye to all the other issues that Maggie's had to face in keeping the town going. We've both been working around the clock for months. My partner is about ready to throw me out if I don't spend more time at home," he concluded with a rueful smile. "And I know a certain veterinarian who is feeling neglected." He raised an eyebrow at Maggie.

Maggie knew the time had come to make her pitch. "This would be an opportunity to put some of your academic ideas to the test in the real world," she entreated Upton. "And you wouldn't be dealing with tiresome faculty committees. I remember from my days as a college president's wife that you professors get frustrated with the slowness of everything. You wouldn't be subjected to that here. We need to make changes now."

Professor Upton draped one arm over the back of his chair and studied the anxious faces across the table. "Anything else that you'd like to add to tempt me?" he asked.

"There *is* one more thing, Professor," Maggie replied. "We have no money in the budget to pay you, so your stipend would be one dollar. And the eternal gratitude of an entire community."

A smile emerged beneath the professor's neatly cropped gray mustache. "In that case," he said, "you'd better start calling me Don, which is what all my colleagues call me. Let's order lunch and get started."

Chapter 3

Glenn Vaughn leaned back into the leather booth at Pete's Bistro and idly ran his fingers up and down through the condensation on his glass of iced tea. He stretched his long legs under the table, content to wait patiently for his female companions as he had done scores of times during his seventy-seven years. Gloria Harper was in the ladies room and his granddaughter would be along shortly.

It was odd, he reflected, that Gloria, his late wife's best friend, and Cindy had never met. Gloria and Nancy, before she died, had both faithfully volunteered at the daycare center for special needs children located in the church next to Fairview Terraces. They spent most weekday mornings together rocking babies and sharing their lives' current tidbits and detailed histories, forming the kind of deep friendship that women are so good at.

Nancy had made friends with almost everyone in Fairview Terraces. What was it she always told people considering moving into the seniors' apartment complex? That it was like being back in a college dorm with all the fun people but none of the boring classes.

Glenn shifted in his seat. Despite living at Fairview Terraces for more than ten years, he hadn't made any firm friendships. Most of his connections, including Gloria, had come through Nancy. He'd had a very busy career as a civil engineer, and when he retired, Nancy's companionship had been enough for him.

These days he didn't even see his granddaughter Cindy much. A physician's assistant whose work always seemed to spill over into her personal life, she routinely ran herself ragged, which all too often rendered her unavailable for family time. Glenn was half afraid that she would cancel on this luncheon at the last minute. Gloria would be so disappointed, although he knew she would be too well mannered to show it.

From Fairview Terraces all the way to the restaurant, Gloria chatted excitedly about presenting Cindy with the baby blanket she had finished knitting for the young woman's soon-to-be-born first child. Nancy had started the blanket for her great-grandbaby, but she knew she probably wouldn't be able to complete it. When her death had suspended the project mid-row, Gloria had taken up the project just as she promised Nancy she would.

Glenn turned when he felt a hand on his shoulder.

"Sorry to leave you waiting. When I came out of the ladies room, I saw my friend Laura Fitzpatrick, and we got chatting about her baby. I'm surprised at all of the young mothers I know. I think I'll get some yarn and start knitting another blanket in anticipation of the next baby gift I'll need," Gloria said.

She settled herself across from him and regarded him thoughtfully. "How are you doing these days, Glenn?"

"I'm adjusting," he responded with a sigh. "I always expected that I'd be the first to go, since I was so much older than Nancy. I've gotten over being mad about that—well, most days I'm over it—and I'm trying to fill my time with the things I told myself I'd do when I retired."

Gloria nodded. She'd been a widow for over fifty years. Being left with nine young children to raise, she never had to worry about how to fill her time. Now that they were all finally grown and gone, she had grown accustomed to being on her own. When asked why she had never remarried, she always quipped that no man in his right mind would ever want to date a woman with nine children.

"Nancy told me you were a scratch golfer back in the day."

"She exaggerated a bit," Glenn said. "I was all right. My game was consistent. I play a couple of times a week now—that fills up the best part of two days. I've always liked to build things, and I've got a model ship going on the dining room table. I'm a voracious reader, and I've started to dabble in—" He broke off suddenly as his cell phone chirped and scrambled to wrangle it out of his pocket.

"Sorry. It's Cindy," he said, with unmistakable tension in his voice. As he listened intently, a relieved smile lightened his expression. "She's pulling into the parking lot now. She'll be right in."

Gloria positioned the fancy gift bag she had purchased the day before at Celebrations, her favorite shop on the square, so that her gift sat proudly at the end of the table. She and Glenn turned toward the rear entrance from the parking lot as Glenn's radiant—and very pregnant—granddaughter burst through the back door and hurried to their table.

"So sorry I'm late. I hope you haven't been waiting too long. I'm Cindy Larsen," she said, holding out her hand to Gloria. "Gramma always said so many nice things about you. I know that you were wonderful friends. I'm delighted to finally meet you."

"The pleasure is all mine, young lady," Gloria replied, squeezing Cindy's arm. "Nancy thought the world of you, and I know she was over the moon about your pregnancy. How are you feeling? When is the baby due?"

"I'm feeling great; this has been a super-easy pregnancy. I'm due in six weeks. Still, I have to admit I'm getting tired of being pregnant—I'm ready to have this baby," she said as she slid into the booth next to her beaming grandfather and leaned over to kiss his cheek.

"What's all this?" she asked, eyeing the gift bag in front of her.

"Always curious about presents, aren't you?" Glenn chided. "You were the grandchild who snooped for Christmas gifts. Let's order, and then we'll get to that," he said, signaling to their waiter.

"Okay," she replied good-naturedly as she picked up a menu.

With their orders placed, Gloria glanced at Glenn. He cleared his throat and turned to Cindy, but the words didn't seem to come. Seeing his distress, Gloria quickly interceded.

"As I said, Nancy was overjoyed about the fact that you were expecting. She was an expert knitter and had already created the better part of this lovely blanket for your baby when she passed. It would have been such a shame for it to remain undone, so I picked it up and finished it off for you," she said as she slid the gift bag toward Cindy. "Besides, I promised Nancy I would. I'm not the knitter that she was, but it turned out nicely."

Cindy regarded Gloria with damp eyes and withdrew the blanket wrapped in a cloud of tissue. With shaking hands, she held the delicate white-lace pattern woven with yellow and green ribbons high above her head. She stared at it in admiration, and then hugged it to herself as she turned to Gloria.

"I don't know what to say," she choked. "This is incredibly beautiful, and immeasurably kind of you to do this for me. And for Gram. I'm sure she's up there and is grateful. So am I."

Although clearly gratified by this reaction, Gloria modestly waved away the compliment. She glanced at Glenn and realized that he, too, was on the verge of tears. "I'm delighted that you're so pleased," she said quickly in an effort to get them back onto an even emotional keel. "And don't be afraid to use it; Nancy and I didn't go to all of this effort for it to sit in a drawer, you know."

Their entrées arrived and they spent the next hour and fifteen minutes in easy conversation centered on Cindy's hopes for her baby and her plans to juggle her family and her career. Gloria bit her tongue several times. She knew that women today wanted to do things their own way and didn't want advice—no matter how well founded—from an old crone like her. Still, she had taken a shine to this earnest young woman. When Cindy looked at her watch and gasped, realizing that she was running late to meet her husband, Gloria took her hand in both of hers.

"I know that you're perfectly prepared to care for your baby, but sometimes things don't go according to the books. If you'll permit me one piece of advice, go with your instincts. They won't let you down. You'll know your child better than anyone else. And if I can ever help you think anything through, you know where to find me. There probably isn't much I haven't seen, raising nine kids."

"Oh, Gloria," Cindy said, awkwardly leaning over the table to give her a hug, "I was hoping you'd offer. And I can never express how grateful I am to you for finishing Gram's blanket.

"Gramps," she said as she gave Glenn a kiss on the cheek, "you are the best. Thank you for this. Will you stop by after church on Sunday? Tom needs help putting the crib together—correctly at least."

Glenn nodded and she swept back out the door.

"She's an absolute delight," Gloria said as they settled back into the booth. "She'll make a fine mother."

Gloria studied Glenn intently. This outing had done him a world of good. His color was better and his eyes sparkled.

"Let's see what Laura's Pie of the Day is today, shall we?" he asked. He was stuffed from lunch, but was enjoying himself so much that he wasn't ready to leave.

"I've never met a pie I didn't like. That's a capital idea!" Gloria replied.

Over two slices of peach pie, Glenn and Gloria delved into topics from art to zoology. They were discussing Glenn's interest in poetry and Gloria's lack of knowledge on the subject when the waiters began resetting the restaurant for the dinner crowd.

"Good grief, it's almost four o'clock," Glenn exclaimed. "And I remember that you wanted to be home by two," he added sheepishly. "I'm so sorry that I've kept you so long."

"Not at all," Gloria hastily reassured him. "I had no idea we've so much in common. I can't remember a better afternoon. And I want to hear more of your views on poetry; I'm intrigued. I think I'll pick up a volume from the library."

"I'll do you one better," Glenn replied. "I'll drop a couple of my favorite anthologies at your front door. Maybe we can go to lunch together again to discuss them."

Gloria smiled. "That's a grand idea."

With the promise of an encore in hand, they reluctantly left the restaurant.

Chapter 4

Maggie glanced up from the spreadsheets strewn across her desk at Town Hall and checked the time. Three o'clock. She'd been up to her elbows in figures all day and still wasn't any closer to making sense of them. At least she'd be seeing John tonight. The thought brought a smile to her lips and she leaned back in her chair, taking off her reading glasses and tossing them on her desk.

Meeting John Allen, DVM, was possibly the best thing that had ever happened to her. The long-divorced local veterinarian had been so kind and gentle with both her and Eve, the stray terrier mix that adopted Maggie on her first morning at Rosemont. How could she not start falling for him?

She'd left California with the firm conviction that relationships weren't for her. By the time Paul died in the cardiac ICU, their relationship had soured. What she learned after his death made her wonder if she'd ever really known the man she'd been married to for more than twenty-five years. Not only had Paul embezzled more than two million dollars from Windsor College, he had maintained a mistress in grand style in the posh Arizona suburb of Scottsdale. Then in a final bizarre twist, Maggie had inherited Rosemont from Paul. Even now, almost a year after moving into the manor, she still couldn't believe that he had concealed its existence from her for a decade after it had been left to him.

Maggie stood and stretched. She walked to the window and leaned against the sill. How nice it would be to go away with John for a long weekend. They needed to spend time together. Maybe a mini-vacation would get him out of the doldrums, a side effect of his recent and long-overdue knee replacement surgery.

Maggie knew that John hated being away from his veterinary practice, especially since his patients—both human and not—relied on his wisdom and gentle manner. He hated even more being dependent on others to chauffeur him around. A better doctor than a patient, he'd set his recovery back by ignoring doctor's orders and pushing himself too hard. The fact that he wouldn't be able to resume driving for another six weeks had rendered him inconsolably irritable.

Maggie smiled. She'd pick him up at physical therapy and take him out for a nice dinner. Maybe they'd even stop for his favorite dessert—butter pecan ice cream—on the way back to his house. She'd been late the last three times she'd collected him from therapy. She'd surprise him tonight and be waiting when he stepped out the door. She needed to treat him like the priority he was.

Maggie's phone began to ring and she quickly returned to her desk, answering on the third ring with a cheerful "Maggie Martin."

"You certainly sound chipper, Ms. Mayor. But then you're not a pensioner whose checks may bounce."

Maggie sank into her chair. This call was going to take time. She knew from experience that it probably wouldn't end well.

R

By the time she managed to get off the phone, she was shocked to see that it was already dark outside. Her conversation with the retired town worker who was concerned about his pension had taken far longer than she would have liked. He'd been furious with her answers, and who could blame him? No one wanted to find out that their retirement nest egg was half of what had been expected. She listened to his complaints and sympathized with his frustrations. Maybe he was right; maybe she should turn the job over to someone else better qualified to deal with the financial mess. She certainly hadn't come up with any solutions.

Maggie quickly checked her watch. Ten minutes after seven! She logged off her computer, snatched her purse from her desk drawer, and hurried to the elevators. She fished her cell phone out of her purse and dialed John's mobile phone number as soon as she exited the elevator on the ground floor.

"Hi, John," she said as soon as he answered. "I'm on my way. I should be there in about twenty minutes. Are you all done?" she asked, hoping that he hadn't been waiting for her. "You are? I know I was supposed to be there at seven. And I'm so very sorry. I got a call from—" She stopped as he cut her off.

"You're right. It's no excuse. I know I'm making a habit of it." Maggie listened attentively as she approached her car.

"The exception is getting to be the rule. You're right. I know you're tired after physical therapy and that you're anxious to get home. I'm truly sorry. Can we talk about this later? I want to concentrate on heading your way. I'll see you shortly," she said, punching off.

She had to admit he had every right to be furious with her. How had she let this happen again?

She hovered by her car door and pulled on the handle, but it wouldn't open. "What in the world?" she muttered as she churned through the contents of her purse like a cement mixer, looking for her keyless remote. A tide of panic rose as she set her purse on the hood and pulled out her wallet, makeup bag, and other miscellany searching for her keys. No mistaking it; they weren't there. It was after hours and Town Hall was locked up tight as a drum. She didn't remember seeing anyone else on her floor on the way out.

Now she'd really be late. How could she be so stupid as to lose her keys? She circled around to the back of the building and noticed lights in one office on the top floor. The office of Councilman Frank Haynes.

It was unusual for Haynes to be in his office at Town Hall, let alone to be there in the evening. She found his number in her contacts and placed her call. He picked up on the second ring.

"Why, Mayor Martin, is it? To what do I owe the pleasure?" he said, dripping cordiality that didn't quite ring true.

"Hi, Frank, how are you? Listen, I'm in a bit of a pickle. I seem to have misplaced my car keys. I'm here in the lot at Town Hall. My office key is on the ring with my car key, so I can't get back into the building to look for them. I see your light is on. Are you at Town Hall?"

"I most certainly am," he crooned. "I'll come to the rear entrance and let you in. On my way."

"Thank you, Frank," Maggie replied, but he had already disconnected. She took a deep breath; she'd have to call John about this further delay. Why did she have to lose her keys tonight of all nights?

Maggie punched in his number. "No, I'm not there yet. I'm still in my parking lot. Stranded for the moment. I can't find my keys." She winced. He was tired and upset, and she couldn't blame him.

"I'm not sure where they are. Probably fell out of my purse into my desk drawer. Fortunately, Frank Haynes is working late and is coming down to let me in so I can look for them. I'll call you as soon as I find them and am on my way." Maggie paused and listened.

"I don't want you to take a cab. I'm going to take you to get a bite to eat." Her shoulders drooped as she continued to listen.

"I understand. You'd like to get home. Yes, we need to talk. Oh," Maggie turned as Haynes approached across the lot. "Frank's here to let me in. I've got to go. Can I call you later?" Maggie listened. "No, you're right. Don't wait up for me. If you have to be up early, just get to bed. We can talk tomorrow. Goodnight, John." Maggie took a deep breath. "And please know how sorry I am." She rang off without the satisfaction of any reassurance from him.

Haynes gave her a quizzical look and smiled sympathetically. "Sounds like someone might be in the doghouse," he said.

Maggie ignored his unsolicited observation and turned toward the entrance. Truthfully, her conversation with John had unnerved her she realized as she and Haynes silently walked toward the elevators. She couldn't bear the thought of losing him.

The elevator stopping at their floor jolted her out of her reflection. Haynes held the door. "Housewares and appliances," he said in an attempt at humor. Maggie smiled weakly and headed toward her office.

"Thank you so much, Frank. I'm glad you were here tonight." She stopped and turned to face him. "Why are you here so late? What are you working on?"

"Just catching up on paperwork and correspondence to my constituents," he replied, obviously irritated by her inquisitiveness. Here he was, doing her a favor. She wasn't his supervisor. *Nervy broad*, he thought. *Some things never change.*

Maggie eyed him thoughtfully and nodded. "You answer all your own mail, don't you? I've heard that. I know that you're very busy with your franchise businesses. But you're also dedicated to your district. You put in a lot of time as a councilmember. That's admirable. You should be very proud of your service."

In spite of himself, Haynes flushed with pleasure. This woman confounded him. Just when he had her firmly placed in the enemy camp, she did or said something genuinely nice. He shook his head slowly as Maggie retreated to her office.

R

As anticipated, Maggie found her keys in the corner of her desk drawer. She thought fleetingly about firing her computer back up and working for another couple of hours, but firmly dismissed the idea. The mountain of work could wait. Attending to her relationship with John Allen could not.

Maggie got into her car and set off to procure a carton of ice cream.

Have butter pecan in hand. Are you up for dessert? Maggie texted John.

She waited for a return text. When none appeared, she started her car and pulled out of the grocery parking lot. Instead of heading directly to Rosemont, she decided to take the long way home—past John's house—in case he replied.

When she reached the stop sign at the entrance to his street, she paused. Should she drive by to see if his lights were on? And if they were, should she park across the street and call him? March up to his door and ring the bell? She was reminded of Susan during high school. Her daughter had driven by her boyfriend's house incessantly to keep tabs on him, which only led to information that made her miserable. And now, fifteen years later (and many years older than Susan had been at the time), she was doing the same thing.

Maggie turned onto John's street. She was here, so she might as well drive by. Lights were on. *He's still up,* she thought happily. She punched his number in her cell phone, with a cheery invitation on her lips. Her smile faded as the phone continued to ring and finally went to voicemail. She hadn't been prepared for this. In a panic, she punched the end button without leaving a message. Reluctantly tearing her attention away from his house, she headed home.

Chapter 5

Professor Lyndon Upton downloaded the spreadsheet and documents Maggie Martin had emailed him and began the laborious task of sorting through the numbers. Truth be told, he loved this sort of project—it was like putting together a jigsaw puzzle of about a million pieces. His mind returned to her comments about Frank Haynes.

Although he hadn't told Maggie that he knew Haynes when the opportunity had presented itself during their lunch meeting, Upton actually considered himself to be in the man's debt. Upton's late wife had been Haynes' cousin. When her treatment and care during her long illness threatened to bankrupt Upton—who by then had tapped out both emotionally and financially—Haynes stepped in and quietly paid the hospital bills along with their youngest son's college tuition. Upton presented Haynes with a promissory note and the deed of trust on his home to secure repayment of the money, but Haynes tore them up. "I don't make loans to family," he said. His support had been a gift and sure enough Haynes never mentioned it again. Surely a man of this character and kindness was not a crook.

Upton shifted uncomfortably in his seat. Why hadn't he mentioned that he knew Frank Haynes? If he called Maggie now to say "By the way, I used to be married to Frank Haynes' cousin and he gave me half a million dollars," his own credibility would be tarnished. Better to let it go. But shouldn't he call Frank to let him know he was under suspicion? When surely there was no truth in any of it? He owed him that much, didn't he?

Upton reached for the overflowing Rolodex on the back of his credenza and flipped through the cards until he came to one yellowed with age titled *Haynes, Frank*. He punched in the number and waited as it rang. He was about to hang up when the vaguely familiar voice answered, "Haynes Enterprises; Frank Haynes speaking."

Upton smiled. "Frank! This is a voice from your past. Don Upton here."

Haynes relaxed back into his chair. "Don. How are you? How are the kids? Are you still a college professor?"

"Fine, Frank, we're all fine. Yes, plugging away in academia. How about you? I see you're still in Westbury. How's business?"

"Not bad. Could always be better. I'm on the town council now, too."

"That's why I'm calling, Frank. This is a courtesy call to alert you to something that might concern you. I've never forgotten your kindness to me and my family. I hate to think what might have happened to us without your generosity."

Haynes cut him off. "That's in the past; you've already thanked me." He stood and paced, tethered to his desk like a dog on a chain. Cold fear settled in the pit of his stomach. What in the world could Upton possibly know that would concern him? "So what's up?"

"I've known Maggie Martin for years; we worked together on a large fraud case some time back. She supplied expert testimony on—"

"And?" Haynes broke in. He remembered how long-winded Upton could be. "What does this have to do with me?"

"She called me recently to solicit my help in untangling the financial mess that Westbury's in. As you may remember, municipal finance is my specialty."

Haynes held his breath. "So, what are you doing? Are you working on the case against Wheeler?"

"No. They've got a special counsel working on that."

"Alex Scanlon. I know that. I didn't know Martin had solicited your help. When did this happen? She didn't inform the town council. I'm not sure she can spend the money to hire you without our approval."

"I'm not getting paid; I'm doing this pro bono. And that's why I'm calling. She didn't tell the town council because she doesn't trust anyone, other than the woman on the council—I forget her name."

"Tonya Holmes."

"Yes, that's it."

"What did she say about the council?"

"I met with her and Scanlon. They're convinced that Wheeler didn't act alone, that he had help from other members of the council. They haven't developed evidence to indict anyone else yet, but everyone is suspect. Including you."

Haynes inhaled sharply. "I'm not involved in any of it, Don. I've made plenty of money from my restaurants and investments; you know that better than anyone."

"You don't have to tell me that. I know you. That's why I'm calling you, Frank."

"What exactly did they say?"

"That others are implicated. She doesn't know what to think about you. She finds you hard to figure out."

Haynes snorted. "Just because I'm not her best friend or supporter, doesn't make me a crook."

"Exactly what I told her." Upton hesitated. "A word of advice, if I may?"

Haynes remained silent.

"Find a way to be on her team. She's floundering."

"That's for sure; she's not qualified to be mayor."

"Well, she is the mayor. And she's a smart and talented person who's doing her best in terrible circumstances. You've got the expertise to help on any number of projects. Volunteer to take something on. She'll see that you're on her side, and you won't be under suspicion anymore. Win-win. Think about it."

Haynes circled back to his chair and sat down. He had to admit Upton was on to something. "Not a bad idea, actually. I've been so busy here that I haven't wanted to take on any more. But I'll consider it. And Don," he added, "if you see anything you think I should take on, or if you hear anything else that I should know, please call me. I really appreciate your reaching out to me."

He leaned back in his chair as he hung up the phone and smiled. Maggie's suspicions were certainly troubling, but having a source of information inside Town Hall was priceless.

Chapter 6

As was their custom, Gloria and her cat sat on her secluded patio early the next morning, Gloria sipping her coffee, and both of them enjoying the hint of fall in the air. She thought she heard a noise at her front door and listened for a knock. Not hearing anything further, she relaxed back into her chaise. Still in her housecoat, she didn't intend to answer her door at this hour of the morning anyway.

She was perusing the Arts & Entertainment section of the Sunday paper when she saw Glenn's car pull out of the lot and onto the main street, heading toward town. *He must go to early church,* she mused. Her thoughts turned for the hundredth time to their engaging lunch earlier that week. "I wonder if he's left me that poetry," she murmured to Tabitha, who stretched and didn't appear the least bit interested in the question.

Gloria tossed the paper aside and scuffed her way to her front door. Checking through the peephole to make sure that no one was about—she really didn't want to be seen in her early-morning state of disrepair—she quietly opened her door. A small parcel wrapped in brown paper and tied with a simple red ribbon greeted her.

She quickly retrieved the package and brought it to her patio. The ribbon was double-knotted, so she had to fetch a pair of scissors to cut it free. On top of two brand-new volumes of poetry—one of classical poets and the other of contemporary—was a clean linen card. In a flowing, masculine script was written:

Some of the best poetry, of course, is found in the Bible. One of my favorite passages is "This is the day which the Lord hath made. We will rejoice and be glad in it." Psalm 118:24. I hope that these poems remind you of reasons to rejoice. ~G

R

Glenn spotted the lanky teen he sought as the youth exited the middle school building's rear door. He waved and extended his hand to him once they were closer. David Wheeler stared at it briefly and then met it awkwardly with his own.

"I'm Glenn Vaughn; you can call me Glenn."

The boy looked away and nodded imperceptibly.

"Do you go by Dave or David?"

The boy shrugged. "My mom calls me David, so I guess that'd be okay."

"All right then. David. I know the court assigned you to this program. I want you to know that I do this as a volunteer because I enjoy it, and I'm looking forward to working with you."

David kicked at a pebble with the toe of his shoe.

Glenn gestured to the dog park across the street. "Let's find a bench over there. We can watch people bring their dogs to play Frisbee or run on the agility course they've set up." Glenn's experience with his own teenagers had taught him that kids open up more readily when you're not sitting across from them, forcing a conversation. "I love watching folks and their dogs, don't you?"

They crossed the street in silence.

"Have you ever noticed how many people actually look like their dogs? There are even look-alike contests." Glenn gestured to an Afghan hound being led by a willowy woman with stringy blond hair. "See. Don't you think they look related?"

A sliver of a smile crossed the boy's lips as he nodded in agreement.

Glenn leaned back on the bench and waited. David pointed to an athletic man with a crew cut, jogging with a yellow lab. Glenn laughed. "Yep, that's a good pair." He turned to David. "Do you have a dog?"

"No. My mom doesn't want to clean up after one, and my dad was too busy," he replied.

Glenn nodded. "I'm sorry about your dad. I know it's been rough on you."

"I'm fine. I keep telling everyone I'm fine."

"If you were fine, you wouldn't have stolen six sets of headphones from the school's language laboratory. You don't need them; they're worthless to you but expensive for the school. And you didn't even try to conceal them. It's like you wanted to get caught."

David turned away from Glenn.

"I reviewed your record. You were a decent student and a good athlete until your dad was indicted. You were never in any trouble. So something is bothering you."

"Maybe I'm just like my old man," David mumbled.

"I don't believe that for one minute. You get to create your own future. Whatever your dad may have done doesn't affect how you live your life," Glenn said. "I'll tell you something else. Your teachers all said terrific things about you."

"So what do I have to do for this court program? Just sit here and talk to you?"

"That's part of it, but there's more. For starters, we get to have fun. What do you like to do when you have a free afternoon?"

"Nothing, really," David replied.

Glenn waited.

"Fishing, I guess."

"Terrific! I've fished since I was a boy. Do you have a spot you like?"

David hesitated. "I've never been. I was just saying it to say something."

"Well, you've said it to the right person. I've got enough equipment for us both. How about we start this Saturday morning?"

"I guess."

"Dress warm and bring an extra pair of shoes and socks. I'll swing by your house Saturday morning at eight."

R

Glenn pulled into the lot at Fairview Terraces late that afternoon, still angered by David Wheeler's situation. Why hadn't his idiot father thought about the effect his criminal activity would have on his son— this decent boy who was looking for his father to show him how to be a man?

Someone had parked in his assigned spot, which didn't do anything to elevate his mood. He found a free parking spot and headed toward his apartment, anxious to shower and get to the dining room so that he might run into Gloria. He wanted to see what she thought of the books he had left by her door that morning.

On his way to his unit he decided to make sure that she had retrieved them. He checked his watch. Even with the quick detour, he'd have time to shower and lie down for fifteen minutes before he had to leave for the dining hall.

R

Gloria preferred the second-dinner seating, but tonight she made sure to arrive as early as possible. She made her way forward after the initial rush of people who surged in when the doors first opened, as if they hadn't eaten in a month, and casually scanned the crowd. To her disappointment, Glenn was nowhere to be seen.

She chose an out-of-the-way table for two with a good view of the door and placed her purse and a magazine on the other side of the table to discourage anyone from joining her. She took her time placing her order and kept an eye on the entrance. After dragging out her meal as long as she could, she finally resigned herself to the fact that Glenn was not having dinner at Fairview Terraces that evening. She'd have to think up some clever way to thank him for his gift—a standard thank-you note would not do.

R

Glenn turned out of bed extra early on Monday morning, annoyed that he had slept through dinner instead of simply taking the catnap he had intended. Since Nancy's death, he'd gotten into the habit of sleeping until almost nine o'clock every morning, unless he had an early tee time. He supposed depression was to blame; he had never needed more than seven hours a night in his entire adult life. Yet despite the increase in sleep, he rarely felt refreshed. Last night he had made himself scrambled eggs and toast when he awoke from his nap, then crawled back into bed. For a change, he slept straight through the rest of the night, without any of the sad and lonely dreams that usually haunted him. Now he felt rested—and famished.

Glenn quickly dressed and bolted out of his room, almost missing the note taped to his door:

Another way to start your day feeling "glad in it" is with a nice, home-cooked breakfast under your belt. Give me a call some morning when you're in the mood for eggs and old-fashioned biscuits and sausage gravy. ~G

Chapter 7

William Wheeler stared through the thick Plexiglas barrier at his wife of almost twenty years. Although still lovely, Jackie was frayed and careworn. The dark circles under her makeup-less eyes and the streaks of gray in her unkempt hair aged her. He used to be irritated by her constant attention to her appearance and her propensity for expensive salons; he now longed for the days when those were his biggest concerns.

He attempted a smile. "Did you miss your hair appointment to come see me?" he asked, trying to sound jovial.

She raised her chin. "What're you saying? I don't look good enough for you? Trying to impress your jailhouse pals?"

"No, sweetheart, no," he replied quickly. "I just meant that you shouldn't give up the things you love just because I'm in here."

"That's easy for you to say," she countered. "But now that you're in prison and I'm working as a receptionist to keep this family afloat, I don't have the time or money to get my hair done."

"Surely it's not as bad as all that," he stated softly. "You found the cash I told you about in the attic?"

"I did. And it's almost gone. Our mortgage is expensive, remember? And they've frozen our other accounts. We're barely hanging on until you're out of here. It'll be soon, right? That's what you said."

Wheeler hung his head and looked at his folded hands.

"Bill, for God's sake," she hissed. "You're getting that plea deal aren't you?"

He couldn't bring himself to tell his wife that according to his lawyer even the best plea deal wouldn't keep him out of prison. A dirty ex-mayor was a big fish; he would have to serve time. Special Counsel Scanlon would see to that.

"We need you home, Bill. David needs you. He's been surly and disrespectful and now he's in trouble at school. I can't control him."

Wheeler brought his head up sharply. "When did this happen? Is that why he hasn't been with you to visit?"

"Yes. He's refused to come." Tears rimmed her eyes. "It's been building for a while. I thought I could handle it, but then he stole some stupid headphones from the school. Hid them in his locker, where they would be found. Now he's in a court-ordered diversion program. His mentor is an old guy—really nice. David seems to like him. If he finishes it, he won't have anything on his record."

Wheeler rubbed his hand over the stubble on his chin. His sweet, good kid was running off the rails. His beautiful wife looked like a charwoman. And they'd soon run out of money and lose the home they'd worked so hard to create. All because he'd been a greedy idiot and had gotten mixed up with Delgado and his cronies. And now he was stuck. If he gave up information about them, there wasn't a prison in the state where he'd be safe. He could only hope that his time served awaiting trial would satisfy the prison component of the plea deal. That's why he had opted not to get out on bail. He knew that if he couldn't cut a deal to get out, he might as well be a dead man. In fact, death would be a relief.

Wheeler forced a smile. "This'll all be over soon. Not much longer now. Tell David I love him and that he needs to finish this diversion program and get back on track." He sighed. "And spend some of that money to get your hair done." He held her gaze for a long moment. "Don't ever forget how much I love you both and how very sorry I am about all this. No matter what it takes, I'm gonna fix it."

Chapter 8

Maggie worked distractedly all morning, sifting through the arcane legalese of the 130-page ground lease. According to clause 12(D)(4)(iii), the landlord had the right to surcharge the tenant—which in this case was the Town of Westbury—for certain items. There followed pages of definitions and escalation clauses tied to LIBOR. Sorting through it all and verifying the landlord's calculations and charges was making her cross-eyed. This ground lease had been in place for years, and the town hadn't been assessed any surcharges until the original landlord had sold the property—and the related interest in the ground lease—to a limited partnership owned by a limited liability company managed by a corporation. Even the digging she'd done hadn't revealed who was behind all of these entities. All she knew for sure was that if the landlord's figures were correct, Westbury owed a lot of money. And Westbury didn't have a lot of money.

Maggie rested her head in her hands. The sublease to Fairview Terraces did allow the town to pass the surcharge along to the residents of Fairview Terraces, but they were all retirees living on fixed incomes. They wouldn't have the money either. And it didn't seem right to spring this on them, like the landlord had done to the town.

She had to find some way out of this, but boy did she need help. This wasn't Upton's specialty, but Frank Haynes had leased a lot of space for his restaurants. Maybe she'd ask him to take a look at the ground lease and the landlord's calculations.

Maggie turned from her computer to the stacks of papers on her desk, all the while keeping an eye on her cell phone. Why hadn't John called or at least returned her text? Maybe he hadn't seen her missed call. It wasn't like him not to respond.

By lunchtime, she was totally unnerved. She was waiting in line at Pete's Bistro to pick up a salad to take back to her desk when she heard the familiar ping alerting her to a new text message. She tore her purse apart until she found her phone and opened his curt text: *Thank you, but I turned in early.*

That's it? she thought. *And it's not even true. I saw his lights on.*

Her appetite suddenly gone, she stepped out of line. She was weaving her way through the crowded restaurant when she felt someone grab her elbow from behind. She turned and found herself face to face with Hal Green, editor of the *Westbury Gazette*.

"Mayor Martin. Wondering if I could get your reaction to this morning's feature article about your 'qualifications' to be mayor. Maybe you'd like to amplify your statement of 'No comment'?" he said maliciously.

Maggie pulled free of his grasp. Her face flushed, and in spite of the chilly day, beads of sweat formed in her hairline. "I'm late for a meeting at Town Hall. Excuse me."

She was certain he had laughed derisively as she pushed through the door and stepped onto the sidewalk.

R

Meetings with the utilities commission at Town Hall tied up Maggie's afternoon. It was almost five thirty when she could finally let out an increasingly uneasy sigh. What was she going to do about John? Did she really want to do anything about him? Upon moving to Westbury, she had decided to live a solitary life. Maybe that wasn't such a bad decision after all.

Maggie had two beautiful children with Paul. And she had inherited Rosemont from him. Her gratitude for both, however, did not make up for the betrayal and heartbreak she'd suffered at his hands. She had vowed to never again get into a situation where she'd be so vulnerable.

Maggie's heart pounded as she recalled that day, before she had moved to Rosemont, little more than a year ago, when she sweltered in the rental car outside the home of the "Scottsdale Woman," as she dubbed her. The private investigator she had hired to report on Paul's embezzlement had uncovered this most unwelcome association. Against her better judgment, Maggie had made the short daytrip to Arizona from her Southern California home to get answers. What she got was a glimpse of a tall, beautiful young blonde pulling her Escalade out of the driveway of the biggest house on an exclusive street, apparently transporting her two children to some afterschool activity. After getting violently ill on the spot, Maggie had torn up her return plane ticket and driven the rental car back to California as fast as she could—the one-way rental surcharge be damned.

She turned her chair to look out at the growing dusk. What was it her mother always told her? Make decisions based on how they feel in your gut. Well a decision to let John slip away from her felt terrible. Maggie's stomach had been in knots all day. She pushed away from her desk and headed to Westbury Animal Hospital. If she rushed, she could be there in time to give him a ride home.

R

34

"Okay, Juan, I'm ready to go if you are," John Allen said as he rounded the corner into the reception area of Westbury Animal Hospital. He stopped short when he saw Maggie, the only other person in the room. "Maggie," he stated simply.

"Hi, John," she replied as brightly as she could. Maggie rose from her chair and crossed to where John was standing. "Juan said to tell you he's in the back. I thought I'd give you a ride home. Maybe take you to dinner? I want to make amends for last night. I'm so sorry, John."

"Don't be silly," he said. "We've all locked ourselves out of our cars. I'm sorry I was so short with you about it."

"Thank you. After that curt text from you today, I thought you were still angry." Maggie sighed in relief. "So are you hungry? Where would you like to eat?"

John hesitated, but he held her gaze. His eyes broadcast such deep sadness that Maggie felt her heart crumple like a used paper napkin. "This isn't working, Maggie. You're a wonderful woman. I admire you and everything you've done for the town. I'll always support you. But I'm second fiddle for you. I spent my entire first marriage that way, and I'm not going to do it again." He held up a hand. "Let me finish. I've been struggling with this for weeks. I'm sorry, but last night was the last straw for me. I'm not interested in changing you. And I'm not going to allow myself to fall any deeper in love with someone who can't make me a priority."

Maggie stared at John as tears pooled in her eyes. How in the world had they come to this point? He was right—she had neglected him horribly. But why couldn't he be patient a little longer? Things would settle down. She would change, starting now. At least he had said that he'd fallen in love with her.

Despite her tears, Maggie smiled at the thought. She rummaged in her purse for a tissue and collected herself. "I'm such an idiot, John. I'm so very, very sorry. You mean so much to me, too. Can't we give it more time?" She trailed off as he shook his head.

"You've made your choice, Maggie, and it isn't us," John answered. "I need to focus on rehabbing my knee and getting my life and practice back on track. I wish you well."

Maggie gulped and nodded. "If that's what you want." She succeeded in composing herself long enough to blurt out yet another apology. "I'm so sorry. I hope you change your mind." Then she fled.

Chapter 9

Loretta Nash repositioned the final packed box in the rear compartment of her Escalade and quickly closed the hatchback before anything could slide out of place. Her three-year-old was crying, and her two older children, also in the backseat, argued over the last snack cracker. Worn out, irritable, and anxious to be out of this place, she nonetheless walked up the driveway to take one last look at the elegant house she had called home until the foreclosure two days ago.

"Paul, you complete ass. How in the hell did you let this happen to us?" she whispered to herself.

She wiped a tear from her sweaty cheek and turned toward the car. That would be the next thing to go. Her salary as a front desk clerk at a chain hotel didn't stretch far enough to make the payments on the Escalade. She was surprised it hadn't been repossessed already. The repossessors might not find it right away at the modest apartment they were moving into. Maybe she'd catch a break for a few days.

"You kids stop fighting right now," she growled as she slid into the driver's seat. She leaned back to hand a Sippy cup to Nicole in her car seat. In response to the older kids' continued quarrel, she snatched the almost empty box of crackers with one swift motion, powered down her window, and chucked it onto the driveway. Both children became instantly silent.

"There. Problem solved," Loretta snapped, fighting back tears.

"Geez, Mom, you didn't have to get all crazy and do that," Sean huffed.

"Yeah, Mom. You littered," Marissa muttered.

Loretta exhaled deeply and leaned her forehead on the steering wheel. Only the hiss of the car's air conditioner could be heard.

"Sorry, Mom," Sean said. "You okay?"

"You're scaring us a little," Marissa added.

Loretta lifted her head, put the car in reverse, and backed out of the high-end Scottsdale home's driveway for the last time. She had been a fool when it came to Paul Martin. She had been young, poor, and desperate for someone to help her and her two kids, since their lowlife father never paid his child support and was nowhere to be found. Paul had swooped in. Everything had been great until she got her degree and wanted him to make good on his promise to leave the "Ice Queen," as he referred to his wife, and marry her. The relationship had started to unravel as soon as she pressed him on his plans.

Then she got pregnant.

That had not been intentional, no matter how much he doubted her. But with yet another child on the way, she had forced him to provide for them all by threatening to file suit and expose him. So he had bought the car and the house, telling her they were both paid for.

Now she was right back where she started, except with one extra mouth to feed. She had an education, but in this economy her hotel/restaurant management degree only landed her an entry-level job.

"You'll be secure while I work out my plan to move Maggie to the little home I inherited in Westbury," he had told her. He would keep his precious job at the college, and Loretta would gradually be introduced as his new girlfriend. Everyone would accept her then, he assured her.

It had all been a lie.

"Okay, guys, Mommy's tired. When I ask you to do something, I mean it, understand?" she said, locking eyes with each of them in her rearview mirror. "Taco Bell or McDonald's for dinner? You choose."

R

Loretta shifted from her aching left foot to her aching right foot as she forced a smile for the next person in line. She hated manning the front desk alone. Why couldn't they find a replacement when someone called in sick? Working check-in during the late afternoon was no picnic. People were tired from travel, impatient to get their key and get to their room. She did her best to move through the line as fast as she could, incessantly murmuring, "So sorry for the wait. Checking in?"

An hour and forty-five minutes later, she finally found herself blissfully alone as the last guest headed for the elevator. She snuck her cell phone out of her pocket—her kids were supposed to text when their babysitter picked them up. She nodded when she saw the expected message, then noticed a voicemail message. Cell phone usage during working hours was strictly prohibited, and she knew she should wait until her break to listen to it. But she never got voicemails anymore. Not since Paul had died.

Loretta scanned the lobby and walked to the end of the counter where she could see the curb outside the entrance. No activity anywhere. She knocked a pile of brochures onto the floor behind the desk and bent down to pick them up, tapping the phone to retrieve her message. She abandoned the scattered papers and listened to the message a second time. Then she rocked back onto her heels and exhaled slowly as she slipped the phone back into her pocket.

37

A recruiter wondered if she would be interested in other jobs within her industry. The hotel-and-restaurant business was booming in the Midwest and eastern United States, and employers were finding it difficult to secure qualified candidates. One of her former professors had recommended her. "Maybe sleeping with most of the faculty will pay off after all," she muttered under her breath.

A change of scenery might do them all good. God knows she wanted to get out of here. Running into anyone from her old neighborhood was almost a daily embarrassment. Their quizzical looks and phony expressions of sympathy didn't fool her. They had always assumed that Paul was her sugar daddy; that she was beneath them; that she was now getting just what she deserved. How had her life taken this turn, anyway? When she met Paul, who seemed like such a nice, upstanding man, she thought that she had finally overcome her affinity for bad boys. *You fool,* she thought. *You settled on a married man. You fell for the oldest line in the book.*

Maybe in a new job far away from here she could press the reset button on her life. Maybe she could be a mother that her children could look up to. Her résumé would be in the hands of this recruiter by the time he got to his office the next morning.

Chapter 10

Frank Haynes logged off his laptop and rubbed his eyes with both hands. He glanced at his Rolex and saw that it was almost midnight; he was knocking off early by recent standards. Ever since those idiot Delgado brothers had screwed up their creative investments with the pension fund assets—potentially exposing them all to criminal charges—Haynes had assiduously managed his financial affairs. There was no telling when Scanlon might subpoena his records. No trail would lead from his fast-food franchise businesses to the pension fund.

But he couldn't keep working like this forever, especially since he suddenly had to actually show up at his Town Hall office on a regular basis and do more work there. Now that he had things well covered up, maybe it was time to hire a bookkeeper. He leaned back in his deeply tufted leather chair and steepled his fingers as he considered the possibility. He'd need to have someone trained before the busy holiday season. He didn't want to run an ad in the local paper. An employee connected with someone affected by the pension fund problems might be inclined to dig around in his books. An out-of-towner would be just the thing. He'd get someone with a restaurant/management degree. Haynes smiled his private Grinch Who Stole Christmas grin. He'd contact an employment agency the next day.

R

By midmorning, Frank Haynes had engaged a recruiter to find him a bookkeeper and had placed orders for next week's inventory. He needed to tackle the payroll, but for the first time in weeks was feeling ahead of schedule. He swiveled in his chair to look out the window at the lush Indian summer day. When was the last time he'd actually been outside in the sunshine? Haynes pushed himself back from his desk, tossed his jacket over his arm, and locked up Haynes Enterprises. He'd just take a short drive in the country—no more than an hour—and would be back in plenty of time to submit payroll.

Haynes opened the moon roof on his Mercedes sedan and turned his car in the direction of Rosemont, just as he did every day. With Maggie Martin firmly ensconced there, his dream of owning the place was further away than ever, but old habits die hard.

The trees surrounding the estate were in glorious color, deepening his sense of envy. He forced his eyes back to the road and took the turn toward the Shawnee River on the outskirts of town. Maybe he'd even stop in at The Mill for a bite to eat. He was accelerating into a curve when a stray dog lunged into his lane. Haynes braked sharply and swerved. The fine German engineering responded to his skilled hands, and he narrowly avoided the animal. Frightened, the dog skittered to the berm.

Haynes pulled into a large grassy area just ahead and shut off the engine. He grabbed a Forever Friends Animal Shelter leash and a handful of treats from his glove box and went in search of the stray. Forever Friends received animals found along this stretch of road all the time. *Probably some poor creature whose owner had brought him here and dumped him when he didn't want him anymore. Damn those fools,* he thought. *Why didn't they just bring the dog to Forever Friends?* Isn't that why he had started the shelter in the first place?

He found the stray pacing along the berm a half-mile down the road. Hesitant at first, the hungry dog finally succumbed to the treats, and Haynes was able to loop the leash around his neck. He crouched down and ran his hands over the animal. His ribs showed and his hair was matted and dirty; he'd been on his own for quite a while.

"No worries now, buddy," Haynes spoke softly. "We'll find you someone who will take care of you; you won't have to live like this anymore."

Haynes and the dog trudged back to the car, where the backseat contained a kennel that Haynes regularly used for strays. It felt good to stretch his legs on such a sunny day. He allowed the dog to sniff and mark as many spots as it wanted along the way. They were no more than thirty feet from the Mercedes when a black sedan with darkly tinted windows pulled into the grassy area and blocked their progress.

Haynes groaned inwardly as the portly form of Chuck Delgado emerged from the car.

"Frankie boy," Delgado called. "What you doin' out here walking that piss-poor mutt?"

Haynes ignored the question. "Why are you here, Charles? I thought we agreed it would be safest for everyone if we kept our distance except when we were both present for town council meetings."

"Somethin's changed, Frankie."

Haynes raised an eyebrow.

"Wheeler may be crackin'. Sources on the inside say he's tryin' to cut a deal with that pansy Scanlon."

"We always knew that was a risk. He doesn't know anything that would link us to him."

"The boys don't like it, Frankie. They think it may be time for Wheeler to have an accident. Maybe an assisted suicide."

"Damn it, Chuck. We can't go around murdering people. For God's sake, he's got a wife and kids. I hear his thirteen-year-old son is having a terrible time. We should be helping his family, not trying to kill him."

"Don't go gettin' soft on me here, Frankie. You're in this up to your ass, like the rest of us. When he talks, we all go down."

"If he has a suspicious death, that'll put the spotlight on this whole mess even more. Are you guys clueless? That's what happens with cover-ups. We were careful. Wheeler doesn't have any information to trade for a plea deal. Did it ever occur to you that Scanlon might have started this rumor to get us to do something stupid?"

Haynes could see this possibility hadn't occurred to Delgado. God, what a moron the guy was. How in the hell had he ever let himself get mixed up with this bunch of goons?

"Okay, Frankie, I'll talk to the boys."

"I'm out, Charles. I'm done with all of you. This is our last meeting in private. Don't contact me again."

Delgado lunged and grabbed Haynes by the lapel. "You're out when—and if—we say you're out. You got that Frankie?" He released Haynes with a shove that sent him stumbling to keep his balance.

Haynes watched silently as Delgado swaggered back to his car and pulled away, the stray dog whimpering at his side.

Chapter 11

By the end of the week, Gloria hadn't run into Glenn at the dining hall or received a call from him. *Probably thinks I'm making a pass at him, the old fool,* she thought with a trace of irritation. She knew that other women swarmed the widowers at Fairview Terraces. She had never chased after a man and was not about to do so now.

Gloria picked up one of the volumes Glenn had dropped off and turned again to Walt Whitman. She read a poem each morning, right after her daily Bible study. Knitting and poetry—what an odd combination of things he'd brought into her life, she mused.

Across the complex, Glenn again checked his watch. He had been up and out before six every morning this week helping to set up the new food pantry at his church—way too early to take Gloria up on her offer of breakfast. The whole idea was ridiculous, really. He didn't even like biscuits and gravy. But he longed for someone interesting to talk to. Not that his children and grandchildren weren't interesting. And God knows they had kept close tabs on him since Nancy died. But he wanted someone who shared the perspectives of his generation.

The hour hand finally clicked to seven o'clock, and Glenn reached for the phone and dialed. It took Gloria six rings to answer. He almost gave up, fearing she might still be asleep and he'd be waking her. When he heard her steady "Hello, this is Gloria," he was suddenly speechless.

"Hello," she repeated.

"Gloria," he replied, before she could hang up. "It's Glenn. I hope I'm not calling too early?"

"Not at all. I've been up for hours. Was just reading Walt Whitman, as a matter of fact. Thanks to you."

"That's great. Glad to hear it. Are you enjoying him?"

"Enormously. I'm so grateful you shared your books with me."

"Those books are for you, Gloria. I wanted to thank you for finishing the blanket."

"That was my gift to Cindy—and Nancy. No need to thank me. And now I've found that I enjoy knitting. So the blessing was all mine."

Glenn found himself smiling.

"I'd like to discuss some of these poems with you," Gloria added. "Did you get my note about breakfast? Would you like to come over tomorrow morning?"

"I did. And I'd love to. But please don't fuss; I'm easy."

"I'll see you at seven thirty. It'll be fun to fuss for a change." Gloria replaced the receiver, hoping that she still remembered how to make sausage gravy.

R

Glenn's windshield wipers were going full blast on the drive to church and the sky was gray in every direction. *Blast!* he thought. He loved to stretch his old Cadillac on the country roads and had suggested a drive in the county to Gloria during yesterday's breakfast. She'd readily accepted, but it wouldn't be worth doing in a pouring rain. He entered the sanctuary feeling downright forlorn.

The sermon ran long and Glenn had tuned the pastor out before the midpoint. Anxious to see if the weather had cleared up, he shot out of his seat as the final chords of the closing hymn hung in the air and hurried to the front of the receiving line to greet his pastor. With an uncharacteristically curt "insightful message" comment, he shook his pastor's hand and quickly strode out the large double doors of the narthex. A cloudless blue sky and receding puddles on the walkway greeted him, reflecting a brilliantly sunny afternoon.

He fired up the Caddy and headed toward home.

R

Gloria had anxiously watched the weather all morning, too. Pleased when the midmorning sun finally began to peek through the clouds, she turned positively tickled when the wind died down to a gentle breeze after eleven o'clock. What a perfect day for a drive. She put her sweater and a rain jacket (just in case) on the chair by her front door, turned to a chapter of Carl Sandburg's poems in the anthology Glenn had given her, and read until she heard a knock at the door.

She answered his knock and they set off for the lush countryside surrounding Westbury. Fields had been harvested, and the leaves were near their peak. Glenn turned the radio to the local classical station. They were content to remain silent, taking in the brilliant afternoon to the accompaniment of Haydn.

Glenn pointed to the sky and recited, "The geese flying south, in a row long and V-shaped, pulling in winter. Sally Andersen."

Gloria smiled and nodded. "That they are. Well put." She turned to him. "Have you heard anything about an ecumenical prayer breakfast on Thanksgiving morning? Some of the nursery staff were talking about it yesterday when I was at the daycare."

Glenn glanced at her briefly. "I didn't know that you'd gone back to rocking babies. I'm glad to hear it."

"I just started again. It's been hard since Nancy's no longer there with me."

Glenn nodded.

"I'm sorry, Glenn. You know that better than anyone."

Glenn cleared his throat. "I know about the breakfast; my church is one of the sponsors. They're planning to make it an annual event. And I hope they do. It'll return some of the emphasis of the holiday back to its origin and away from food and football."

"I'd like to attend, if I can get myself there."

"That won't be hard," he replied. "They're going to have it on the lawn at Fairview Terraces."

"Really? I hadn't heard that. What a wonderful idea."

"I couldn't agree more. It'll be good to host our Westbury neighbors on our campus."

Gloria leaned forward in her seat to read a small roadway marker. "If my memory serves and if it's still in business, there should be a farm down the next lane that sells apples by the bushel and all sorts of lovely fall produce. If I can get my hands on good apples, I'll bake you a pie. I'd like to make up for those dreadful biscuits yesterday."

"They weren't dreadful," he lied. "Best I've had in years." At least the latter part of his statement was true—he hadn't had biscuits in years. "We'll find this place. I definitely want to send you home with apples for a pie. Nobody in my family knows how to bake. Everything comes out of the freezer these days."

"I know. And it's so easy and so much better to make from scratch. Plus, it's a lot of fun. We'll find apples, don't you worry."

Gloria's memory was spot on. Before long they had piled a small wagon with varieties for applesauce, pies, and eating, along with acorn squash, Indian corn, and decorative gourds. Gloria was almost giddy. She couldn't remember the last time she'd enjoyed these fall delights.

R

Gloria rummaged around in her kitchen for her apple peeler and rolling pin, wondering why in the world she had opened her big mouth and offered to bake a pie. Just like sausage gravy, it had been years since she'd last made a pie. Still, once she'd assembled the ingredients and tools, she found she had retained her touch. She rolled out a thin crust and filled it with sliced fruit, tossed in cinnamon, sugar, and nutmeg. Soon the aroma of the baking pie caressed every corner of her apartment.

At four o'clock on Thursday afternoon, Gloria set her treasure in a wicker basket lined with a tea towel and left it in front of Glenn's door. She attached a card on which she had penned:

> Earth's increase, foison plenty,
> Barns and garners never empty,
> Vines with clust'ring bunches growing,
> Plants with goodly burthen bowing;
> Spring come to you at the farthest
> In the very end of harvest!
>   ~The Tempest, Act 4, Sc. 1

R

When Gloria arrived at the dining hall at her usual time for the second seating, she spotted Glenn parked in one of the chairs by the entrance.

He beamed as he got to his feet and greeted her. "I almost stepped in the best-looking apple pie in the county when I left for dinner tonight! Will you come over for dessert to share a slice? Thought I'd wait here to see if we could sit together at dinner."

Neither realized at the time, but Glenn's invitation would officially mark the start of their romance.

Chapter 12

Maggie rose from her seat at the conference table in the council chambers on the top floor of Town Hall.

"Thank you all for coming on such short notice," she said to the town council and Special Counsel Alex Scanlon.

"It was a bitch gettin' through those protestors," Chuck Delgado said. "Dumbasses. Like that's gonna do any good."

"They were very vocal and downright mean. Chanting 'Get rid of Martin!' I was uneasy walking past them," Tonya Holmes said. "How long has this been going on, Maggie?"

"They've been out there consistently for the past several weeks. Today's crowd was larger than the usual handful."

"You need to request extra police presence if this continues," Tonya replied. "Maybe you need a police escort."

"You might be right. I'll think about it. I've been coming in early and leaving late to avoid them."

"One thing's for sure, we won't get re-elected if we don't fix this mess," Councilman Russell Isaac stated. "We may all get impeached from office."

"No point in speculating on all of this. Protestors or not, we've got a serious matter to address during this executive session and a short fuse to contend with before this thing blows up. As you know, Westbury's pension fund subleases property to Fairview Terraces on a long-term lease. The fund is in year twenty of a ninety-nine-year ground lease of that property. And the pension fund is in default on that lease. The lessor started a foreclosure proceeding last week. We have a short window—maybe four months—to bring the lease current or reach a deal with the lessor." Maggie paused to let this take root.

Isaac was the first to speak up. "Are you sure about this? Maybe there's something wrong with the lessor's accounting records."

"We've looked at all that. We're in arrears."

"Have we been collecting from Fairview?" Delgado asked. "Maybe those old fogies are behind."

Tonya spun on him. "Honestly, Councilman. Have some respect. We may be in executive session, but we're still conducting official business."

"Relax," Delgado returned. "It was just an expression."

"Tonya's right, Chuck," Frank Haynes spoke up. Delgado glared at the reprimand. "I'd like to know the answer to his question, though," Haynes continued. "Is Fairview current?"

"Yes, they are," Maggie answered. "We've recently been hit with a fee under the ground lease that hasn't been passed through to Fairview. That's why we're short."

Alex broke in. "Has anyone reviewed the ground lease? Maybe we can dispute the increase. We should be able to go back to Fairview to collect the shortage under the sublease."

"Won't that amount to raising rents with no notice on all of those senior citizens? We won't get re-elected doing that," Isaac remarked.

"Not to mention it's the wrong thing to spring on people with fixed incomes," Tonya noted dryly.

"We need to work on this from all angles," Maggie interjected. "We've got two areas of attack—the legitimacy of the increase under the ground lease and a possible increase in the sublease. The ground lease documents are two inches thick; we'll need to hire our outside law firm to assist us. I asked Bill Stetson for an estimate. He told me it would cost at least $20,000 for his firm to handle the matter."

"This town is broke; has he forgotten that? We don't have an extra twenty grand in the budget," Isaac sputtered.

"I'm not sure we have much choice," Tonya said.

"I'd like to lead the effort to tackle this problem," Haynes volunteered. All heads snapped toward him. "Most of my restaurants are leased, so I've got a lot of experience beating up landlords. So to speak," he added quickly. "Let's hold off on engaging Stetson & Graham."

"This will require a lot of your time over the next few weeks, Frank," Maggie replied. "Aren't you already working too much? Are you sure you want to take this on?"

"Quite sure. And if it gets to be too much, we can hire the firm. Let me take a crack at it first."

Maggie relaxed into her chair. "Terrific. Thank you, Frank. You're the ideal member to handle this. I'm sure we're all very grateful to you."

Haynes shrugged as everyone around the table nodded their assent. "Fairview Terraces is in my district. If we have to raise their rent, things could get sticky for me."

"Working with Fairview and the senior community will require a delicate touch," Isaac noted. "I think that Councilwoman Holmes and Mayor Martin are the best suited for that job."

Tonya turned to Maggie. "I'm willing if you are."

"We've got a plan, then," Maggie replied. "Let's get busy."

Chapter 13

Frank Haynes pulled the résumé off the stack and checked his watch. He still had two minutes before his phone interview with Loretta Nash. He sighed impatiently. Her time zone was three hours behind his, and he'd stayed at his office late so that they could talk after the conclusion of her workday. If he hired her, this would be the last concession he would make for her. Still, her background and experience were just what he was looking for.

Haynes punched in her number and idly tapped his pen on his desktop. He was about to hang up when she answered on the sixth ring.

"Loretta Nash," said the pleasant voice on the other end of the line.

"Frank Haynes, Ms. Nash. I believe you were expecting my call? Is this still a good time to talk?" he said with manufactured solicitude.

"Yes it is. Thank you."

"Good. Let me start by telling you a bit about my company and what we're looking for." He launched into his now-familiar interview script and ran through his part in record time, ending with the requirement that the successful applicant must relocate. He asked if she knew anything about Westbury.

After a long pause Loretta replied, "I believe there's an estate there known as Rosemont. That's about all I know about the place."

Her answer brought him up short. He struggled to recover and sputtered, "You're right. There's a Rosemont here. How do you know about that? What do you know about it?"

"Nothing, really. I've never even seen a picture. A friend of mine inherited it several years back."

"Ah … so you know Maggie Martin?" Haynes asked. If she were a friend of their mayor, this interview would be over in a heartbeat. No way would he allow her near his business.

"No," Loretta said. "I was a friend of Paul Martin."

Haynes' head snapped up so fast it bounced off the back of his leather chair. This was the most tantalizing piece of news he'd heard in months. His Cheshire cat grin spread across his face, and his voice oozed friendliness. "Is that right?" he crooned. "I'm sorry for your loss."

"Thank you," Loretta murmured.

Haynes wasn't sure where to go with this information. He needed time to investigate Loretta Nash. "Ms. Nash," he said, resuming a businesslike demeanor, "I've very much enjoyed our conversation. It's getting late and I have another appointment, but I'd like to discuss this opportunity with you further. May I have the recruiter set up another call in a few days? Good. I'll look forward to it. Thank you for your time. Have a pleasant evening."

Haynes immediately punched his speed dial button. "I've got another investigation for you," he stated as soon as the other party answered. "In Scottsdale, Arizona. I want you out there by noon tomorrow."

"Hold on, Frank. I can't drop everything I'm workin' on."

"I want a report on Loretta Nash on my desk by the end of the week. If you've got a problem with that, I'll find someone else."

"Not a problem, Frank. Not a problem."

Haynes replaced the phone on the receiver. This Loretta Nash knew Paul Martin and not Maggie? What were the chances of that? Paul had inherited Rosemont and never told his wife, which was very odd. He had kept that secret from her. Maybe he had kept others as well. Frank Haynes was going to find out. He'd always believed the old saying that knowledge is power; he was going to get power over Martin, one way or another. He leaned back in his generous leather chair and smiled.

R

The report came in a day earlier than expected. He quickly opened the email and downloaded the attached photos and documents. They'd hit pay dirt. Loretta Nash had been Paul's mistress, supported handsomely until he died and it all fell apart. She was now living a hand-to-mouth existence. Tough to get tossed out of a big, fancy house in Scottsdale and have the car repossessed. He laughed out loud at the mental images. Still, she wasn't a bad-looking woman. He wondered why she hadn't latched onto some other accommodating old fool. Women like that usually did.

The pièce de résistance was her young child. Was it Paul's? If so, why hadn't she tried to get a piece of his estate? Had she even thought of that? She would be entitled to support for the child *if* it was his. *A big if,* he realized.

Haynes paused and stared unseeing out the window. This Loretta Nash opened up all sorts of possibilities. If she was a decent bookkeeper, that would be icing on the cake. If not, he had seen enough to make him want to have her right here in Westbury, regardless of what she could contribute to his business.

R

Loretta Nash relaxed as she buckled her seat belt and made sure her tray table was locked in the upright position. It had been ages since she had been away from her kids, not at work, and all on her own. Not since before Paul died. The break would do her good. Frank Haynes seemed nice enough even though there was something a bit odd about him. She couldn't put her finger on it, but for now she didn't care. He was paying for this trip and she was going to enjoy herself. He was even paying her neighbor to take care of her kids while she was gone overnight. Things would either work out with Haynes Enterprises or they wouldn't. Contented, she drifted off to sleep.

R

Loretta surveyed herself in the hotel room's full-length mirror. She looked good in the Neiman Marcus charcoal suit Paul had bought her. Thank goodness it was still in style and she was able to squeeze into it after starving herself for the past week. She'd never be able to afford a suit like this again, she thought sadly. Still, she had it now. She picked up her purse and headed downstairs to meet the cab Mr. Haynes sent for her.

Meanwhile, Frank Haynes was pacing in front of the window in his office, waiting for Loretta Nash to arrive. He knew he was pulling out all the stops to impress her. Airfare, hotel, a *babysitter*—all for a simple bookkeeping job? *Ridiculous. Didn't she see that? Was she that naïve?* he wondered. Or would she sense that his interest in her wasn't purely professional and drive a hard bargain? *On the other hand, it wasn't easy to outsmart Frank Haynes,* he reminded himself.

He saw the cab turn into the driveway in front of his building and went out to meet her. It was time to turn on the charm. Haynes stepped off the curb to introduce himself as she emerged from the backseat. He paid the driver and ushered her into the suite occupied by Haynes Enterprises.

"Did you have a pleasant trip?" he asked, offering her a seat in his most solicitous fashion. "Hotel to your liking?"

"Yes, everything was fine. Thank you."

"How do you like Westbury?" he pressed on, taking his place behind his desk.

"I haven't been here long enough to tell," she responded. "It was dark when I arrived last night, and I came straight here this morning. All I can really tell is that it's very green and pretty. That makes it a nice change from Arizona."

Haynes nodded knowingly. "Well, we'll want you to see more of our beautiful town." Thankfully, it was going to be a perfect day, with the fall colors just a day or two past their peak. He couldn't have asked for better weather. "When we're done here, I'll show you the sights, if you'd like," he offered, knowing he'd enjoy nothing less.

She smiled at him coyly. "I'd really like that, Mr. Haynes."

A wave of revulsion swept through him. *Good God,* he thought. *She's coming on to me. She must assume she can put every man under her spell. Let her think that, but it's not going to happen with me.*

"So," Haynes continued, "I've reviewed your résumé and it's very impressive. I run several fast-food franchises and we need a bookkeeper. We want someone with industry experience. You've got exactly what we're looking for."

This is going too easy, Loretta realized. *This guy isn't flirting back, so he's not looking for that ... Maybe he's gay? No. There's something else.*

Even though she wanted this job, she decided to test the waters. "I thought you were looking for more than just a bookkeeper. I thought you wanted a financial analyst with industry experience. I've got a hotel/restaurant management degree; I can do a lot more for you than just bookkeeping."

Haynes snapped the pencil he was holding in half. *Who in the hell did this little slut think she was?* He opened his mouth to speak and thought better of it. He needed to compose himself. He forced a smile and held her gaze.

She broke the uncomfortable silence. "I've got a family to support, Mr. Haynes. I was hoping for more," she said.

"Of course, of course," he replied, believing that she was being sincere. "We pride ourselves on promoting from within here at Haynes Enterprises," he lied. "I'm sure we can consider an expanded role after the probationary period."

He rose to his feet to forestall any further conversation on the subject. "Let me show you the office. Then we can do some sightseeing around town and have lunch before I drop you at the airport. You have a four o'clock flight, is that correct?"

R

Haynes kept up a steady chatter on their drive around Westbury. It was clear he loved the town and knew every nook and cranny of it. As far as Loretta was concerned, it looked old, small, and not the least like beautiful Scottsdale, Arizona, where she lived—or, rather, used to live. Her current circumstances were much reduced, she reminded herself. If this guy wanted to pay her decent money to move her here, she would consider it. Still, she wasn't wowed like she'd hoped to be.

Sensing her low enthusiasm, Haynes pulled out his ace in the hole. "You mentioned Rosemont when we talked on the phone a while back. Would you like to drive by? It really is something to see."

Her head whipped up to face him, and he knew he'd hit his mark.

"I'd forgotten all about Rosemont," she said even though the house that Paul's former wife lived in was never far from her thoughts. "If we can, I'd like that."

R

By the time they turned into the parking lot at The Mill for lunch, Haynes knew he had her. Loretta Nash tried to cover up her awe at seeing Rosemont, but he knew better. Thank God it was a weekday and Martin was at Town Hall. He'd driven up the driveway and stopped in front so she could get a good look. He almost felt sorry for Loretta. Whatever Paul Martin had told her about Rosemont, he obviously hadn't characterized it as a gorgeous stone manor house. He could practically see the wheels turning in her head as she tried to figure out what might be in this for her.

After barely looking at the restaurant or its patrons, Loretta absentmindedly ordered a chicken Caesar salad without even opening the menu.

"I want to offer you the job as financial analyst," Haynes announced. If the title would entice her, what the hell did it matter to him?

That caught her attention.

"Your duties will focus primarily on the accounts, of course. But I'm sure you'll be able to use your degree and experience. I'll pay your moving expenses, and you'll have a car allowance. Plus the usual medical and dental benefits." He knew he was offering too much, but he wanted to seal the deal. He made sure her starting salary doubled her current income.

To her credit, she didn't pounce on his offer and accept immediately. *Maybe she has some moxie after all,* he mused.

"This is a very good offer, Mr. Haynes. I need time to think about it," she said, knowing that her decision had been made. "May I call you after I've had a chance to sleep on it?"

"Certainly," he said, suppressing his annoyance. "But don't wait too long. We have other candidates." He could tell by the look on her face that she didn't believe him.

Chapter 14

The notice from the mayor's office, copied and slipped under every resident's door, caused quite a stir. Gloria called Glenn the minute she got it.

"What does this mean?" she asked. "Increase in fees? I've got a five-year lease. How do they think they can just come in here and charge more? That's what I want to know."

"I've never seen anything like this," Glenn replied. "There must be something in the fine print of our leases that allows this. I've been trying to find my copy. Nancy kept all the files. I don't know where she put it," he said with a hint of frustration.

"If they're going to do this anyway, why have a meeting?" Gloria wondered.

"They probably want buy-in from all of us residents. They're afraid they'll have a mutiny on their hands. Unless I miss my mark, we're very good tenants. I'd be willing to bet that everybody here pays their rent on time."

"You know they do!" Gloria responded. "I'm going to that meeting, that's for sure. I've read good things about both this new mayor and Councilwoman Holmes. I'm sure everything will be fine. But it's hard not to worry."

"I agree. I'll swing by your place tomorrow and we can walk over together."

Over the prior few weeks, one shared meal turned into many as Glenn and Gloria explored memories from their pasts and discussed current events and interests, both finding the allure of genuine friendship and compatibility irresistible. Gloria had worried about the gossipy locals branding them a couple, a concern she shared with Glenn since he might find the rumors hurtful as a recent widower. For his part, Glenn had never taken much stock in people's opinions and was only uneasy about anything disrespectful of Gloria. In the end, the comfort they both took in their developing friendship had carried the day, and they had quickly become a daily fixture in each other's lives.

Gloria and Glenn arrived at the dining hall twenty-five minutes before the scheduled meeting with the mayor and Councilwoman Holmes. All the seats had been taken, and the maintenance crew was setting up folding chairs. Glenn ushered Gloria to the last available folding chair and took a spot along the sidelines.

Mayor Martin and Councilwoman Holmes arrived right on time. The mayor stepped to the podium and addressed the residents of Fairview Terraces. "Thank you all for coming here this morning. My office has been swamped with calls and emails, and I'm sorry I haven't responded. We felt it would be best to talk to everyone at once." She scanned the anxious faces of the residents. Decent, hardworking people who had lived up to their obligations all of their lives and now wanted a peaceful retirement. *Who could blame them?* Maggie swallowed hard and continued with her difficult message.

"We haven't come here to alarm you, but I can see that you're concerned. Nothing I'm about to tell you will happen right away. But we have decisions to make.

"Let me get to the point," she continued. "Fairview Terraces is a nonprofit corporation, organized to own and run this facility. It subleases the real estate that your apartments are located on from Westbury's pension fund. The fund holds the property as the tenant on a long-term ground lease. For years, the payments we received from Fairview Terraces—the sum of your rental payments—have been enough to make the payment on the ground lease." She scanned the crowd and glanced at Tonya, who nodded encouragingly.

"Several months ago, the lessor increased the rent under the ground lease and the pension fund has not been able to make the increased payment. In response, the lessor has filed a foreclosure action against the fund. I've called this meeting because the lessor will be posting foreclosure notices on the property tomorrow. I didn't want anyone to see them without knowing what's going on." Maggie paused to let this sink in. She was greeted with a sea of puzzled faces.

This is as dreadful as I thought it would be, she realized. "If the lessor forecloses, your leases may be terminated and you will be forced to move out." This remark hit home, prompting a collective gasp from the audience. The residents turned to their neighbors in disbelief. Hands shot up all over the room.

Maggie motioned for quiet, which quickly ensued in a room full of people who were by nature courteous and polite. "We believe that the ground lease provision regarding the increase is ambiguous. We've been in contact with the lessor and the pension fund is prepared to file suit if necessary. The foreclosure won't go forward during the pendency of the suit. We're also looking at ways to raise the money, both for the arrearage and on an ongoing basis if the increase is valid."

"Won't you look to us for the extra money?" someone in the back asked. "Aren't we the only ones with a vested interest in this place?"

At this point, Tonya Holmes rose and approached the podium. "Not necessarily," she stated. "A rent increase is one possible solution, sure. And it will probably be part of the solution."

"How can you do that?" an elderly gentleman interrupted, gesticulating with his cane before leaning on it again for support. "We've got leases. You can't just start charging us more rent."

"Your leases contain a clause that allows the pension fund to pass on increases in the ground lease," Tonya replied. "But we assure you that this is a last resort. And we'd raise rents as little as possible. We're going to fight the lessor on this increase."

"We came out here today so that you'd hear the facts instead of just rumors," Maggie reiterated. "And our very last resort will be to exercise our rights to raise your rent. You have my word on that."

Glenn raised his hand. "If you're not successful in defeating this increase and you don't want to raise our rents, where else could the funds come from?"

"That's a very good question," Tonya responded. "We're exploring options. We could charge fees to the vendors that supply goods and services to Fairview. We could hold a fundraiser." Tonya smiled at Maggie. "Our mayor is good at that."

Another hand shot up, and a diminutive woman stood. "You won't see me if I don't stand," she joked. "I'd like to suggest that we lease out our recreation room for events and parties. We've got a really nice facility and we don't use it very much. I've thought that for years. We could raise some money that way."

"That's a terrific idea," Tonya stated.

"Any other ideas come to mind?" Maggie asked.

Gloria chimed in. "We could open a small gift shop. We have the space, and we've got residents who turn out gorgeous arts and crafts."

"And maybe once a month we could hold a bake sale," added the woman on her right. "We could advertise it around town. Hold it on Saturday mornings."

"We could hold a farmers market on our front lawn," called out a man standing in the back. "Charge a fee to each vendor."

"That'd be a lot of fun," agreed two women simulta-neously.

Maggie and Tonya exchanged a relieved glance. These people were resourceful.

"I'm inspired by your can-do spirit. I want to encourage you to keep thinking of ideas to generate income." Maggie's eyes swept the audience. "Most of all, I don't want anyone losing sleep over this. We've got a long way to go. You had to be informed. For now, the attorneys and

Councilman Frank Haynes are working with the lessor to get this issue resolved. Fairview Terraces is in his district, and I know he's very devoted to you. I've seen him working late into the night at Town Hall. His business experience makes him uniquely qualified to tackle this issue." She noted with satisfaction the nods of approval from the crowd.

"If you have any additional questions after all this sinks in," she concluded, "you know where to find me. Councilmembers Holmes and Haynes and I are available to you at any time. And keep generating those inspiring suggestions!"

Chapter 15

Maggie reluctantly logged off her computer shortly after six. Now that she wasn't giving John a ride home from physical therapy anymore, there was no reason to leave the office any earlier. At least Eve would be waiting to greet her, wagging her tail, and turning in circles at the sound of Maggie's key in the door.

As she headed for the elevator, Maggie noticed that Frank Haynes was working late again. She bypassed the elevator bank and headed toward his office. He was bent over a pile of documents strewn over his desk, making notes on a legal pad. He hadn't heard her approach and started when she spoke.

"Burning the midnight oil, Frank?"

He looked up and ran his fingers through his thinning hair. "This ground lease thing is a mess. The factors that play into the rent increase are extremely complex. I'm going through the lessor's calculations, but can't verify their figures."

"Thank you, Frank. That's exactly what we need to have done. Can anyone in accounting help you?"

"Honestly, no. They've tried. Nobody understands this. Alex is also working on it."

"I'm sure the two of you can get to the bottom of anything."

"Actually, we were hoping to put our conclusions together and run them by you. You're an accountant after all."

Maggie nodded. "I'd be happy to go over them."

He rested his head in his hands.

"Frank, you look exhausted. I think you need to go home and get some rest. Why don't you walk out with me?"

Haynes met her gaze. He straightened his shoulders and paused, as if weighing a momentous decision. Maggie raised an eyebrow. "Come on, Frank. This will all be here tomorrow."

"I guess you're right. I wasn't making any progress, anyway. I'll pick it up first thing tomorrow," Haynes replied with a tired smile.

The evening air felt chilly when they exited through the rear door; there would be frost on the grass in the morning. Haynes loved this time of year. Impulsively, he turned to Maggie. "Are you on your way to pick up the good doctor?"

"No," Maggie sighed. "I'm not doing that anymore." Haynes noted the sadness in her voice. *Trouble in paradise?* he wondered.

"If you don't have other plans, why don't we grab a bite to eat?" he suggested tentatively.

Maggie regarded him thoughtfully. "Thank you, Frank. Can I take a rain check? I've got to head home to feed and walk my dog. She's been inside all day."

Frank looked genuinely disappointed, she realized. "Will you be at Town Hall tomorrow? Maybe we could grab lunch?"

"No," he replied stiffly. "I've got business meetings all day. That's okay—just a thought."

"You understand about dogs," Maggie said, referring to his well-known status as the founder and principal funder of Forever Friends.

"Yes, that I do," he conceded.

Maggie decided to press the point; if she had an opportunity to forge a cooperative professional relationship with Frank Haynes, she needed to seize it. "The next time you're at Town Hall during the day, please let me know and I'll buy you lunch. I'll rearrange whatever's on my calendar."

Haynes smiled in spite of himself. "If you insist. I'll be back before the end of the week."

"Terrific. Just give me a call," she said as she reached her car. "Have a good night. And Frank, thanks for working so hard to get things straightened out for the residents of Fairview Terraces."

No need to tell her that he couldn't have cared less about them, he thought as she drove off. He was just following Upton's advice to get on her good side.

R

Maggie slung her purse over her shoulder shortly after one o'clock on Friday. She had been waiting all week for Frank Haynes to accept her offer to buy lunch, but he hadn't contacted her. She had misgivings about the whole idea anyway since she still resented the way he had taken credit for the Easter carnival at Rosemont. It could have been an innocent mistake and, frankly, what politician didn't try to steal the limelight whenever possible? But after how much work she had put into the event, it still raised her hackles.

She rounded the corner of Town Hall to find Frank Haynes pulling into the lot. She momentarily considered darting into the trees along the sidewalk and pretending she hadn't seen him. *For heaven's sake*, she scolded herself. *You're not in kindergarten. Act like a grownup. You offered to have lunch with him, so march on over there and ask if he's hungry.* If she were lucky, he'd already have eaten and would turn her down.

"Hello, Frank," she said as he retrieved his briefcase from the backseat. "I was hoping to run into you. I'd still like to take you to lunch."

Haynes looked startled and hesitated before responding.

He doesn't want to spend time with me any more than I want to spend time with him, Maggie realized. That's why he hasn't been around all week and got here so late today. His reluctance intrigued her. She pressed him again before he could reply. "Come on, if you've already eaten, you can keep me company. I was just going to walk over to Pete's for a quick bite."

Trapped, Haynes nodded. "Sure. And no, I haven't eaten. Sorry I haven't been back all week. I've been busy. But I could spare thirty minutes for a sandwich."

They made the short walk to Pete's Bistro in silence. Pete looked at Maggie quizzically when she asked for a table for two. After the unlikely pair had placed their orders, Haynes launched into a summary of his findings on the ground lease issue. Maggie held up a hand to interrupt him.

"That's terribly important and I know you've done an incredible amount of work to get to this point. I want to hear what you've uncovered, but not now. We've only got a few minutes to eat, and I'd like a break from thinking about all of this. I want to get to know you better."

Haynes drew a deep breath. "Not much to tell that you don't already know," he replied gruffly. "Born and raised here. Own a conglomerate of fast-food restaurants and other investments. Member of the town council. That's it."

"That's definitely not it," Maggie smiled. "You're the force behind Forever Friends, such a wonderful thing to have done for the community. Tell me about your pets. Have you always been a dog lover? Eve is my very first dog. I can't imagine how I'd ever live without a dog again."

Haynes smiled with genuine pleasure. *That's his soft spot,* Maggie realized.

"I rescued a stray when I was ten," he said. "A big mutt of indiscriminate pedigree. He was a grand dog—healthy as a horse—who died at the age of seventeen, when I was in college. I've had at least one dog ever since. Always strays. Pretty soon I was collecting them right and left. Decided I needed somewhere to take them. So I set up the shelter."

Maggie nodded. "What do you have now?"

"I've got a Border collie mix. She's a marvelous dog. I've also got an oversized calico cat. She adopted me about five years ago, just moved right in."

"I've heard cats do that sometimes. I'm surprised one hasn't adopted me. I found Eve in that snowstorm when she escaped from Forever Friends. I'd say she adopted me."

"And that's how you met your boyfriend? Dr. Allen?"

"That's how I met him, yes, but we're not seeing each other anymore. How about you? Have you been married? Do you have children?" she asked before he could inquire further about her relationship with John.

"I'm divorced; have been for a long time. We didn't have any children," he answered gruffly.

Maggie looked at him thoughtfully. "You've got to be one of the most eligible bachelors in town. Have you wanted to remarry? Or just having too much fun playing the field?"

Haynes blushed in spite of himself. "I don't have time to play the field. Between Haynes Enterprises, the town council, and Forever Friends, I don't have much free time."

Maggie smiled. "I know what you mean. With Westbury's financial crisis, being mayor is all-consuming. Besides, I'm not so sure I want to remarry. And I don't know how I'd meet someone, anyway."

She glanced at her watch. "We'd better get back," she said, signaling for the check. "This has been fun. I've enjoyed getting to know you better. Thanks for joining me."

Frank Haynes smiled and realized he couldn't remember the last time anyone had treated him to lunch.

Chapter 16

A week had gone by since the disquieting meeting with the mayor and Councilwoman Holmes, and the residents at Fairview Terraces were still abuzz with chatter about the predicament they found themselves in through no fault of their own. Many simply wanted to complain, but a surprising number wanted to help.

"You know what?" Gloria said as she sat back and observed the other diners. "There's more energy in this room than there's been in I can't remember when."

"That's one way of putting it," Glenn remarked.

"I'm serious. When was the last time you felt you were working on something that really mattered? It's been a long time for me. That baby blanket was a start, but nothing like this. Look around you. We've got people talking to each other who haven't spoken in years."

"You're right about that," Glenn said upon consideration. "Gives us all something to rally around. But I haven't seen anything productive come of all this. We don't have any direction."

"What do you want to happen?" she asked.

"I'd really like this whole problem to go away. For Councilman Haynes to straighten this out."

"Me, too," Gloria replied. "But I *would* like Fairview Terraces to set up a gift shop or craft co-op or something like that. I'd be willing to volunteer. I think it'd be fun."

Glenn smiled at her. "That blanket got you going, didn't it? I've seen your knitting basket by your chair when I pick you up."

"I have to admit that project brought lots of good things into my life," she replied. Glenn hoped she was referring to him. "What would you like to do if we need to raise money?"

"I've been giving that some thought. Renting the unused space would be the smart thing to do. It wouldn't inconvenience any of us. In fact, it could bring in customers for your gift shop."

"It just might," she replied

"But none of this is likely to happen. Nobody is doing anything concrete, as far as I can see."

"Then why don't you make it happen?" Gloria challenged. "You've got the business acumen and experience. You're well known and well liked around here. And you're always talking about how much time you have on your hands. So fill it with this project. Whether we wind up needing the money or not, it's a good idea."

Glenn scanned the dining room as he considered her suggestion. Maybe she was right. He'd always been a good organizer. He turned back to her and nodded slowly.

R

Chuck Delgado paced in his office above his liquor store. Noticing that he was sloshing whiskey out of his glass, he exchanged his glass for the bottle on his next pass by his desk. He might own a liquor store, but there was no point in wasting the stuff.

It had been months since Frank Haynes had requested—no, demanded—one of these clandestine meetings in the wee hours. After the indictment of that idiot William Wheeler, they had agreed to keep their distance. Go dark for a while. Let the trail grow cold. As far as he knew, no one had linked any of the councilmembers to the fraud and embezzlement that had almost bankrupted Westbury. What had stirred Haynes up?

Delgado started at the rap on the door downstairs. He pressed the entry button and settled himself behind his desk while Frank Haynes methodically climbed up the stairs to Delgado's lair.

Haynes paused inside the door, allowing his eyes to adjust to the low light. He scanned the sofa and chairs for a place to sit and decided to remain standing. "I see you haven't bothered to straighten anything up in here," he sneered. "I think those are the same hamburger wrappers that were on the floor the last time I was here."

"What do you care? You call me here to lecture me about cleaning my office? Go to hell," he slurred.

"No, Charles, that's not why I'm here."

I hate it when this bastard calls me Charles, Delgado thought.

The two men stared at each other.

"What's up?" Delgado finally asked, breaking the silence.

"The lease on Fairview Terraces. The increase in those phony fees. You're squeezing the town for the arrearage. Threatening foreclosure?" he snarled. "Are you nuts?"

"It's the landlord, Frankie. And it's all in writing. It's in the lease. Legit."

"I've done some digging. I know that the landlord is you and your greedy cronies. It may be in the lease, but do you want to put a spotlight on yourself? Now?"

"I know why you volunteered to straighten this mess out with the landlord. Those old geezers at Fairview are your constituents, and it's hard to get re-elected when the seniors are against you, ain't it, Frankie? You might have to campaign and spend some money like the rest of us."

"I'm working on their behalf, yes. This isn't just about re-election, you moron. We don't want anyone digging into anything even remotely related to us. Scanlon's interested in it, and they've got some professor from a university consulting on how to get Westbury out of the financial mess it's in. Lots of eyes are going to be all over this."

"Damn. That ain't good," Delgado replied, suddenly sounding a lot more sober.

"No, it's not. For now, Scanlon isn't suspicious of anything and is so busy that he's willing to let me handle this. I need to make this problem go away, fast, before anyone looks in this direction. Do you understand?"

"You want us to back off for you, Frankie?"

"That's exactly what I want you to do. But let me handle it all."

"You want to be the hero?"

"Exactly. I'll string this along a little bit. Have meetings at Fairview where we get people scared and all stirred up."

"Then you ride in on your white horse and save them? Beat down the big, bad landlord. The great, compassionate Frank Haynes?"

"Would that be so bad? It'll get me re-elected for sure. And we need as many of us to stay on the council as possible. We don't want any more nosey councilmembers like that bitch Tonya Holmes."

Delgado straightened in his chair. "Not a bad plan, Frankie."

"So you'll get the landlord to stop the foreclosure on the ground lease and quit trying to collect from Fairview Terraces?"

Delgado nodded slowly. "I can try. I'll make some calls in the morning."

Haynes stood.

"I'll do my best with the boys, Frankie," Delgado extended his hand.

Haynes reluctantly took it and shook on the agreement. He hurried down the stairs to his Mercedes sedan parked in the shadows and reached for the hand sanitizer as soon as he opened the glove compartment.

Chapter 17

Rain pelted the windows of the Town Hall conference room where the finance committee had convened to hash out solutions to the town's growing budget crisis. They were to be joined, for the first time, by Lyndon Upton. The professor's plane had been delayed, rendering him conspicuously absent from the meet-and-greet luncheon Maggie had arranged to introduce him to the committee. When Russell Isaac grumbled that he didn't have all day to wait for this "know-it-all professor," Maggie decided to start the meeting without him or Frank Haynes, who had been delayed as well.

Lesson one in politics, Maggie had learned, is to obtain support for any change in the status quo, no matter how deserving. Professor Upton's help had already proved invaluable. He'd suggested practical solutions they could easily implement. Considering that he was working for a stipend of one dollar, his collaboration should have been gratefully embraced. Instead, the committee had greeted the news of his involvement with tepid acquiescence.

Maggie turned toward the door as Professor Upton burst through, tossing his rain-soaked trench coat on a spare chair. "So sorry to be late," he said as he confidently circled the room, shaking hands and introducing himself. Maggie felt a chill settle on the already skeptical group.

"Let's see where we are, then," Professor Upton began as he pulled a chair up to the table.

Oh boy, Maggie thought. *I've got to rein him in, fast.* She intervened as Upton bent down to retrieve a stack of papers from his briefcase.

"Here's an agenda, Professor," she stated, sliding a paper down the table. "We're on item five, Fairview Terraces. I believe you're familiar with the issues?"

Upton was about to speak when Frank Haynes entered the room. "Oh, good," Maggie continued. "Let me introduce you to Councilman Frank Haynes."

"Nice to meet you, Professor," Haynes said, finding a place at the table.

Maggie continued. "Councilman Haynes has a lot of expertise in leased properties and has done a thorough analysis of the documents. He's been negotiating with the lessor. Councilman, would you like to report on your progress?"

Everyone turned to Haynes. Upton caught his eye and raised one brow.

Haynes scanned his notes and began. "The lessor has the right to an increase in our ground lease rent. His calculations are incorrect, however, and he's conceded that. We haven't come to a final agreement on the amount of the increase. I'm meeting with the lessor's attorney next week and hope to reach a final agreement then."

"So we'll need to raise the rent at Fairview?" Isaac asked.

"Of course we will," Chuck Delgado interrupted. "The citizens of this town can't subsidize those old folks."

Haynes let out an exasperated sigh. "Yes, we'll need to raise some revenue, Chuck. How we go about that is what this committee needs to decide. Raising rent isn't the only option. In fact, it's probably the worst idea."

"That's just because those old geezers are in your district, Frank," Delgado prodded. "You're worried about your re-election."

"There's no call for this sort of accusation, Councilman Delgado," Maggie interceded. "Councilman Haynes has worked long and hard to help us resolve this situation. He's doing a fine job for both his constituents and the town." She turned back to Haynes. "Were you finished?"

"No. Thanks, Mayor Martin," he replied, adopting her formality. "I expect the lessor will take a discounted payment for the past-due amount." A hint of pride tinged his voice. "We just have to finalize what that sum will be."

"That's just grand, Frank," Delgado snarled. "Beating up an honest landlord."

"Lay off him, Chuck," Isaac said. "I think you're doing a great job, Frank." He swiveled in his chair to face Haynes directly. "But I'm not sure where we're going to get any of this money."

Tonya Holmes raised her hand and Maggie nodded to her. "Mayor Martin and I met with residents at Fairview Terraces recently. They're full of good ideas to raise funds on an ongoing basis. With a bit of assistance from us, I think they'll be able to handle an increase in their sublease payments. Without raising rents for the residents."

"That's the point, Tonya," Delgado stated dismissively. "The town doesn't have money to give them."

"I'm not talking about monetary assistance, Councilman Delgado," she answered sharply. "Assistance with the permitting process for a gift shop or licensing for a farmers market. We can ease them through the red tape and bureaucracy at Town Hall."

Delgado shrugged and looked at his hands.

"She's right," Haynes interjected. "We can do all of those things. And a private donor might step forward to pay the past due amount."

Delgado's head snapped up. "Like you, Frankie?" he asked. "You're the only private donor we've got in these parts."

All eyes locked on Frank Haynes. He remained silent, sorting his notes.

Maggie cleared her throat. "Thank you again, Councilman Haynes, for your excellent work. We'll look forward to your next report after you meet with the lessor's attorney."

She rose and walked to stand behind Professor Upton's chair. "I'd like to formally introduce you to Professor Lyndon Upton. As you know, he specializes in municipal finance. I've worked with him professionally during my career as a forensic accountant. I have the highest regard for him and am thrilled that we were able to persuade him to assist us in getting our finances back on track. The fact that he's helping us for free is nothing short of remarkable."

She patted the back of Upton's chair. "The Town of Westbury will be forever in your debt."

Looking back to the assembled councilmembers, she resumed her address. "Professor Upton has joined us today to give us his preliminary conclusions. He's put together a comprehensive review for us, and has recommendations that I've found most encouraging."

This last remark snagged the committee's attention.

"Would you like me to pass these out?" Maggie asked, picking up the pile of neatly stapled copies stacked next to him.

Three and a half hours of deep concentration on the exhaustive analysis presented and suggested resolutions followed. By the time the committee adjourned, those in attendance had reached consensus on a proposal to present to the entire council.

Chapter 18

William Wheeler sat on the edge of his bunk, alone in his cell. He had at least an hour before his cellmate would return from the meeting with his lawyer. Enough time to do the deed.

He rolled the small capsule around in his fingers, feeling oddly exhilarated. With one small swallow, he'd join the ranks of other notorious people who'd chosen this way out: Eva Braun, Heinrich Himmler, Hermann Göring, and even Adolf Hitler (before firing his pistol into his right temple) had poisoned themselves with cyanide. Over 900 devotees of the Peoples Temple in Jonestown, Guyana. And countless fictional characters—from the novels of Agatha Christie to William Styron's *Sophie's Choice*—had followed this path.

He slipped the capsule carefully into his pocket. His cell was cold and damp; he'd spent his last night shivering in his cot. He straightened his blanket and pillow, indulging his almost-compulsive tendency to be neat.

He'd read that cyanide poisoning is often undetected, as detailed in a story about a forty-six-year-old lottery winner in Illinois who died the day after he collected his winnings. He'd fallen ill and was pronounced dead at the hospital, with death ruled a result of narrowing and hardening of the coronary arteries. Absent suspicious circumstances, the Chicago medical examiner didn't perform autopsies on people older than forty-five. When the dead man's relatives insisted that the case be reopened, the Cook County coroner's office confirmed he had been the victim of cyanide poisoning.

Given Wheeler's age and the fact that he was a smoker, he prayed fervently that they'd assume he'd had a heart attack. He didn't want to further shame or embarrass his family; he wanted his death to firmly and finally close this chapter from which there was no way out. The life insurance money would generously provide for them all—more than he would ever be able to do with a felony on his record.

He thought about how easy it had been to obtain the drug. One thing he'd learned in his time in jail—controlled substances were readily available. His supplier hadn't even been surprised at Wheeler's inquiry. As if anticipating Wheeler's request, he'd had the drug on hand.

Wheeler lay back on the cot, resting his head uneasily on the pillow. He reached into his pocket with a shaking hand and withdrew the means of his escape. He turned to the photos of his family, stuck to the wall beside his bunk, and drank them in. Tears streamed freely down his cheeks as he placed the tablet in his mouth and bit down. Death quickly silenced his final prayers.

Chapter 19

Mayor Maggie Martin and Councilmembers Tonya Holmes and Frank Haynes sat at the makeshift head table at the front of the community room at Fairview Terraces. The rain that had settled upon Westbury for the past two weeks had turned to sleet during the drive out to the center. Despite the inclement weather, the room was packed and uncomfortably warm. Not a good way to start what promised to be a long evening.

As Maggie scanned the crowd, she noted that almost everyone was equipped with a pen and paper. A couple she remembered seeing at the first meeting was seated in the center front, and the man held a three-ring binder open on his lap and appeared to be running his finger down a list on the first page.

Frank Haynes leaned over, interrupting her reverie. "It's time to start," he said softly. "These folks never arrive late."

"You're right," she replied as she got to her feet and moved to the podium.

"Ladies and gentlemen, residents of Fairview Terraces, thank you so much for turning out in this awful weather. I know that we delivered distressing news the last time we were here. You received it with a great deal of grace. I understand that you've been busy exploring options to raise money, and we want to hear all of your ideas."

She smiled across the crowd.

"We've been working on our end," she continued, "analyzing legal documents and negotiating with the lessor. Your councilman spearheaded these efforts, and I think you'll be pleased to learn what he's accomplished. Councilman Haynes," she said, extending her arm to him as she stepped aside.

Haynes approached the podium with papers in hand, and adjusted the microphone. The sooner he delivered the bad news and got out of there the better. They might come up with a plan to raise money going forward, but they'd all have to contribute to the past due payment. People on fixed incomes always hated that, but it couldn't be helped. He had tried, he really had. He'd finally convinced the lessor to take twenty cents on the dollar. However, that still left someone writing a big check, bigger than he cared to write himself.

"We've been able to negotiate an eighty percent discount, but that leaves a large arrearage." *Might as well just rip the Band-Aid off.* "That arrearage must be paid by all of you."

He glanced up, expecting to find an angry and agitated crowd with hands waving in the air to protest and criticize. Instead he found himself looking out at a sea of earnest and encouraging faces. He rocked back and contemplated the gathering. A tall man in the center of the front row raised his hand and asked if he could address the group.

He stood and turned to his audience. "I'm Glenn Vaughn. I think you all know me by now. I've been thinking about this since the last meeting. I've put together a business plan for a gift shop, a farmers market, and I've done a pro forma for the money we could make renting out this room plus a couple of others for community use," he said, holding up his notebook. "I think we can pay our way going forward, no problem. If the lessor could give us time to come up with the arrearage, we should be able to raise that, too. Do we need to pay it right away?" he asked, turning back to Haynes.

In spite of himself, Haynes liked this pragmatic, resourceful older man. He glanced at the clock on the back wall. Maybe it wouldn't hurt to hear these people out. He turned to his colleagues at the front table, then back to Glenn. "I think we'd all like to know more about your plans."

Haynes held Glenn's gaze. He surprised even himself with what he said next. "And if you've got a plan that would repay the arrearage over time, that's fine. I'll take care of it now and you can pay me back, when you can."

As Glenn started toward the podium, applause, starting as a trickle and ending in a crescendo, spread through the room. *I'll get re-elected yet,* Haynes thought. As he returned to his seat to make way for Glenn, he realized the lightness in his heart might not have anything to do with the prospect of an electorate voting him back into office.

R

A handful of residents stayed after the meeting to voice their concerns, but eventually the room emptied. Only Frank Haynes remained locked in conversation with the older gentleman who appeared to be the spokesman for the seniors interested in working toward a solution with the town officials. Maggie and Tonya collected their purses and signaled to Haynes. He nodded in acknowledgement.

Maggie followed Tonya out the door, pulling the collar of her coat up against the wind. Chief Thomas' car was pulled into the fire lane by the exit. He was out of his car and upon them before they could reach the side of his car.

"Chief Thomas," Maggie called. "What brings you here? Were you providing security detail for the meeting? Surely no one thought that was necessary?"

"No. Nothing of the sort. Something else's come up." He glanced at Tonya.

Tonya looked from the chief to Maggie and back again. "I'll say goodnight and leave you two to it," she said hastily, turning away.

"No. Don't go," Chief Thomas replied slowly. "You'll hear it soon enough. You may as well hear it from me."

Alarmed, both women faced the officer. Maggie nodded for him to continue.

"William Wheeler was found dead in his jail cell about four hours ago."

"What?" Maggie and Tonya gasped in unison.

"He was alone in his cell when he died, which would put it between three and four o'clock this afternoon. His cellmate returned to the cell around four and thought Haynes was asleep. No one realized he was dead until they tried to rouse him for dinner."

"He was in his early fifties, for heaven's sake," Maggie replied. "People that age don't just up and die. What happened?"

"We don't know yet. There aren't any signs of foul play. He wasn't hanging from a noose. He was lying in his cot, dead. The medical examiner will follow protocol and perform basic toxicology screening for opiates, cocaine, and carbon monoxide. If they come back negative, he probably had a heart attack."

"He was a chain smoker," Tonya said. "But he always seemed healthy to me."

"Heart disease is the silent killer," Chief Thomas murmured. Frank Haynes' exiting through the front door cut further discussion short.

"Frank," Maggie called. He turned in their direction and nodded as Chief Thomas signaled him to join them.

"What's up?" he asked. He listened intently as Chief Thomas repeated his report. "I don't know what to say," he finally managed to choke out. "I've known him all my life; we went to school together."

Maggie rested her hand on his arm. "I'm sorry, Frank, truly. You knew him better than the rest of us."

She turned to Chief Thomas. "How is his family taking it?"

"Pretty bad, as you can imagine. His son's devastated. He's been in trouble since Wheeler was arrested; this won't help matters."

"Where are they? I'd like to go to them. I know what it's like to lose your husband."

"They're at home. With all due respect, ma'am, I don't think she'll want to see you. You have her husband's old job after all."

"You're right. What was I thinking?"

"I'll go," Haynes interjected. "I've known Jackie as long as I've known William. Maybe I can help."

Chapter 20

Gloria was ready and waiting when she heard the familiar knock on her door just before dinner the day after the meeting with the bigwigs from town. It was overcast and gray, but the rain had subsided. She shrugged into her jacket in anticipation of their walk to the dining room and opened her door.

"Hello there, Mr. Fairview Terraces," she greeted him as she closed the door behind her. "I've been anxious all day to tell you how impressive you were at the meeting."

Glenn blushed. "I wasn't the only one who put thought into how we could save Fairview Terraces."

"No, but you were articulate and organized. Your ideas were well thought out. Everyone's been saying as much. And the mayor and councilmembers certainly thought so. That was plain as day."

"It did go rather well, didn't it," he admitted with pride.

"And you could have knocked me over with a feather when Councilman Haynes offered to loan us the arrearage. I must admit I'd pegged him all wrong. When he started to speak, I felt like he wanted to say what he came to say and get out of there."

"That's how I saw it, too," Glenn said. "But he was the one who wanted to hear more. He gave me his card and wrote his personal cell phone number on it in case we have any problems as we move forward. I think he's really concerned about us."

"He's a sharp businessman, from what I understand. You should take him up on his offer."

They entered the dining room and headed for their usual table by the windows. Halfway across the room, two couples sitting at a table for six motioned them over.

"We're sorry to intrude on your date," said a heavyset woman, with extra emphasis on the word *date*. "But we have questions about some of these ideas of Glenn's." The man to her right nodded vigorously. "Would you mind joining us?"

Glenn was about to object when Gloria responded. "We'd be delighted to. And you're not interrupting a date; we're just friends." Out of the corner of her eye, she noticed Glenn's shoulders sag. Or was she imagining that? "I'm sure you're going to find that Glenn has considered his proposals from every angle. If there's a problem, he's thought of a solution," she stated firmly.

The woman gave her a wan smile.

"And we'd love to hear *your* ideas for getting us out of this mess," Gloria added with a touch of malice.

"I'm sure you've put a lot of work into your proposals," interjected one of the men, directing the conversation toward Glenn. "We were most impressed with your presentation last night. We just want to hear more. Let's go through the line and get our food. Then we can settle in and talk."

R

Two hours later, after discussing and defending his ideas so intensely that he hardly had a chance to eat his meal, Glenn walked Gloria across the complex to her place.

"You look tired, Glenn," Gloria noted with concern. "You're not twenty anymore, you know."

Glenn smiled. "I'm fine. And believe me, I know I'm not twenty. I wouldn't want to be young again, would you?"

"Only if I could know then what I know now. Otherwise, no."

They continued in companionable silence.

"Seriously, Glenn. Don't let these folks exhaust you; don't let them use you up. What you're doing is wonderful and noble. And I know you're finding it very satisfying. Which is fine. But you need to set some boundaries. Maybe you should go out for meals for a while? Until this blows over."

Glenn stopped and turned to Gloria. "I'd miss your company, unless you went out with me," he said simply.

"That would really get tongues wagging in this gossipy old place!" she replied.

"Who cares what people say. Aren't we finally old enough to be beyond all that?" he asked.

"Not me, Glenn. We're just good friends and it rankles me that people are branding us as a couple. Doesn't it bother you?" she asked. "It never occurred to me that people would pay any attention to us," he replied. "I honestly never thought about it."

"Well, you might want to consider it if only for my sake," she replied as they reached her door. "I don't want to be the clichéd old widow pouncing on the recent widower. Now go on home and get a good night's sleep."

R

A good night's sleep was not in the cards for Glenn. He tossed and turned, replaying the earlier conversations with the other residents and thinking of the things he should've said. Gloria's statement that they were just good friends played loudest in his mind.

They *were* good friends, to be sure. He loved sharing the day-to-day bits with her, keeping someone up to speed on the mundane details of his life. And he valued her opinions and observations. But he was increasingly aware that his feelings ran deeper. Was it possible, at this age and stage of his life, that he was falling in love again?

He pushed himself out of bed and padded to his favorite leather chair by the window, the one where he read poetry every morning. He picked up a pen and pad and began another note to Gloria.

Was he insane to be proposing this? Would he ruin their friendship which had brought him so much peace and pleasure in recent weeks? Would his overture turn their companionship into an awkward mess for both of them?

He paused, pulling aside the curtain to gaze out at the dark, cloud-filled sky. He'd never been a coward, and he wasn't going to act like one now.

He returned to his paper and began.

R

Gloria slept late the next morning and might have stayed in bed until noon had Tabitha not insisted on her breakfast. Scrounging up a peanut butter and jelly sandwich for lunch, she opened her door to retrieve the paper. Sitting beside it on her doormat was a small bouquet of mums arranged with ribbons and berries in a hollowed-out pumpkin accompanied by an envelope addressed in Glenn's now-familiar hand.

She brought the offerings inside and found a spot for the flowers on her kitchen island. She propped the card against the pumpkin and stared at it, not sure if she wanted to read it or not. She knew that her remarks about their gossipy neighbors had surprised Glenn. Why in the world had she mentioned that to him? She loved things just as they were and would be heartbroken if they discontinued their daily ritual of shared meals. What did it really matter what other people thought? Nothing. So why did she still care about their opinion of her?

Gloria reached for the envelope, turned it over in her hands, and then quickly set it back down. She would read it before he called for her at dinnertime, but she wanted to collect herself first.

An hour later, after dressing and wrangling her unruly hair into a more-or-less presentable bun, she summoned the courage to confront the note. What she read both delighted and confused her:

My dearest Gloria,

You are correct when you say that we are good friends. In fact, I look upon you as one of the best friends I have ever had in this life. Since I've been alive almost eighty years, that's saying something. I've come to realize over these last few weeks that my feelings have grown beyond friendship. After Nancy died, I never expected—or even wanted—to feel this way again. Although our outsides may show some wear and tear, our insides tend to remain untouched by time. I'm still a young man in my mind. And I'm falling for you. Head over heels. After much thought—I've been up most of the night—I would like permission to court you. Come out in the open with this thing. Frankly, I don't give a damn (pardon my French) what anyone else thinks.

I know that you may not feel the same way about me. The hardest part about writing this note is that I might damage our friendship. That's the last thing I want. I'm writing this to you instead of telling you in person, which I'd very much like to do, so that I don't put you on the spot. If you don't return my feelings, or if you don't want to pursue anything beyond friendship, then please just ignore this note. No need to respond. If I don't hear anything from you, we'll continue on as friends, like before, and I'll consider myself blessed.

If you'd be my gal, I'd be honored.

Yours faithfully,
Glenn

R

Gloria clutched the note, which she'd read at least a dozen times, with shaking hands. She hadn't entertained the idea of a suitor in decades. She was in her mid-eighties. Was this the time to risk her heart on such an unlikely romance? How did she really feel about him? It wouldn't be fair to start down this path if she couldn't return his affection. And what about their age difference? She was almost eight years older than Glenn. Although she was in good health, that could change on a dime. She'd just watched him care for Nancy during her long illness; she didn't want him to go through that again with her.

Gloria wandered to her bedroom and sank slowly to the edge of her bed. After yet another read, she returned the note to its envelope and placed it carefully on her nightstand. He would be here in ten minutes to pick her up for dinner. She needed time to decide. For now, she'd remain silent and he'd have to accept her continued friendship while she became sure, in her heart, of her answer.

R

On the other side of Fairview Terraces, Glenn Vaughn fidgeted like a schoolboy fearing he'd be caught passing a note to a girl. Which, of course, was exactly what he had done. He had felt good about the whole idea at seven thirty this morning when he had finally thrown on some clothes, headed to the supermarket to buy flowers, and placed the bouquet and note by Gloria's door. He had even felt pleased with himself when he returned home and stretched out in his recliner for a morning nap following a sleepless night.

Upon waking in midafternoon, however, he was filled with misgivings. What in the world had he done? He didn't doubt his feelings for Gloria, but why had he risked their friendship by trying to change things? Wasn't the status quo enough? Why had he been in such an all-fired hurry? They weren't getting any younger, that was true. But why was he trying to rush into something new? What they had was good enough for him.

He showered and shaved, nicking himself twice. *Blast!* He tried to settle into a Sudoku puzzle, but could not force himself to concentrate. He puttered around his home office until it was finally time to walk over to Gloria's. He checked his reflection in the mirror by his front door before he left. *Get hold of yourself,* he admonished. *You're being a ridiculous old fool. The die is cast; now it's time to see what happens.*

He knocked on her door at their usual time, to his ears a little too loudly. She was on the phone when she opened the door. Smiling at him and holding up her hand, she gestured with her thumb and index finger that she would only be a moment longer. Since she hadn't motioned for him to come inside, Glenn waited patiently on her doorstep.

"Yes, yes, that's right," he overheard her say sweetly to the person on the other end of the line. "Okay, I've got to go now." She paused to listen then stated firmly, "I really must get going, my friend is here."

Friend, he thought. He felt himself droop.

"We'll talk tomorrow. Bye now," Gloria said as she hung up and rushed through the door. "Honestly," she huffed as they set off for the dining hall. "You just cannot get some people off the phone. They don't take the hint. Drives me crazy.

"How are you?" she asked, glancing up at him.

"Just fine, couldn't be better," he said, forcing his familiar reply. He had fervently hoped that she would open her door and tell him immediately that she felt the same way about him. He had worked out several such scenarios, all with happily-ever-after endings. Still, she was here and friendly, and was walking to dinner with him as before. He worried briefly that she might not have received his flowers and note before dismissing the fear as ridiculous.

Gloria smiled at him. "Good to hear it. I'd be better if I hadn't spent all afternoon listening to my cousin drone on and on about her family and all of their problems. Honestly, they could be on one of those reality television shows. I'm not proud to admit they're relatives."

Glenn cocked an eyebrow and gave her a quizzical glance. Apparently, they were to remain as friends. He'd have to get over his disappointment and be grateful for what he had.

"Sounds pretty titillating. Care to elaborate?" he asked.

Gloria occupied the entire mealtime with a detailed description of her cousin's lineage, their shared "people," and a thorough cataloging of her cousin's many relationships. Glenn couldn't keep it all straight and soon stopped trying. Gloria was on a roll, and he only needed to nod or grunt knowingly from time to time. She finally turned to Glenn.

"So? What do you think I should tell her?" she asked the ultimate, open-ended question.

Glenn hadn't focused on the details and was caught short. He didn't want to appear uninterested in Gloria's family, so he answered tentatively, "What do the kids say these days? 'She sounds like a hot mess!'"

To his relief, Gloria laughed. "That's an understatement, for sure. I'd love to say that. I'm going to tell her to give her kids a big, life-changing gift—the gift of financial independence. Get them off the payroll, for heaven's sake. They're in their forties and fifties now. It's way past time." She looked expectantly at Glenn.

Emboldened, he responded, "Absolutely. She's doing them no favor by continuing to support them. They'll figure things out. And gain some pride and self-respect in the process. There's no reason she should be helping to support them."

"Good. I'm glad you agree," she replied. "I promised I'd call her tomorrow. I'll tell her that I've discussed this with you."

"Does she even know who I am?" he asked as he helped her with her jacket.

"Of course she does," Gloria said, as they walked back to her place. "I've told her all about you."

Glenn's step lightened. He hoped that Gloria would elaborate, but she remained silent. They reached her door and Glenn stood quietly as she unlocked it. "Goodnight, then," he said with a sigh, turning to retreat to his house. Gloria reached out and touched his elbow.

"Before you go, Glenn," she said gently, "I want you to know that I was deeply moved by your note and that I'm thinking about what you asked. I'm not being coy. I value your friendship too much for that. I just need time to consider your offer—carefully. Do you understand?" she asked, with a soft, inquisitive look.

He met and held her gaze. "Indeed I do, Gloria. I meant every word of that note. I'm in no rush. Take your time. I'm content with that," he assured her as he rested his hand over hers and held it briefly.

Gloria nodded and let out a sigh of relief.

With renewed hope, Glenn turned toward home.

R

Gloria shifted the phone from one ear to the other. Her cousin had called every day for the past week. The woman just wore her out. The voice on the other end stopped abruptly.

"Gloria. Are you all right?"

"Yes, fine. I've had a lot on my mind recently."

"That's a first. I've never known everything *not* to be perfect in your world."

Then you haven't been paying attention, Gloria thought. *I was a widow with nine children—how perfect could that have been?* She kept these feelings to herself and said, "There's turmoil about the leases here. And Glenn wants to be my boyfriend, if you can believe that."

The other woman let out a low whistle. "Why didn't you say so? That's big stuff."

"I know," Gloria replied. "The lease will get worked out, I'm not really worried about that. It's Glenn. I'm not sure what to do."

"I can tell you one thing. You're crazy about him."

Gloria laughed. "Why in the world do you say that?" she asked.

"You talk about him every time I call. I can't remember you doing that with anyone else. Ever."

"That's just because we've become such good friends."

"Nonsense. There's something different in your voice when you talk about him. You gush. Takes seventy years off your life. Truth be told, I thought you were already going together."

"I really do care for him," Gloria conceded. "Don't you think it's sort of ridiculous for us to start a romance at our ages? Aren't we past all that?"

"Evidently not," she replied. "And a good thing, too. I've hoped for—prayed for—this for years. Gloria, if you can live out the rest of your days in love with a good, kind man like Glenn, you'd be crazy not to."

"You really think so? This is such foreign territory for me."

"I do. Quit sitting on the fence. Let him know, okay?"

Gloria paused. "You're right. I've got to go. I need to make myself presentable before dinner."

R

Glenn tapped on Gloria's door as usual. It had been a week since he made his overture to her. Other than that initial response, he had heard nothing more. Disappointed, he was resigning himself to the fact that they would just remain friends. At this point in his life, he knew he was lucky to have that.

Gloria stepped across her threshold and he caught a whiff of a familiar heady fragrance. He couldn't put his finger on exactly what it was, but he liked it. "Whatever perfume you're wearing smells nice," he remarked.

Gloria beamed. "Glad you approve. I always like putting on scent when I go out on a date," she replied as she slipped her hand in his.

Glenn stopped and turned to her. Their eyes met and they stood quietly as the happy realization washed over Glenn. His smile mirrored hers. He brought her hand to his lips and brushed it with a gentle kiss.

Hand-in-hand, they proceeded to dinner.

Chapter 21

Maggie strode through the lobby of Town Hall an hour before the town's administrative departments opened. Given the bad press she had been barraged with recently, she liked to get to her office before the building filled with constituents who had questions or—as was happening more and more frequently—wanted to give her a piece of their mind. She noted the tall man lingering outside of the juvenile court department and was surprised when she got close enough to identify him as the activist from Fairview Terraces. *Glenn something, wasn't it?* If she was going to be a politician, she'd have to get better at remembering names, she chastised herself.

She approached him, holding out her hand. "Good morning. I didn't expect to see you here this early in the morning. Is something scheduled concerning Fairview?"

"Mayor Martin," he said, shaking her hand warmly. "Glenn Vaughn. Nice to see you again. No. I'm not here on Terraces business. I'm hoping to meet with one of the juvenile court case workers."

"Oh … I see," Maggie said, attempting to conceal her bewilderment.

"I'm a mentor in the court-ordered diversion program, and the boy I'm working with is having a very difficult time."

Maggie regarded him thoughtfully. How many people at his age had the energy and willingness to work with a troubled young person? Glenn Vaughn was gaining in her estimation at every turn. "That's admirable, Mr. Vaughn. The juvenile court doesn't open until eight. Is there anything I can do to help?"

Glenn shook his head. "I was so anxious to talk to somebody that I jumped the gun. Maybe you can point me to the coffee machine?"

Maggie smiled. "I'll do better than that. Ride the elevator upstairs with me, and I'll make us coffee in my office."

"You don't have to do that; I don't want to be a bother."

"Nonsense. I'm making a pot for myself, anyway. Come on," she insisted, steering him to the bank of elevators.

"You know," he said as they stepped onto her floor, "maybe you can help me. This boy is a good kid—very intelligent. His life has been turned upside down through no fault of his own. He feels betrayed by the person he looked up to most, and now that person has died. He's feeling rudderless, and he's acting out in destructive ways. I want to break that cycle before he gets himself in too deep."

Maggie nodded. "William Wheeler's son?" she asked.

"That's supposed to be confidential," Glenn said. "But, yes."

"I've heard that he's having a terrible time with all of this. Who can blame him? It's a lot for a thirteen-year-old to handle. What do you have in mind?"

"He needs a project of some sort; something active to do with his mind and his energy. I'm supposed to be leading him through a workbook of lessons. It's a terrific tool, but studying a workbook won't help him now. He's smart enough to answer all the questions correctly and get back to making mischief or worse. I want him involved with others less fortunate than himself—he needs to have someone depending on him. Something to care about. I think he'll rise to the occasion."

"How do you think he'd like to work with stray animals at a shelter?"

A smile slowly erased the worry from Glenn's brow. "I think that just might be the ticket."

"Did you know that Frank Haynes is the founder of Forever Friends? And, of course, he knows David Wheeler. Ask him if the boy can volunteer at the shelter."

Chapter 22

Maggie made her way through her back door, wrangling her purse on her shoulder, her briefcase on her arm, and a bag from the supermarket in her hands. Raindrops trailed across the tile floor as she shuffled her way to the kitchen island and deposited the load in a jumbled heap on the counter. It was good to be home early for a change. The caustic email she'd received midafternoon from yet another disgruntled pensioner had convinced her that she needed to take a break. If he wanted to start a movement to get her impeached, more power to him.

She instinctively bent down to pet the ever-effusive Eve, but her dog was nowhere to be found. Maggie abandoned her groceries and walked to the dining room.

"Eve? *Eve?*" she called. "Mommy's home!"

Her pace quickened and her voice became a shrill cry as she rushed through Rosemont. Eve had never failed to greet her return home with unrestrained affection.

Maggie's panic mounted as she turned to the stairway that swept up the side of the living room. She started climbing, taking the stairs two at a time, when she heard the plaintive whine. *From the library?* She had already looked there.

Maggie tore into the room. This time she noticed a bulge under the long drapery by the French doors. She pulled the fabric aside and fell to her knees. Eve lay on her side, eyes wide and scared. She lifted her head a fraction and wagged her tail infinitesimally.

"Oh, sweetheart! What's happened to you?" Maggie whispered softly as fear wedged into her chest. "No, don't try to move." She stemmed her tears as she gently stroked her beloved companion. "We've got to get you to the doctor."

Maggie rose to retrieve a towel to use as a stretcher. Eve dutifully tried to follow her master. "No," Maggie commanded a bit too shrilly. "You stay. I'll be right back." Her tone was firm and Eve obeyed.

After placing Eve gently onto a towel and carefully carrying her to the car, Maggie set off for Westbury Animal Hospital and the capable hands of Dr. John Allen, DVM. Seeing John might be awkward. She had wondered if she should find a new veterinarian following their breakup, but right now her only concern was getting the best care for Eve. Without question, that would be John.

Maggie pulled into the parking lot shortly before closing. She didn't have an appointment, but she knew John would see them. She gathered Eve into her arms and was grateful when another pet owner held the door for her. She rushed to the counter. The receptionist was checking out a patient. Maggie hailed a technician.

"Eve was in this terrible state when I got home a few minutes ago. I don't know what's happened to her, but something's terribly wrong."

"Dr. Allen just left; there's nothing we can do for you here," he said, looking at the miserable creature lying in Maggie's arms. "She definitely needs to be seen right away. There's an emergency animal hospital about thirty minutes from here. Take her there. I'll give you directions."

"No. That won't do. She needs help before then." She reached into her purse, pulled out her phone, dialed John's cell phone, talking right over his greeting when he picked up.

"Eve's terribly sick. I'm here at your office. Please, please, John, come back. I'm so scared. I don't think she'll make it to the emergency hospital."

Maggie looked at the technician. "Your technician is shaking his head," she choked out the words. "He thinks I'm right."

Maggie put her head in her hands and listened.

"He's coming back, isn't he?" the technician asked.

Maggie nodded. He disappeared into an examining room with Eve while Maggie sat in the reception area for what seemed like an eternity.

R

Waiting in a hospital for news of a loved one—human or not—was a lonely experience. She quietly prayed for her sweet companion. The animal that had adopted her upon her arrival those months ago and had, in truth, turned Maggie's life in a new direction. Introduced her to Dr. John Allen. Brought her comfort as she started over.

A door finally opened and John emerged looking tired and serious. Maggie steeled herself for the worst. He took a seat on the bench next to her. "She's resting comfortably. I believe she's going to be fine, but we'll need to keep her here for a few days for observation. And when she goes home, she'll need a long course of antibiotics."

Maggie released the breath she had been holding. She tried to talk but found herself sobbing instead.

John reached over and took her hand. "I think she'll be fine in a few days," he reiterated.

"What happened to her?" Maggie choked.

"Looks like she was bitten by a spider and it got infected. The infection had taken hold."

"I should have noticed," Maggie cut in. "I've been so negligent." She was crying harder now.

"That's not true," John quickly reassured her. "There really aren't any signs that you could have seen. It comes on fast. Was she eating and acting normally?"

Maggie nodded.

"Then you couldn't have known. Don't beat yourself up over this."

She nodded again.

"Eve knows you love her," he continued gently.

Maggie lifted her eyes to his and attempted a smile.

"Infections in animals are like infections in people these days—they can be resistant to antibiotics. We'll keep her here until we're sure that the antibiotic is working. Then we'll send her home." He squeezed her hand before he let go.

R

Maggie stepped through the back door at Rosemont and hung her purse on its usual peg by the door. She trudged to the laundry room and tossed the towel she had used as a makeshift stretcher into the hamper.

Exhaustion and hunger were both vying for her attention. She leaned into her open refrigerator, looking for something appealing. Nothing presented itself. She retrieved an egg and decided to fix an egg sandwich. Her bread looked dubious, so she settled for a scrambled egg and saltines. Halfway through the meal, she chucked it down the disposal.

The sterility of the house without Eve's companionship settled on her like a shroud. Maggie took the stairs to her room slowly. *She's going to be fine,* she repeated to herself. *John's got her; she'll be fine.*

R

Maggie was hard at work at her desk at Town Hall when her cell phone rang. The caller ID showed Westbury Animal Hospital. She punched the answer button and brought the phone to her ear, expecting to hear the technician who had called her daily with positive reports about Eve's progress. Her eyes widened when she heard Dr. John Allen say, "Maggie. It's John."

She smiled. "I recognize your voice, John."

He hesitated, and then continued. "Eve's all set to come home. She's done very well. You'll have to give her antibiotics for another week, but that's all. She's fine."

"Oh, John, that's such great news! You can't believe how much I've missed her. I hate being at Rosemont without Eve. When can I pick her up?"

"Anytime today. Just stop in and the technician will go over her medication with you."

"So I won't be seeing you?" Maggie asked, unable to hide her disappointment.

"No, you don't need an appointment."

Did his voice suddenly seem a bit brighter or was she imagining that?

"Okay. Well, then," she stammered. "John, thank you so much for coming back to the clinic to see Eve and for taking such good care of her. I'm convinced she wouldn't have made it without you."

John smiled. He didn't tell her that he didn't think she would have made it either. He had spent that first night at the clinic with Eve when things had been touch and go. Her fever, left untreated, would have killed her. John simply replied, "You might be right. The main thing is, she's fine now."

He hesitated and Maggie waited, hoping he would continue. John finally drew a breath and said, "Call if she has any problems. Goodbye, Maggie."

Chapter 23

Maggie leapt out of bed the next morning at the first buzz of her alarm. Eve didn't seem anxious to do the same, and Maggie rushed to her side. She stroked the shaggy head gently as Eve thumped her tail against the bed and slowly stretched. Eyes now bright, she jumped down and circled. "Just tired from being in the hospital?" she asked as they headed downstairs. "Well, I didn't sleep well without you, either."

Maggie let Eve out into garden while she retrieved her paper. A cold blustery day had been anticipated, but the weather was calm now. It being Saturday, she didn't have to rush out the door. She and Frank Haynes had planned to discuss the Fairview Terraces matter, but they weren't due to meet until midmorning. She'd throw on some old clothes, feed Eve, and take her for a walk. Maybe even do some yard work if the weather held.

By the time she returned to the kitchen, leash in hand, Eve was fast asleep in her basket by the breakfast nook. Maggie stood quietly and watched the steady rise and fall of her chest, broken by the occasional deep sigh and snuggle into her blanket. *She deserves this rest,* Maggie thought. *I'll leave her be.*

Maggie stepped outside; an icy wind swept her hair from her face. She exhaled and her breath crystallized, hanging expectantly in the air. Winterizing her garden could wait. The weather might be better later that afternoon. Or tomorrow. She retreated to the warmth of Rosemont.

She had at least two hours before she needed to get ready to meet Haynes. She headed upstairs, intending to find her winter boots, when her eyes fell on the small, recessed door to the third floor and the attic beyond. Sam Torres, her faithful handyman, had taken her up to the attic shortly after she had moved in, but she hadn't been up there since.

She drifted over to the door and turned the knob. Nothing. She gave it a solid push, but it still wouldn't yield. Determined, she leaned into and shoved the door until it finally gave way. A cold draft hit Maggie; she'd have to remind Sam to replace the seals on the windows.

She had a vague memory of the attic being loaded with the discarded treasures belonging to prior occupants of Rosemont, remnants of lives well lived in days gone by. *I'll just go upstairs for a few minutes,* she told herself. *Just to take another look around and get an idea of what's up there.* That way she'd know if it was all junk that some overly thrifty owner hadn't been able to part with—cooking utensils and discarded furniture, and old records and papers—or whether there might be something of value, either historical or monetary.

She found a flashlight in the drawer of the secretary in the upper hallway and cautiously ascended the steep stairs. At the top, she flipped the switch for the bare bulbs positioned erratically throughout the space. Their scant illumination provided a theatrical effect, as if items within the pools of light were on stage while those in the shadows observed from the audience.

Maggie edged her way cautiously through the clutter on the front side of the house along a pathway that someone had cleared long ago. Her sneakers left footprints on the dusty floor. The grimy windows rattled in the wind. She shivered. *This feels like the point in a movie when the heroine is creeping along and the audience is mentally shouting "You idiot! Get out of there! Run away!"* she mused.

She carefully trained her flashlight around the room, making sure she was alone, even though she felt foolish for doing so. As the beam of her flashlight rounded the final corner, Maggie caught a quick flash of something metallic. She slowly retraced the light's trajectory and was about to give up when she found the object she sought. There was definitely something shiny in the far corner.

Making her way to it would be quite a chore. She really should wait until Sam was there to help her, she told herself reasonably as she began gingerly picking her way across the detritus, sliding aside a stack of boxes and crawling over an old trunk that proved too heavy to move. Curiosity had always gotten the better of her.

Maggie's jeans were covered with dust when she reached the spot where she had seen the reflection. There, hidden by an old tarp, was a stately mahogany secretary with an intricate filigree key protruding from its lock. The key must have caught the light. This piece alone would be worth a tidy sum. Excited, she propped her flashlight on a nearby box and worked the key until the lock finally yielded and the door swung open.

She gasped and stood in stunned silence. Shelves crammed full of silver serving pieces—pitchers and urns, gravy boats and trays, and an entire row of champagne buckets. Her hand trembled as she carefully dislodged a small creamer near the front, careful not to cause the contents of the entire shelf to tumble to the floor.

She reached for her flashlight and examined the piece. The stamp was unmistakable; this was solid sterling. For the second time since her arrival at Rosemont, the discovery of a treasure left Maggie feeling faint. She had just stumbled upon a collection of vintage and highly collectible silver. All of it was badly tarnished. She'd have to consult an expert before she attempted to clean any of it, she thought as she began to cautiously pull additional items from the cabinet.

Finally checking her watch, Maggie realized that she'd lost track of time and was running late if she was going to get herself pulled together to meet Haynes. The wind, which had picked up, howled around the dormers. She'd much rather stay safely inside and continue exploring her marvelous attic. She'd call him and cancel, she decided.

Maggie reached for her phone, then realized it wasn't in her pocket. She must have left it in her bedroom. She'd have to run down to get it. She reluctantly pulled herself away and attempted to retrace her steps, this time paying more attention to the items in her path. What other gems might be laying under these layers of dust and debris?

She reached the top of the stairs just as a blast of wind hit the house, forcing a draft up the stairway. The door at the bottom slammed shut with a resounding thwack. Maggie glanced nervously over her shoulder then carefully made her way downstairs, fighting the urge to race down as if the bogeyman was at her heels. Suddenly she noticed that the door was missing a knob on the inside. The skin at the back of her neck began to tingle. She shoved her hair behind her ears and resolutely reached into the opening where the knob should have been. Her attempt to turn the outside knob using the exposed mechanism failed. With mounting panic, she yanked and pulled at the door, but it wouldn't budge. No two ways about it, Maggie was locked in her attic. All of a sudden, it didn't seem like such a marvelous attic. And she didn't have a phone.

Maggie kicked at the door savagely, but the solid construction of the old house held firm. Startled by the racket, Eve began to bark downstairs. Maggie slumped onto the bottom step and sagged against the banister.

She knew that she wouldn't die in this attic; she had enough appointments and commitments on her schedule that someone would notice her absence and come looking for her when she couldn't be reached. Frank Haynes might even raise a hue and cry when she didn't show up this morning. She'd be out by dinnertime—tomorrow afternoon at the latest. Sam and Joan would worry when she wasn't next to them in the pew at church. But what about Eve? She would become increasingly agitated as it got dark. And she'd miss the doses of her medicines. Would that set her back? *How could I be so stupid?* Maggie berated herself.

She hoisted herself to her feet and returned to the attic. If she was going to be here for a while, she should clear a space to sit near one of the front windows. She needed to be able to hail any vehicle that might approach on the driveway below.

With the howling wind as her only companion, she tested the locks on the windows along the front and found that the third one unlocked easily and the pulley operating the window was intact. With a concerted effort, Maggie managed to push the lower pane open six inches from the sash. *Enough to shout through,* Maggie thought with satisfaction.

She considered leaving the window open so that she could better hear anyone outside, but quickly abandoned the idea. Although it wasn't raining—yet—the wind was cold. Maggie pulled the sleeves down on her thermal shirt. For the first time, she noticed how chilly it was in the attic. She'd remain close to the window and stay on lookout duty.

She glanced wistfully over her shoulder at the collection of silver in the corner. Only moments ago she had happily contemplated spending the afternoon sorting through it all. The idea still held a lot of appeal, and she started in that direction. Before she was halfway to her destination, she realized that she wouldn't be able to quickly dart back and forth to the window. She'd also need to use her flashlight and she had no idea how fresh the batteries were. Being stuck all night in this inhospitable space was a possibility. She didn't want to be without a working flashlight.

Maggie spent the next hour making short forays into the attic and returning to the window every few minutes. She planned to open the window as soon as she spotted a car and wave her shirt like a surrender flag.

By four o'clock, she had finished sorting and stacking the boxes closest to the window. She'd found tax returns and household ledgers from the 1920s and 1930s. They would be interesting to go through when she wasn't imprisoned in a cold, dark, creepy attic. The set of ancient golf clubs and the decrepit croquet set would be discarded.

The light began to fade as an early dusk descended on the cloudy day, and Maggie reluctantly abandoned her efforts to restore order to her attic. She set her sights on an overstuffed leather armchair in the middle of the room and shoved aside a stack of banker's boxes, knocking the lid off the top box and sending file folders tumbling to the floor. She moaned and glanced in their direction. Based upon their cleanliness, they looked to be of recent origin. She'd have to go through them some other time. She tidied them into a stack, not noticing the thin file folder labeled *F.H./Rosemont* that had slipped to the floor.

Maggie wrestled the overstuffed leather chair to the window. If she sat just right, she could avoid the springs poking through the seat cushion. She focused her attention on the driveway and tried to summon up something productive to think about. Maybe she'd benefit from some quiet time to consider the myriad of problems she faced as the mayor of Westbury. The only thing she could think about, however, was how miserable and afraid she was. The tears she had been fighting broke free.

She quickly stood and stamped her feet for warmth. *This is ridiculous,* she chided herself. *I'm safer and more comfortable in this attic than ninety percent of the world's population is in their homes. Why am I feeling sorry for myself?* The niggling worry at the back of her mind surfaced—what if no one came for her? Then she wasn't so safe, was she?

She drew a calming breath and told herself to focus. Someone would come looking for her on Sunday. At this point in the afternoon, she had to accept that Frank Haynes hadn't been alarmed by her absence. He was probably annoyed that she stood him up for their meeting, but he wasn't worried about her. If he had been, someone would have been here before now. She would have heard them, wouldn't she? No one was looking for her, but someone would be tomorrow. The most sensible thing was to stay put and wait. Still, she'd better come up with a plan B—just in case no one came on Sunday afternoon.

Maggie pressed her forehead to the windowpane. She was on the third floor and the first two floors had high ceilings. She calculated that she was at least thirty feet from the grassy area below. *Thank God, this window is over grass and not the driveway,* she observed. Dropping this far would be fatal, she knew. She'd have to tie sheets or clothing together to make a ladder to climb down. *There must be old linens and clothing up here,* she thought as she glanced at the shadowy attic. *Maybe even a rope.* She'd have to use the skills she had taught her daughter's Girl Scout troop when she was their leader. Still, they'd never really used them, had they? Never really tried them out. It would be scary and dangerous to climb down a makeshift ladder from this height.

She might have to. *Tomorrow,* she decided. She didn't have any water with her, so she wouldn't be able to hold out for a second night. If no one came for her by two o'clock, that would mean that Sam and Joan weren't concerned and no one would arrive to save her. She'd have to save herself. As soon as it was light in the morning, she'd search for materials and make her ladder.

She was turning away from the window to settle into the chair when a flash through the trees below caught her attention. She stood; her eyes riveted on the driveway as a late-model Mercedes sedan emerged from the trees and slowly approached Rosemont. Maggie tore off her shirt and threw open the window in a single movement. She screamed and waved her shirt through the small opening as Frank Haynes emerged from his car, a large envelop in hand.

Haynes looked right and left, unsure where the commotion was coming from. Maggie drew a deep breath and yelled, "Up here, Frank! Frank, up here!"

Haynes tilted his head back and quickly brought his hand up to acknowledge that he'd seen her. He stepped forward and cupped his mouth with his hands.

"Maggie, is that you?"

She withdrew her hand from the window and pressed her face to the opening. Fighting to control tears of relief, she struggled to make herself heard over the wind.

"Yes. I'm locked in the attic. Can you get in and let me out?"

"Are any of the doors or windows unlocked?" he yelled in reply.

"I don't think so. Maybe the kitchen door. Windows are all locked," she shouted.

Haynes turned to walk to the back of the house.

"Wait. There's a key hidden in the flower pot to the right of the garage door."

He nodded vigorously to signal that he understood and disappeared around the side of the house.

Maggie shoved herself into her shirt and slammed the window shut. She grabbed the flashlight and flew down the stairs at breakneck pace. Eve suddenly started barking wildly, and just as quickly quieted. *He must be petting her,* she realized with a surge of tenderness. Within moments, she heard his rapid steps on the stairs.

R

John Allen decided it was time to wrap it up for the week. He'd had a busy Saturday, as usual. Clinic hours had been over more than ninety minutes ago and his last technician had just left. He had his favorite college football game recorded on his DVR. He'd pick up a bucket of chicken on the way home and eat in front of the TV.

Now that Eve was back home, they had no dogs overnighting at the clinic. He sighed. Eve had been touch and go that first night. Thankfully, she'd pulled through. As usual, he made his rounds to check that all of the doors were locked. On his way through the waiting room, his foot connected with a prescription bottle and it skidded across the floor, pills rattling inside. He switched on the lights and found the culprit. *Someone dropped their pet's medications on their way out,* he mused. If it were something important, he'd have to call the pet owner.

He checked the label; it was an antibiotic for Eve. She couldn't go the weekend without it. He still knew Maggie's number by heart and reached for his cell phone. In spite of himself, a smile crept across his face as he waited for her to pick up. When his call went to her voicemail, he intended to leave a message directing her to a box around back where he would leave the prescription for her to pick up. Instead he heard himself telling her that he would stop by Rosemont and bring it to her. He picked up the prescription bottle and headed out the back door.

John's pulse quickened as he made the familiar drive to Rosemont. He had to admit he missed Maggie terribly. He was trying to distance himself from her, but she continued to dominate his thoughts. Maybe this lost prescription was a sign. Maybe fate was throwing them together. Maybe he should give it another try. He stepped on the accelerator.

He rounded the corner and emerged from the trees to find Rosemont silhouetted against the late afternoon sky. A lone car was parked in front and all of the lights were out except for one on the upstairs landing. As John pulled up to the front door, he recognized the familiar Mercedes sedan. He sat in stunned silence as his imagination took him places he didn't want to go. The house was silent; it was obvious that Maggie and Haynes were alone. On the second floor. His stomach lurched and his mouth went dry.

He wanted nothing more than to get away from there. His dedication as a doctor forced him to quietly get out of his car and leave the bottle by the front door. He'd send Maggie a text message that the medication had been delivered, he thought as he hastily retraced his steps and drove away.

R

"Over here, Frank," Maggie yelled hoarsely from inside the attic.

"I've got it," he replied. "You'll be out in a jiffy." Turning the knob, he shoved the door open in one firm movement.

Maggie tumbled out, almost knocking him over. She bent over, hands on her knees, and breathed deeply to steady herself.

"Sorry about that, Frank," she gasped and tried to stand.

Haynes recovered his balance, and put his arm around her shoulder to steady her. She leaned into him.

"How long were you up there?" he asked.

"Since early this morning."

"I almost didn't come out here. I figured you forgot about our meeting. Frankly, I was angry. I was bringing you a bunch of paperwork to review—on your own."

Maggie nodded and straightened. "I was certain I'd spend the night up there," she said with a shudder. "I didn't have any water and figured I'd have to make a ladder out of whatever I could find if no one came for me by early afternoon. And I've been so worried about Eve because she just got out of the hospital and needs antibiotics."

Haynes gave her a quizzical glance.

"She had a spider bite that became infected and was really sick. But Dr. Allen fixed her up," she replied.

Haynes nodded. In all his days, he'd never been in a situation like this. Saving a damsel in distress was a task he was totally unprepared for.

"Well, you're okay now," he stated the obvious. "How did you get locked in?"

"That damn door is missing a knob on the inside. I left it open when I went up to the attic, but it's drafty and a big wind gust slammed it shut. And there I was."

Maggie switched on the chandelier on the landing, throwing light onto the stairway and the driveway from the window.

"What's up there?" he asked, his interest in this house, which he had coveted for so long, once again piqued.

"Just a bunch of old junk, really," Maggie stated dismissively. "I found some old ledgers and records from the twenties and thirties. Those might be fun to look though." She turned to him. "Frank, I can't thank you enough. You're my white knight. You saved me from the most terrifying night of my life, for sure, and maybe from much worse. I don't know if I could have climbed all the way down a makeshift ladder. And I don't know if Eve would have survived. I'm so very grateful to you."

Haynes smiled, his earlier annoyance with her evaporated.

"Let me run up and lock the window," Maggie said, starting toward the stairs.

"No, I'll get it," Haynes replied firmly. "You've had enough of that attic for one day." Maggie nodded. Taking the flashlight from her, he quickly ascended the stairs and made his way to the window that Maggie had hailed him from. He secured the lock then turned to head back toward the stairs when the flashlight's beam caught a file folder lying on the floor. He stopped short to avoid stepping on it and stooped to pick it up. He was about to toss it on top of a stack of banker's boxes when he noted the title. Shock waves coursed through his body. He hesitated, wondering if he could stash the file inside his coat, when he heard Maggie's tread on the stairs.

"Frank," she called. "Did you get it?"

Haynes quickly shoved the file into the closest box, vowing to somehow, someway retrieve it.

"Got it," he called as he intercepted her at the top of the stairs. "You propped that door open, right? So we don't get locked in?"

Reassured by Maggie's assertion that the door couldn't slam shut again, he turned and slowly led them both down the stairs with the flashlight.

Neither of them noticed the car in the driveway as they walked to the front door. The taillights disappeared into the trees as Haynes stepped through the front door and Maggie stooped to pick up the prescription bottle propped on the doormat.

Chapter 24

Maggie opened a can of soup for dinner and tried to force herself to review the documents Frank Haynes had brought her. After plowing through one section for the fourth time—still with no understanding—she replaced the cap firmly on her highlighter and tidied up the stack of papers.

"Eve, I'm exhausted, aren't you?" Eve thumped her tail in reply. "I guess being locked in a drafty old attic all afternoon really took it out of me. I think it's time to get ready for bed."

Maggie reached for her phone and lazily checked her messages. Her heart leapt when she saw John's name in the list. She read and reread his curt text. He must have been the one who had dropped off Eve's medicine. She'd send a warm, appreciative response and see if she couldn't get things going again between them. He still felt something for her, she was sure of it. The spark was there that day at his clinic when she brought Eve to him.

Maggie settled onto her stool at the kitchen island, and Eve curled up at her feet. She sat, fingers poised over her keypad, deep in thought.

Looks like Eve & I have been recipients of your kindness again. Thanks so much for delivering her medicine. Sorry I didn't answer the door—was occupied. Would like to tell you about it. And thank you properly. May I take you to dinner this week?

Maggie contemplated what she had written. Was dinner too much, too soon? Would it turn him off? Should she start with something smaller? Yes, that would definitely be safer. She erased the last line and typed: *Can I buy you coffee this week?* ☺

There—that sounded friendly and not pushy. Satisfied, she pressed send. "Okay, Eve," she yawned. "Now we really need to get to bed."

R

Maggie kept a close eye on her phone all day Sunday as she waded through the Fairview Terraces paperwork, hoping for a response from John. She pushed aside her disappointment, rationalizing that he might be out on an emergency call and unable to respond to a social text, but by dinnertime, she was thoroughly discouraged.

Maggie spent the evening watching episodes of *Upstairs Downstairs* on DVD—her son, Mike, had given her the entire series for Christmas the prior year—and doing her nails. She was just about to turn out the light on her nightstand when his reply came in: *Not necessary. Call office if you need anything.*

Maggie felt her heart plummet. *That's it,* she realized. *He's done. I was mistaken.* She nestled into her pillow that was soon wet with her silent tears. Sensing the change in her master, Eve abandoned her familiar spot at Maggie's feet. She sniffed and wagged, and licked Maggie's face until Maggie was compelled to smile.

"It's okay, girl," she whispered as she moved Eve to a spot next to her. She turned on her side and snuggled her furry companion. "I've always got you."

She forced her mind back to the financial data she had spent the afternoon analyzing and was soon asleep.

R

A cold front settled on the Midwest, bringing with it freezing rain and gusty winds. Both Maggie and John were in a funk by quitting time on Wednesday. *Comfort food,* Maggie decided as she turned out of the Town Hall parking lot. *I'm sick and tired of salads; I need something that will stick to my ribs. One night won't ruin my diet.* She spun her car around and headed to Pete's.

Meanwhile, John Allen had parked his car in the No Parking zone outside the back door of Pete's and run in to pick up the nightly special to go. He had been doing this for so long that he didn't need to call in his order anymore or stop to pay; he called if he wasn't coming, and they had his credit card on file. The arrangement suited him perfectly.

Maggie parked at the far end of the lot, positioned the hood of her coat as far over her face as she could and held it firmly in place while she dashed to the back door. She pulled the door open and collided with the veterinarian, sending his take-out boxes to the floor.

"John," she exclaimed, laughing with embarrassment. "I'm sorry. I was just trying to get in here out of the rain. Here, let me help you." As she bent to retrieve one of the Styrofoam boxes, her heart felt happier than it had in days.

"Not necessary," he said, snatching the box before she could reach it.

"How are you?" she continued, eyeing him carefully and willing the conversation to continue.

"Fine, thanks. Goodnight," he said brusquely as he opened the door without meeting her gaze.

Maggie watched silently as the door shut behind him.

R

It was irretrievably over, Maggie thought morosely as she picked through the fried chicken, mashed potatoes, and corn she brought home from Pete's. She'd almost finished the humongous piece of chocolate cake that came with the special—what on earth was she thinking, eating all of this?—when Susan called.

"Hi, honey," Maggie answered without enthusiasm. "What's up?"

"Well, aren't we chipper? What's got you down? Are those crooks at Town Hall still up to no good?"

Maggie smiled in spite of herself. "I'm sure they are. Who knows? That's not what's bothering me."

"Okay," Susan replied. "Then what? Come on, Mom, no secrets. Spill the beans. You and John are fine, aren't you?"

Maggie sighed. "That's just it. We're not. I think it's definitely over."

"What? When did this happen? Why didn't you call me?"

"I was hoping it was all a tiny misunderstanding and it would blow over. Until last week, I knew he still liked me. But that's not why you called. What's up with you?"

"Not so fast, Mom," Susan replied.

Maggie could picture her lying back on her sofa, phone to her ear, just as she had done as a teenager. Susan was in the mood to talk and there would be no denying her.

"Give it all to me, Mom."

"Not much to tell, really. I was late picking him up from his physical therapy several times and missed a session or two—he had to take a cab."

Maggie heard Susan wince.

"That's pretty bad, Mom."

"I know, I know. He's absolutely right to be angry. I was trying to make it up to him, but he said that he couldn't do it anymore; he'd been second fiddle to his wife, and he wasn't going to be second fiddle in a relationship again. That was pretty much it."

"Have you seen him since? How has he acted?"

"That's the thing. I have. Eve got very sick from a spider bite, and I rushed her to his clinic. He was so kind and concerned, I thought we could start talking and then begin again."

"So why hasn't that happened?"

"I have no idea. The last time he dropped by Rosemont was the day I got locked in the attic."

"You what?"

Maggie launched into a recap of her afternoon in the attic. After a period of joint speculation about the vintage silver collection, they returned to Maggie's more pressing concern and concluded that John's attitude had completely cooled to her immediately thereafter.

"How odd," Susan commented. "Makes no sense. But if you're absolutely sure that it's over, then you might as well sign up with an online dating service and meet someone that way."

Maggie snorted. "That's ridiculous. No way would I do that. That's your thing, not mine."

"So it's good enough for me, but not you. Apparently you don't really believe all that encouraging stuff you tell me about meeting someone online? Seems a wee bit hypocritical, doesn't it?"

She's nailed it, Maggie realized. She drew a deep breath and was about to mount her defense when Susan continued.

"Mom. I think you might be scared. We all are. But online dating can be a lot of fun. I'll help you with your profile, and we'll be able to talk about the men you find out there. Just like we do for me. It'll be fun to do this together."

"Honey, I'm not so sure I even want to date anyone."

"You're not making a lifetime commitment here," Susan teased. "Just give it a whirl. If you don't like it, you can quit. As you're always telling me, you can't hit a home run if you won't get up to bat!"

Maggie laughed. "You win. I surrender."

She could hear Susan get up off the couch.

"Perfect. I'm getting my laptop and going online. You do the same. We'll get you going right now. No time like the present."

Knowing when she had been defeated, Maggie retrieved her computer and they began.

R

Across town, John Allen disposed of the Styrofoam containers that held his dinner and searched for something interesting to watch on TV. He replayed running into Maggie in his mind—and her recent text message—for the hundredth time. He still cared for her. Had he been too hasty in calling it off? He didn't think so. He kept falling for the wrong kind of woman—he didn't want a workaholic who put her career ahead of him. And he definitely didn't want to have coffee with Maggie so she could tell him that she'd gotten together with Frank Haynes. If they had become an item, he'd have to get used to that. But he didn't have to listen politely while his heart was torn in two.

He had to admit he was lonely. He'd never dreamed it would be this difficult to find the right person to spend the rest of his life with. Of course, he hadn't exactly been trying very hard of late since he never went out anywhere to meet anyone. At this rate if "the one" didn't walk through the doors of Westbury Animal Hospital—as Maggie had done those months ago—he wasn't going to meet her.

Where did a person go to meet someone these days anyway? Over the years he'd tried bars and church and the dog park, but had never met a soul he was remotely interested in dating. John turned his attention back to the TV and resumed channel surfing. He suddenly switched it off and tossed the remote aside. *You're sitting here feeling sorry for yourself and acting like the couch potato you never wanted to be,* he thought. *This is ridiculous.*

He propelled himself from his semi-prone position and grabbed his laptop. He'd register with an online dating service and get back in the game. There were sites for people with specific interests; he'd overheard his receptionist talking about one for dog lovers. He'd check it out. If he didn't find anyone, he could always quit. And who knows, something just might happen for him. That kind of thing occurred all the time.

R

Frank Haynes hit "save" and closed out of the spreadsheet he had been working on in Excel. His numbers looked good; he was a very wealthy man. But what good did it do him, really, if he didn't have anyone to share it with? Would he be one of those people who died and left a fortune to their dog?

He sighed and turned back to his computer. It couldn't hurt to check out an online matchmaking service. Surely they'd changed in the years since he'd been on one. What did he have to lose?

R

In response to her daughter's constant reminders, Maggie checked her account on DogLovers.com daily. Susan called each night and together they analyzed all possible matches. After a week even Susan had to admit that there was no one suitable for Maggie. Until the following Sunday afternoon. When she found a profile that caught her attention:

> *Dogs—and other animals—have been a major part of my happy, satisfying life. I'm in my late fifties, healthy, and independent. I'm still working in a job I love and have no plans to retire. I'm an avid sports fan, enjoy fine dining, and I'd like to travel. I'm looking for a serious relationship to share the large and small joys of life. DogLover7718*

Sounds interesting, Maggie thought. *And normal.* It'd be nice to see what he looked like, but the site didn't allow photos, advising that you couldn't judge a book by its cover. She supposed they were right.

Then Maggie found a second profile that caught her eye:

> *Successful business owner looking for an intelligent woman to spend time with. I enjoy European cars and the occasional movie. I'm an animal*

100

lover and have a soft spot for strays. My career is demanding and I'm looking for an independent woman with her own interests. DogLover7719

He's not as intriguing as DogLover7718, but he fits the profile of what I'm looking for in a man. She reached for her cell phone to solicit Susan's advice. *That's interesting,* she mused as she waited for Susan to pick up. *I'm DogLover7717.*

"Honey," she said, "call me when you can. I think two of the matches look interesting. Now I need to know what to do next!"

R

John scrolled through the profiles on DogLovers.com. Maybe this whole idea had been a mistake. How in the world was he going to weed through all of these people? Four profiles were interesting, but he kept returning to DogLover7717. Something about her intrigued him:

Lifelong dog lover finally has her perfect canine companion. Forging a new life with my dog at my side. I'm a homebody—I like to cook and garden. Avid reader when I have time. I've travelled widely and plan to do more in my free time. Honesty, integrity, and open communication are the cornerstones of a relationship. I'm looking for a long-term commitment that will fulfill and nurture us both.

Sounded right on the mark to him. He'd contact her. He typed his message, deleted it, retyped, reread it, and finally hit send. There—he'd done it. Made a start. Satisfied with himself, he shut his laptop and whistled to his Golden Retriever. He suddenly felt like checking out the dog park.

R

Maggie busied herself in her garden all Sunday afternoon. It felt good to be doing something physical where she could instantly see the results of her efforts. She was almost finished when Susan returned her call.

"Can I call you back in a few? I want to finish up outside before it gets dark."

"No way, Mom. You're procrastinating. And I want you to get messages to these guys. It'll only take a nanosecond. I'm on my way out the door, so we can't talk long."

Maggie sighed. She could use a short break anyway. She opened her laptop and logged on to the website. Susan was prattling away in her ear, dictating possible messages. Maggie interrupted.

"Wait a minute—I've got two messages."

"Good going, Mom. Let's check 'em out."

101

"They're from DogLovers 7718 and 7719! How about that!"

"Ohhhh. Interesting. So … what do they say?"

"7718 has proposed a double date. The two of us and our dogs at the dog park. Next Sunday afternoon. Says he works on Saturdays. That's weird—who works on Saturdays?"

"I work most Saturdays, Mom. Don't start finding reasons not to like him. I do that, and you call me on it every time. So here's a dose of your own medicine."

Maggie laughed. "You're right. This is good. Now I don't have to figure out how to make the first move. So what do you think? Do I say yes?"

"Of course you say yes! You and Eve get to go for a walk, and if you don't like him, you can get away fast. It's not like you'll be trapped in a restaurant making small talk while you wait for your food. This will be easy. Brilliant, actually. Maybe I should get a dog and join this site."

"How's this sound? *Great plan. We'd be delighted to join you. I'll meet you by the south entrance at 2 p.m. If the weather is wet, we'll wait under the bandstand. If you can't make it*—Do I give him my cell phone number?" Maggie asked.

"No way. Too soon. If he can't make it, tell him to send you a message through DogLovers. You'll just need to check the site before you head out. If he's a no show, you and Eve can simply enjoy a walk.

"Sounds good. I've added that to my reply."

"Press send. And you've done it! I'm proud of you, Mom. What about the other guy?"

"Okay," Maggie replied. "He says, 'We have some common interests. Would you like to meet for coffee?' That sounds a bit formal and drab, doesn't it?"

"Everybody doesn't bounce off the page with enthusiasm. He might be nice. It's just a cup of coffee. Like you always tell me, you have time for that."

"I suppose you're right."

"I'm right. Email him to set up a meeting, okay? You should suggest the time and place."

"Why don't I wait until I see how it goes with DogLover7718 first?"

"It doesn't work like that, Mom. Answer him. You're not going steady with 7718; you haven't even met him yet."

"All right. Will do."

"Good. I've really got to go now. We'll talk later about what you're going to wear when you meet these guys."

Maggie set the phone on her desk and leaned back in her chair. Good lord, she had really done it. When she signed up for the online dating service, she didn't think she'd actually go out with anyone. Now what had she gotten herself into? She glanced out the window; dusk was fast approaching. She heaved herself from her chair and headed back into the yard to finish her gardening.

Chapter 25

Gloria took a seat on the bench to the right of the large double doors leading into the town council chamber. It was shortly before noon, and the doors were locked. The zoning hearing was at one o'clock, and no one else had arrived yet. Glenn paced, nervously shuffling his note cards and practicing his speech. He was making the presentation to the town council on the proposed zoning variance that would allow Fairview Terraces to operate moneymaking ventures on their campus.

"Why don't you sit down and relax?" Gloria encouraged. "You know what you're going to say. You're prepared."

Glenn sighed, "I know. But it's been a long time since I've done anything like this. I don't want to mess up."

"You won't," Gloria reassured. "You're going to knock their socks off. I read all of it with a critical eye. If anything were unclear or missing, I'd have told you. Besides, Councilman Haynes will be there, and he's going to vote for us and persuade the others. He told you so."

Glenn sat and reached for her hand. "We're first on the agenda," he said, gesturing to the notice posted on the door. "At least I can get this over with soon."

Gloria sighed and toyed with the idea of suggesting that they step across the street to get a bite to eat—they had plenty of time—but decided against it. She may not have known Glenn Vaughn long, but she knew him well. And she was sure that he needed to stay right where he was, perfectly prepared and ready to go, an hour early.

R

Two and a half hours later, Glenn, Gloria, and a handful of other residents from Fairview Terraces exited the town council chamber in high spirits. A neighboring apartment complex had opposed their variance, but with the addition of parking restrictions and other concessions, the town council approved their request by a narrow margin. Councilman Haynes had been as good as his word and had pushed the matter through.

"I think we need to celebrate," Glenn said to the group. "Why don't we head over to Pete's? Gloria and I got here so early, we didn't even eat lunch. Anyone else care to join us?"

The group made its way to the lobby and Glenn pushed the button to summon an elevator. When the doors opened, Mayor Martin stepped out.

"Why, hello," she said, smiling at Glenn and Gloria. "Did you just come from the zoning hearing?" Without waiting for an answer, she added, "By the look on your faces, I think you've had good news?"

"Yes," Glenn replied. "It passed. Just barely. Councilman Haynes was a big help."

"Glenn made a brilliant presentation," Gloria inserted proudly. "You should have seen him."

Maggie couldn't suppress a smile. "I'm sure he did. He was brilliant at the meetings at Fairview. Councilman Haynes told me that it would be tough going, but he thought you'd get a good result."

"Now that we're cleared to operate moneymaking ventures, we need to get them up and running," Glenn continued.

"There's time to think about all that later," Gloria interrupted. "Right now, we're headed to Pete's to celebrate. Would you like to join us, Mayor Martin?"

"I wish I could. I'm running late for a meeting."

"When you see Councilman Haynes, would you please thank him from all of us at Fairview Terraces?" Glenn asked.

"You can thank him yourself; here he comes, now," she said, gesturing over Glenn's shoulder. "Well done, all of you," she said to the group as Glenn broke free and intercepted Haynes.

"Councilman," Glenn said, extending his hand. "Thank you so much for jumping in to answer questions. I thought I had come prepared, but I got in over my head pretty fast. This wouldn't have happened without your support."

"I was only doing my job," Haynes answered with uncharacteristic modesty. "Glad I could be of assistance. You're well on your way to digging yourselves out of this hole. I always like to help people who're trying to help themselves."

Glenn hesitated and looked questioningly at Haynes.

"Is there something else I can do for you?" Haynes asked.

"As a matter of fact, yes. I'm a mentor in the juvenile court system and was wondering if the boy I'm working with could be given a job at your animal shelter—Forever Friends?"

"We're almost entirely run by volunteers. I'm sorry, but we have very few paid staff positions."

"I'm not talking about a paid position. This boy needs something to do with his time; needs the responsibility of someone relying on him."

"Doesn't the juvenile court have programs? We aren't set up for anything like that."

"His case worker has approved my idea; I just need to find someplace for him to intern. You know him, I believe. David Wheeler?"

Frank Haynes' head snapped back.

"Yes, I know David."

He stared at something over Glenn's shoulder. Glenn waited until Haynes slowly turned his attention back to the elderly man. "Yes. I'll make a spot for David at Forever Friends. We'll find something for him to do."

"Thank you, Councilman. You'll be glad you did. It's the best thing for this kid right now. And if I may suggest, let him work with the animals. They'll bring out the kind feelings that he's trying so hard to suppress."

Haynes clapped Glenn on the arm. "Bring him by the shelter on Saturday morning at eight o'clock. I'll be there and we'll set him up. He paused and pointed to the crowd gathered by the elevators. "For now it looks like you've got an entourage waiting for you. See you Saturday morning."

Chapter 26

Maggie returned to her office shortly before six o'clock that afternoon. She had plenty of work to do, but she couldn't muster the energy to dive into it. Running into that sweet couple from Fairview Terraces earlier in the afternoon got her thinking. They were so caring and so genuinely attuned to each other. Maggie wanted that kind of relationship in her life. Had she ever had that with Paul? She didn't think so.

Paul had always put himself first. Anytime he supported her, there was something in it for him. The promotions in her career meant he got to rub shoulders with a new group of influential people. As she grew more successful and independent, Paul became more controlling. The romance had long ago expired by the time he died.

And the Scottsdale family. That younger woman and her two kids. Had Paul really expected he could keep that a secret forever? Maybe. He had certainly covered up his embezzlement from the college for years. *You can't have the kind of love you saw between that elderly couple when you're married to someone as dishonest and self-absorbed as Paul Martin,* she thought.

Maggie spun in her chair and snatched her purse from her drawer. Since she had been elected mayor in the prior year's election, she had been too busy and preoccupied to rehash the betrayal of her faithless marriage. When she did consider her relationship with Paul, her stomach churned and acid rose in the back of her throat. Time hadn't dulled the hurt and resentment that engulfed her each time she revisited her past life.

One thing was for sure, she told herself as she pulled on her coat; she wanted something different for her future. She wanted a happy relationship. She was capable of one and she deserved one. Just like that couple. But she had to stop being a workaholic, allowing her career to distract her from the loneliness of her personal life. Starting now. It was time to head home and figure out what to wear to a dog-park blind date.

Chapter 27

Sunday was crisp and sunny; a perfect day to spend outside. Maggie tried to slip out unnoticed after church but stopped when Sam Torres, her first friend in Westbury and faithful handyman, called her name.

"Hold on there, Ms. Mayor," he called. "Joan and I haven't talked to you in ages."

"I know, I'm sorry," Maggie replied with a rueful shrug. "This mayor business is much more demanding than I ever thought."

"And now you're sneaking out after church. Not to go to the office, I hope."

"No. Not today," Maggie assured him.

She began edging toward the parking lot.

"You're certainly in a hurry to go somewhere," Joan commented, eyeing Maggie curiously.

"I just need to get home to take Eve to the dog park," Maggie replied, realizing how lame that sounded.

"If you're on a scheduled deadline to walk your dog on a Sunday afternoon, we need to do an intervention," Sam teased.

Maggie looked at the concerned faces of this gentle couple who had completely taken her into their hearts.

"To be honest," she relented, "I'm meeting a blind date at the dog park. I need to get home to change clothes."

She watched as their expressions changed from concerned to surprised, and back again.

"Blind date?" Joan managed to croak.

"What about Dr. Allen?" Sam cut in. "Aren't you seeing him?"

Maggie sighed heavily. "I was. In fact, I'm still interested in him. But I really blew it. I was always too busy at Town Hall to spend time with him. I even forgot to pick him up from physical therapy a couple of times. He had to take a cab home."

Sam let out a breath. "That's not good. Not good at all," he said, stating the obvious.

"Have you tried to patch things up, dear?" Joan asked. "I know he really cared for you. We both hoped we'd be going to a wedding soon."

"I've tried. I really have. Thought I was making progress. Then he suddenly shut me out. I don't know what happened. Maybe he met someone else."

"Not that I know of," Sam replied. "But then, he keeps these things to himself. He never told me that you two had broken up. And I've been giving him rides from physical therapy. You'd think he would have mentioned it."

They had been sauntering toward the parking lot while they talked and had reached Maggie's car. She pressed her key to unlock her door.

"Not so fast," Sam stated firmly. "Tell us about this blind date. Who set you up?"

"He's someone I met online."

"Isn't that dangerous?" Joan asked in alarm. "Aren't there weirdoes and perverts online? People disappear all the time and they never find the bodies."

Maggie laughed. "I'll be fine. This is through DogLovers.com. We're meeting at two o'clock today at the dog park. So we'll be in public with lots of people around us. Especially on a nice day like today. I'll have my cell phone with me. And Eve. I'll use common sense. Don't worry about me," she said, giving Joan's arm a comforting pat.

"I'm *going* to worry about you," she stated flatly.

"Don't give him your address or phone number until I check him out," Sam admonished.

"Quit fussing. I'll be careful," Maggie assured them. "Tell you what—I'll call you when I get home. How would that be?"

"I've got a better idea," Joan said. "Why don't you come over for dinner. On the way home. Bring Eve. It'll be like that first time we met when you moved into Rosemont."

"You don't have to do that."

"I insist. It'll make us both feel better. Perfect plan."

"We miss you," Sam added simply.

How could she refuse these people she loved?

Maggie laughed. "Sounds great. I'll pick up a pie from Laura's for dessert. I'll see you later, probably by four," she said as she slid into her car. "And don't worry about me. Everything'll be fine. We'll probably have nothing to talk about, and I'll be out of there in fifteen minutes. See you later."

R

Maggie shivered as she entered Rosemont through her kitchen door. The sun was warm but the air was deceptively cold. "Hello, girl," she said as she patted the squirming Eve. "We've got a date this afternoon. Yes, you're invited. And I'm going to put your new blue-and-white sweater on you. It's cold out there. Maybe I should wear something to match. What do you think?"

Eve wagged her tail furiously. *Good lord,* she thought. *I'm planning an outfit to match my dog? What's happened to me?*

Maggie headed for her bedroom. "Come on, girl. We've got work to do. I need your opinion," she said as they raced up the stairs.

R

After forty-five minutes of rummaging around in her closet and a twenty-minute consultation with Susan over the phone, Maggie settled on her sapphire-blue cashmere sweater and boot-cut jeans—the same outfit she had worn when John took her skating. Did this mean she had a date outfit now? How cliché. Could she help it that the weather had turned so cold and it was the best-looking thing she had? Besides, it matched Eve. Not that it mattered, she told herself sternly.

Maggie surveyed herself in the mirror. She remembered gliding across the deserted rink at The Mill that night, with the cold wind whipping her hair to bits and her hand securely tucked into the crook of John's strong arm. She thought back to the easy flow of their conversation. And how much she wanted him to kiss her goodnight. And how disappointed she'd been that he hadn't; the tragedy of the fires and subsequent chaos had intervened.

All of that led her to where she was today. She had been so sure that John would be part of it all. How had she become careless and preoccupied enough to drive him away? She had to admit that he was right—their split had been her fault. She sighed miserably.

Maggie turned her attention back to her reflection in the mirror. It was pointless to rehash all of this. Crying over spilt milk, as her aunt used to say. She was meeting someone new at the dog park, and it was time to get going. Swollen, red eyes would not help with a first impression. She forced a smile at her reflection.

"Come on, Eve. Time for you to get dressed."

R

John tossed the Sunday paper onto the coffee table and returned his attention to the lackluster football game on the screen. The score remained 3–0 late in the third quarter. He checked his watch. Still a bit early to head out to the dog park, but he was bored and restless waiting around his living room.

"Roman," he called. "Let's go meet this gal. Who knows, she may have a friend for you, too." He was almost out the door when his home phone began to ring. He paused, then pulled his Golden Retriever back into the house with him, and picked up the receiver.

"John," said the familiar voice. "It's Sam Torres."

John instantly snapped into doctor mode. "Sam. Is anything wrong with Rusty?"

"No. Sorry. He's still the best dog on earth. Didn't mean to scare you. I know this is last minute and everything, but Joan was just saying how she never sees you anymore and asked me to call and invite you to an early dinner. Tonight. Are you busy?"

John hesitated, caught off guard. He certainly didn't have any plans other than to stop by Pete's for takeout. Again. He drew in a breath. Why not?

"That's awfully kind of you. I'd love to. What time?"

"Why don't you come by about four? Would that work? We can visit, and you'll still get home at a decent hour."

"Perfect. I've got surgery at six tomorrow morning. That'll suit me just fine. I'll see you later. And please, tell Joan thank you."

R

John arrived at the dog park half an hour early. He let Roman off the leash and allowed him to run; he'd need to work off some steam and sniff everything before he'd be ready to settle down and be sociable.

They circled the park and closed in on the area by the south entrance. He watched the parade of humans and canines pass by, noting the connection between people and their dogs. He could always tell the new, tentative friend-ships from the established, long-term relationships; the ones where commands had to be clearly communicated and the ones where they were intuitively understood. Long-established bonds of love. At least he'd been lucky in that department. If DogLover7717 turned out to be one more in the long line of flaky women he had met online, he still had Roman. The thought, however, gave him little comfort.

His attention was drawn to a very familiar terrier mix wearing a ridiculous-looking blue-and-white sweater, being led by an even more familiar woman in a sapphire-blue cashmere sweater. His heart leapt to his throat. What in the world was Maggie Martin doing at the dog park today of all days? He hadn't seen her here in months. This could get awkward.

He checked his watch. It was five minutes before two. He turned away, hoping she hadn't seen him. If she had, he'd say a quick hello and send them on their way.

Maggie spotted John and Roman just as he noticed her. *Maybe we can just ignore each other,* she thought. *What are the odds of running into him?* She made her way over to the opposite side of the entrance and took up a position under a large oak tree where Eve busied herself sniffing and rooting out a spot to mark. Maggie snuck a look in John's direction and was disconcerted to see that he appeared to be hanging around the entrance, just as she was. She turned away and tried to figure out what to do while still keeping an eye out for DogLover7718.

A squat man with long gray hair pulled into a ponytail and a disagreeable-looking pit bull mix strode through the entrance at two o'clock on the dot and stopped, scanning the area for someone or something. Maggie froze; she didn't want this to be DogLover7718. She hesitated, waiting for him to approach. He shouted to a young boy in the distance who ran to him, crying "Grampa." Maggie sighed in relief.

John and Maggie hovered on opposite sides of the entrance, studiously avoiding each other like competing Olympic skaters warming up on the ice. Roman finally settled the matter by giving a quick bark in greeting and bounding over to say hello to Eve and Maggie. John had no choice but to follow suit.

"Hello. Sorry about that. Roman, come here, boy," he admonished as he produced a leash and snapped it on his collar. His instincts as a vet overcame his impatience to send Maggie on her way, and he bent down to greet Eve. He ran over her with practiced hands and looked into her eyes and ears. "She seems well; back to normal. How is she? Eating and eliminating regularly?" he asked professionally.

"Yes. She's doing just fine. Thanks to you. We had quite a scare."

He waved away the compliment. "I won't keep you. It's a beautiful day for a walk. I'm sure she's anxious to be on her way." He wanted to add "especially since you so rarely take her for walks, with your busy schedule," but he restrained himself. No point in picking a fight. What she did was none of his business.

Maggie sighed. "Actually, I'm waiting for someone. We're going to meet here. At two o'clock." She glanced at her watch. "I guess he's running late."

John drew in a sharp breath and turned suddenly to face her, which struck Maggie as very odd. Why would he care if she were waiting for someone at the dog park?

"I don't want to hold you up. Nice to see you," she said, pulling on Eve's leash in an attempt to separate the two dogs who were happily and inappropriately sniffing each other.

"Actually, I'm meeting someone here at two o'clock, too." They regarded each other steadily, and John was the first to smile.

"Are you, by any chance otherwise known as DogLover7717?" he asked.

As a chagrined smile spread across her face, he extended his hand.

"Allow me to introduce myself. DogLover7718."

Maggie took his hand.

"It looks like fate is telling us to give this another chance," he murmured. "What do you think?"

"I'd be delighted. I never wanted to break up. You were completely right about things. I've changed my ways; I really have."

He tucked her hand into his elbow. With Roman and Eve pulling on their leashes and urging them forward, the pair and the pups began to stroll companionably through the bright afternoon.

"Why were you on DogLovers.com? I thought you and Frank Haynes were an item."

Maggie stopped dead in her tracks. "Are you nuts? I've made a sort of peace with Frank—and he's actually done a few decent things recently—but I still don't trust him as far as I can throw him. Why in the world did you think I was seeing Frank?"

John looked at her solemnly. "Because the night I dropped off Eve's medicine at your front door—that Saturday night—Frank's car was parked in front of Rosemont and the only lights on in the place were on the second floor."

"What? Yes, Frank was there and he was on the 'bedroom' floor, but it is *not* what you're thinking."

She drew in a sharp breath, and he could see she was gathering a head of steam. He instantly regretted bringing the topic up, but he had to know.

"I was foraging through Rosemont's attic that day and got myself locked in—without my cell phone. I was panicked about getting out of there and worried sick about missing Eve's dose of antibiotics. I was even trying to find sheets and curtains to tie together to make a rope to climb down on Sunday afternoon if no one found me by then."

"I had no idea," John muttered.

Maggie cut him off. "I was freezing and miserable when Frank Haynes pulled up. I was supposed to meet with him at Town Hall that morning to go over some documents. When I didn't show up, he drove them out to Rosemont to leave them for me. I was able to get his attention from the attic window. He got in the house with my hidden key and managed to force open the attic door."

"That must have been very frightening. Thank goodness he came by."

"No kidding," she continued. "There was absolutely no hanky-panky."

"No. I realize that now. I've been a fool. I shouldn't have assumed."

"You most certainly should not have," she stated firmly.

113

They resumed walking, John searching for what to say next.

"So that's why you suddenly turned so cold to me?" Maggie asked, glancing over at him.

John nodded.

"You're an idiot," she stated.

John nodded again. "I really am sorry. And I've missed you terribly," he said, tightening his grip on her hand. "We'll need to get that attic door fixed," he added lamely in an attempt to change the subject. "What's up there?"

He sensed the complete change in her demeanor before she answered. "John, you wouldn't believe it. That attic is full of the coolest stuff. Fascinating household accounts and records that probably should go to the Historical Society. And an entire collection of vintage silver."

He had no idea what vintage silver was, but her almost reverent tone indicated how happy the discovery had made her. Just talking about it had lightened her mood and that was enough for him. They walked their dogs for the next hour while he happily learned more than he ever wanted to know about the subject.

They were approaching the south entrance when Maggie checked her watch. "Oh, my gosh. It's almost four! I'm going to the Torreses' for dinner. I'm supposed to be there at four, and I've got to pick up a pie at Laura's first."

John burst out laughing. "When did this get scheduled? Sam caught me on my way out the door this afternoon to invite me for dinner tonight."

"Right after church today. They knew I was meeting a blind date. Joan was so worried I'd be kidnapped and dismembered in a ravine that I promised I'd stop by afterward to show her I was all right. Those little sneaks!"

"They wanted us back together, for sure," John said.

They smiled at each other. "We'd better get going," Maggie said.

"Not yet, young lady," he replied as he pulled her into his arms for a slow, luxurious kiss. Even Eve and Roman seemed to approve as they ceased pulling on their leads and waited patiently.

When the reunited couple's lips finally parted, Maggie rested her head briefly on John's chest before reluctantly stepping back. "We're going to be late. I'm sure Joan is getting anxious about me. Why don't we arrive together?"

"Good plan. I can't wait to see the looks on their faces."

"We're lucky to have such caring friends."

"We're lucky in a lot of ways," John replied as he planted a kiss on the top of her head.

R

As promised, Maggie called Susan much later that night to report on her meeting with the mysterious dog lover. "You've got to be kidding! It was John? No way!" Susan exclaimed.

"You should have seen us hovering by the entrance, stealing glances at each other before we realized what was up."

"Like the plot of a movie with Meg Ryan and Tom Hanks," Susan interjected.

"Exactly," Maggie laughed. "And then it came out that he actually thought I was seeing Frank Haynes," Maggie sputtered, the thought striking her as both irritating and ridiculously funny.

"What? That's preposterous. Haynes is a weasel."

"And you should have seen Joan and Sam when we showed up for dinner together. They were trying to fix us up again. Not too subtle. They loved how it all came together. Sam practically turned himself inside out, grinning."

Susan sighed. "I'm really happy for you, Mom. John is a nice guy. I always thought he was crazy about you. I was so disappointed that you two broke up. But what about the other guy? DogLover7719. What are you going to do about him?"

"I've already sent an email and cancelled. First thing I did when I got home. Now that I'm back with John, I couldn't possibly go out with someone else."

Maggie switched the focus to her daughter.

"What's new on your end? Anyone interesting online for you?"

"Maybe. Maybe not. We'll see," Susan replied with a yawn. "I don't have the energy to get into all of that now. I've been meaning to tell you that Mike and I have decided about the holidays," she stated firmly.

"Oh? And what have you decided?" Maggie asked, bemused. Her children were back to being their bossy selves.

"Mike, Amy, the girls, and I will all come to Rosemont for Thanksgiving. I've got the week off, so I'm coming on the Friday night before, and they'll arrive on Tuesday."

Maggie couldn't hide her delight. "That's wonderful! I thought Mike couldn't get the time off. I can't wait to see the twins. I miss you all so much. It'll be fun to have you here. And it'll be like Rosemont's coming out party," she said in a rush.

"I knew you'd be excited," Susan replied. "Rosemont will be the perfect setting for Thanksgiving. You really need falling leaves and frost on the pumpkin. Not palm trees and sun, even though that's what I've grown up with. Christmas, however, will be here. You'll have to come home to California to be with us. Mike and Amy are adamant that they won't take the girls out of their own home for Christmas."

Maggie felt a pang of regret and instantly felt guilty. What had she expected? She had promised to get out to California every month on business when she moved to Westbury, and hadn't been back once. Granted, she had made that promise before she had been elected mayor of Westbury. Just one more example of how she was letting her work rule her life, she realized. She was changing things with John and she would change this, too.

"Mom," Susan asked. "Are you still there?"

Maggie smiled. "Just lost in thought for a moment. I'll come out to California for Christmas. You can count on me."

Chapter 28

In the end, Loretta Nash accepted the position of financial analyst at Haynes Enterprises. She moved the kids across the country at the beginning of the school year, over their objection, and was completing her second week on the job. The work only involved routine bookkeeping so far, and she hadn't been very busy. When she had asked Mr. Haynes for more duties, he advised her to be patient; he was working her into the business and these things took time.

It was four o'clock and she had finished everything on her desk. Today was Halloween, and her kids were excited about trick-or-treating. Making new friends at school was proving especially hard for ultra-shy Marissa, so Loretta wanted her to have fun tonight. If she could get off work early, she'd have time to fix dinner and help the kids get into their costumes. Marissa was going to be a princess and Loretta would do her hair and makeup.

Loretta glanced warily in the direction of Mr. Haynes' office. Should she ask for this indulgence? She slung her purse over her shoulder and laid her jacket over her arm. She hesitated, then slowly approached his partially closed door and knocked softly. When he didn't answer, she nudged the door open and leaned in.

"Mr. Haynes," she said, clearing her throat.

Frank Haynes looked up and didn't bother to conceal his irritation.

"I'm sorry to bother you. I was wondering if I could leave a bit early. I've finished everything for today."

"Why would you need to leave early?" he snapped.

"It's Halloween, sir. My kids are little. I'd like to get home to help them get ready to trick-or-treat. They've had such a hard time adjusting," she began. Haynes cut her off with a waved hand.

"Certainly you can," he replied his aggravation suddenly dissipated. "I insist upon it. I forgot that it's Halloween. Haven't had trick-or-treaters at my place in years."

He came around his desk and began to walk her to the door.

"You know where you should take the kids, don't you?" he asked solicitously.

"I was going to go out in our neighborhood. And I think their school has something planned."

"Oh, no. You need to take them to Rosemont. I understand Mayor Martin hands out the good stuff—full-sized candy bars and everything. You won't want to miss that."

Whether she did or not, he didn't know or care. He smiled inwardly at the mental image of Martin face-to-face with her husband's mistress. And not knowing it. This was turning out to be a good day after all.

"You remember how to get to Rosemont, don't you?"

"Yes, I think so," she replied slowly.

"Have a good time tonight," Haynes called as Loretta hurried to her car.

R

Loretta's mind reeled as she drove the short distance to her apartment. Rosemont? She might get a glimpse inside the place. And meet Paul's wife. Was she ready for that? She was curious; had been for a long time. She'd be able to size her up at last. For years, Loretta had practiced the speech she'd make to Maggie Martin when they finally met. Tonight with the kids in tow would not be the time. That day would come. For now, she and the kids would make Rosemont their first Halloween stop.

She pulled into her apartment parking lot and called to her children as she opened the front door. "Hey, guys, I'm home."

"Mom! I'm so glad you're here," Marissa exclaimed. "I can't get my costume on by myself. And I want to go out early."

Loretta swept her daughter into a hug. "We will, sweetie. Let me make a quick dinner, then I'll help you get ready and we'll all go. Sean, any homework?"

"No. They can't give homework on Halloween. It's a law or something," he yelled from his bedroom.

"There isn't any such law," Loretta said feeling the need to straighten him out. "But there should be," she concluded when he raced out of his room, wildly brandishing the sword to his superhero costume.

"My boss let me off early and told me the best place to trick-or-treat around here is a big old mansion known as Rosemont. The mayor lives there. She gives out great candy. So we'll start there; what do you think? Let's eat and get out of here," she said, ushering her excited children into the kitchen.

R

An hour later, the entire Nash family approached the massive arched entry to Rosemont. They found a spot to park along the bottom of the driveway and made the long walk uphill in the company of goblins, witches, and Disney characters. Loretta pushed Nicole, dressed as Tinker Bell, in the stroller while Marissa and Sean darted ahead. At the

118

insistence of her children, Loretta had dressed herself in black jeans and a turtleneck, tucked her blond hair into a black cap, and painted her face to become a cat.

The massive door stood open and light from the foyer chandelier poured onto the stone steps. The entrance was lined with pumpkins of various shapes and colors and huge urns of potted mums. Loretta had to admit the house was truly gorgeous.

She could see a nice-looking middle-aged man handing out candy, but a group of tall teenagers dressed as ghouls blocked her view of the person next to him—presumably Maggie Martin. Marissa shrank back at the sight of them and grabbed her mother's hand.

"You're fine, sweetheart," she assured her daughter, not taking her eyes from the spot where she knew Maggie was standing. "Here," she said, thrusting Marissa up the steps. "Those big kids are leaving."

She lifted Nicole from the stroller and pushed her forward as the teens stepped aside.

Loretta and Maggie locked eyes. Something in the woman's expression changed and Loretta's stomach lurched. Had this woman recognized her? Had Paul ever told Maggie about her? Had he shown her Loretta's picture?

She released the breath she had been holding when Maggie glanced down and fixed a warm smile on Marissa, who was inching out from behind her brother.

"Those boys really scared me!" Maggie said. "I'm glad they're gone. I need a nice princess," she directed her remark to Marissa. "And Tinker Bell. Don't you look beautiful," she said, gesturing to Marissa's costume. "I'd like to get a good look at your dress."

In spite of herself, Loretta smiled. Darn it. She didn't want to like this woman. She didn't want her to be so kind to her children. And she hated that Maggie was trim and so pretty. Not at all what she had expected; not all what Paul had described.

Maggie turned to the man just as he was telling Sean how much he admired his superhero costume. "If I can interrupt you two, I think we have treats for everyone."

She reached behind the man and retrieved a large orange bowl filled with virtually every type of candy bar in existence. "Here," she said holding out the bowl. "Take what you'd like."

She turned to Sean.

"Why don't you take one for your mom, too? I'll bet you know her favorite," she continued with a wink at Loretta.

Loretta quickly turned away. This wasn't what she had envisioned at all. She retreated into the shadows.

"Is this a real castle?" Marissa said, her voice breathy with wonder. "Do you live here?"

Maggie laughed.

"It's my house, yes," she replied, glancing up at the tall stone facade. "I'm glad you like it. It's not a castle, but it is beautiful."

Maggie turned back to Marissa before greeting the next group of trick-or-treaters. "We have an Easter carnival on the lawn here in the spring. It's lots of fun. You'll have to come back then."

"Thank you," Loretta's children called as they stepped out of the way of the surging crowd to rejoin her.

R

John made a quick dash for more Halloween candy at seven thirty, and they ran out of that by nine. The crowd had thinned significantly by then. Maggie turned out the porch light, and John secured the cantankerous old lock on the front door.

"How many kids do you think we had?" Maggie asked as she led John to the kitchen where an anxious Eve had been sequestered during all of the excitement.

"I'll bet you had at least three hundred. I've lived here all my life, and I don't remember anyone ever trick-or-treating at Rosemont. You were the main attraction today. Every family on my staff came by."

Maggie smiled; she liked being generous with Rosemont, letting people get close to the grand old house and enjoy it. She would have brought Susan and Mike here to trick-or-treat when they were little.

"I think Rosemont likes having visitors, don't you?" she asked as John put his arms around her and drew her close.

"I don't think houses have feelings," he said softly into her lightly scented hair.

"Then you don't know anything about this house," she whispered in reply.

They remained wrapped in each other's arms, swaying slowly in the silence, relishing their closeness.

"Do you have surgery in the morning?" Maggie asked with a ragged breath.

"Nope. I postponed the one patient on the schedule. I planned to stay here with you until I was sure that the trick-or-treaters were done, and you wouldn't be bothered by anyone."

"That was nice of you," she murmured dreamily.

"I knew you'd be mobbed. Can't be too careful with my best girl."

Maggie smiled into his shoulder. "So when do you think the coast will be clear?" she asked, leaning back and looking into his eyes.

"Are you trying to get rid of me?" he replied, raising one eyebrow.

She shook her head. "Not at all. I'm thinking we really can't be sure that the danger's passed until morning. Who knows what prank one of these older kids might play in the wee hours?"

"Good point," he replied as he pressed his lips to hers. "Exactly what I was thinking."

"Why don't you spend the night with me?"

John took her hand and kissed her open palm, folding it into his own. He turned and, together, they slowly climbed the stairs through the darkened house.

R

Maggie woke the next morning to the tangible comfort of a lover in her bed. She blushed; what a night it had been. She never dreamed that passion in her fifties could surpass the lust of her twenties. She carefully crept out from under the covers and collected her robe from the hook in the bathroom.

With Eve trotting happily at her heels, she headed downstairs and soon returned with a mug of steaming coffee. She set it on the nightstand and watched John slowly wake to its pungent aroma. He opened his eyes and rubbed his hand across his face.

"Well, Mayor Martin. How are you this morning?" he said, reaching for her hand and pulling her onto the bed. "That was my most memorable Halloween ever."

"I'm perfect, actually. I brought you a cup of coffee," she said, pointing to the nightstand.

"Thank you. Haven't had anyone do that for me in a long time. Not sure if anyone's ever done that for me, for that matter. But right now, there's something more important that I haven't done in the morning in a long time," he growled as he slipped her robe off her shoulders and pulled her under the covers.

Chapter 29

Frank Haynes frowned when Loretta announced that Chuck Delgado was on the line. Delgado had made good on his promise regarding the Fairview Terraces matter. As far as Haynes was concerned, there wasn't anything else they needed to discuss. He had gotten his fill of Delgado at the town council meetings.

"Chuck. How goes it?" Haynes said with forced cheerfulness.

"Other than losing money on a legit investment to help out a friend it's goin' great," Delgado rasped.

Haynes remained silent.

"I'm talkin' about you, Frankie boy. And those old geezer friends of yours at Fairview."

"What do you mean?" Haynes spat.

"I heard they was gonna pay you back the money you advanced to the landlord for them. Except you didn't advance no money to us, now did you, Frankie?"

"Oh, for God's sake," Haynes sighed. "I don't have time for this."

"Look here, Frankie. We been talkin' about this. We took a hit to help you out."

"It helped all of us out. You know that. None of us needs Scanlon and company poking around."

"Yeah, but we never thought you'd be pocketing money on the deal. That ain't right, Frankie."

Delgado paused to make sure he had Haynes' undivided attention. "This here's a courtesy call, on account of our long association and all. My guys expect you to turn over any money you pocket from this Fairview thing. You got it, Frankie? No funny business. You don't want to mess with these guys; they ain't nice, like me."

Haynes wiped a line of sweat from his upper lip. "I'm not going to pocket any money on this deal, Chuck. Never intended to. How could I know that those old fools at Fairview Terraces would get a zoning variance and make money from the place? A bunch of senior citizens in a retirement village? That never happens."

"Will wonders never cease? It's happened, Frankie, and we expect to see that money."

"I haven't gotten any checks yet, Chuck. You've got to understand, I may never get any money. I don't expect that I will."

"I believe you, Frankie, I really do. Since we're such good friends and all. I'm out on a limb for you with my boys. Just remember that, Frankie. You owe me one." Delgado disconnected.

Haynes slammed down the receiver. The mob suspected him of cheating them, and now, on top of that, Haynes was in Chuck Delgado's debt. Could this day get any worse?

R

Loretta stamped her feet and hugged herself while searching the patch of road visible through the trees for any sign of the familiar Mercedes sedan. Frank Haynes was late. He was always at the office when she arrived at eight and never left before she did at five. It was now almost nine o'clock; she had gone from feeling annoyed by him to being concerned about him. She'd saved his cell phone number in her contact list; it was time to give him a call. She was fishing in her purse for her phone when he finally pulled into his reserved parking spot.

"Sorry I'm late," he called, hurrying to unlock the door to Haynes Enterprises.

"I was getting worried," Loretta stated truthfully, eyeing him closely. His usual fastidious attention to his appearance was askew this morning—he'd shaved haphazardly, his shoes were scuffed, and his shirt looked rumpled. *Is he a little hungover?* she wondered.

Loretta followed Haynes into the building. Without another word, Haynes proceeded directly to his office, shouting over his shoulder that he didn't want to be disturbed. She nodded mutely as he slammed his door.

Loretta tackled the accounts payable and had a stack of checks ready for his signature by mid-morning. She considered knocking on his door but decided against it. Whatever he was doing in there, she wasn't going to interrupt him.

She leaned back in her chair to think. She was being grossly overpaid for a job that a part-time high-school graduate could do. He wasn't letting her use any of her expertise from her college education. There had been no reason to move her out here from California. And he wasn't interested in her sexually. She had flirted with him enough, without response, to know that wasn't the reason he hired her. Her intuition shouted that things didn't add up. *He's acting like he's got something to hide,* she thought. What was Frank Haynes up to?

Loretta spent the afternoon halfheartedly scrolling through Pinterest and Facebook as she continued to ponder her situation. If she could find out what Haynes was hiding—or even why he hired her—she'd have some very useful information. She was startled from her contemplation when he abruptly flung his door open at three thirty, coat and briefcase in hand. "We're done for the day," he said.

"But it's only three thirty," Loretta replied. "And you let me off early last week. I'll stay until five. In fact, I'll stay until six because we started late this morning," she said, the advantage of being alone in the office suddenly appealing to her.

"No. My fault you started late," he replied curtly. "I need to lock up," he said, motioning for her to get her things.

"I'll do it," she suggested brightly. "Have you got a spare key I can use?"

"I said it's okay," Haynes barked, then quickly apologized. "Sorry. Don't worry. I'll see you in the morning."

He stood at her desk as she gathered her purse and put on her coat, then walked out the door with her, turning to lock the office before rushing to his car without another word.

He was obviously in a hurry—a big hurry. Frank Haynes was getting more interesting by the minute. She'd find out about his little secrets, one way or another.

Chapter 30

David Wheeler had become a regular volunteer at Forever Friends, arriving every day after school. He spent most of his weekends there as well. Frank Haynes couldn't help but notice the similarity to himself at that age. David kept to himself and did what was requested of him without complaint. He'd even begun to show some initiative, cleaning and rearranging the storage room.

The next youngest volunteer was twice David's age, so the boy didn't have much in common with anyone there. The staff appreciated his efforts and was content to leave him alone and let him work. Haynes kept his distance, feeling both guilty for his part in the mess that had been William Wheeler's undoing and inept at offering comfort. Best to leave that to his court-appointed mentor, that kind man from Fairview Terraces.

Haynes swung by the shelter late one evening to pick up the financial report the office manager prepared for him. He was surprised to find David still at work, sweeping the walkway in front of the cages. As Frank watched from afar, David bent down in front of a cage and stuck something through the bars, rousing a mid-sized mutt with only one eye that had been dumped in a ditch and left for dead. Irritation flashed through Haynes. What in the world was this kid doing, teasing an animal like that? Was he just like so many other boys his age, getting his kicks out of torturing some poor creature? Maybe he'd even been with the group that abandoned the dog in the first place.

Haynes bolted down the hall to where David was standing, but brought himself up short when the boy turned and looked up with an expression that Haynes recognized—one of pure love and concern for a helpless creature. Haynes swallowed the harsh words on the tip of his tongue, and David turned back to the dog.

"Nice dog," Haynes uttered lamely. "What're you doing with him?"

David gestured with his head. "He's cold. See, he's shivering. He doesn't have a blanket, like most of the others. And we're out of blankets. So I shoved my jacket through the bars for him."

Haynes nodded. "That's a nice thing to do. Won't you need your jacket to get home?"

The boy shrugged. "Naw. I'll be fine. He needs it more than I do."

"Would you like to take him out to exercise him?"

"Isn't it too late for that?" David asked, poorly disguising the hope in his voice.

"I'm going to be here for a while going over the books," Haynes lied. "You can get him out of his cage. Take your time."

David unhooked the latch and bent onto one knee, gently coaxing the timid animal to him. Haynes picked up the report and took a seat in the now-deserted lobby.

As the pair passed by on the way to the "get acquainted" room, Haynes asked, "Do you have a dog, David?"

"Nope. Never had one."

"Well, maybe it's time we changed that," Haynes muttered under his breath. That boy and that dog belonged together.

Chapter 31

Frank Haynes now drove by Fairview Terraces every day on the way to his office. He didn't know why he did it; the place never changed. Maybe he felt an affinity for these elderly folks, just as he did with the stray animals at his Forever Friends shelter. Or maybe he wanted to curry favor with his voters. Whatever the reason, he kept an eye on the place and was surprised to see the large sign posted on the front lawn. He quickly turned into the main entrance and pulled over to read:

New Home of Westbury West Coast Swing Society
Join Us on Sunday Nights for an Evening of Dancing
Lessons at 4 p.m.
Open Dancing 5 p.m.–8 p.m.
All Are Welcome!
Come Get Your Groove On With Us! What're You Waitin' For?

Haynes smiled. Those seniors were going to make money out of this place after all. His efforts to get them their zoning variance hadn't been wasted.

Haynes started when a man rapped gently on the passenger side window. He swiveled in his seat to see the tall man from the zoning hearing, Glenn Vaughn, bending down to smile at him through the window.

Haynes rolled down his window. "Sorry to startle you," Glenn said. "I saw you looking at our sign. Wanted to thank you again for your help with our variance."

"Looks like you've got your first tenant," Haynes observed, gesturing to the sign.

"We do. They've booked our Great Hall every Sunday night for the next year. They said it's perfect for them. Maybe other dance groups will follow suit."

"That's terrific, Glenn. You should be very proud of yourself. You're the one who made this happen."

Glenn shrugged. "This Sunday will be their first dance. We're going to offer some special refreshments for the grand opening. We're trying to get a good turnout. I'm not much of a dancer, but Gloria and I will be there. She says that's what the lessons are for and I'll be fine." He cleared his throat. "We were hoping that you and Mayor Martin and

Councilwoman Holmes would stop by. To open it up and say a few words? Make it important?"

Haynes groaned inwardly. He hated this part of being a politician. He loved the power but loathed public appearances. Amiable small talk was not his forte. He forced a smile and replied that he'd check his calendar but thought he was already committed elsewhere.

"We've sent email invitations—my daughter says they're called e-vites—and the mayor is coming."

Frank Haynes paused. If Mayor Martin were attending, maybe he would go.

"Let me see what I can do. Why don't you plan on me being there? Now," he continued, "I need your help with something."

Glenn turned to Haynes in surprise.

"I'd be glad to," he answered.

"You're still working with David Wheeler, aren't you?"

"Yes. And thank you, again, for giving him that job at Forever Friends. He's been so much better since he's been working there. I think it's the only place where he feels happy." He added hastily, "Nothing's wrong there, is it? Is there a problem?"

"No. Nothing of the sort. He's doing a great job for us. And I think you're right about it being good for him. That's what I need help with. I think he should adopt one of the dogs."

"That's a lot of responsibility."

"I know that," Haynes replied. "I've watched him with the animals. There's a special bond between him and one of the dogs. I'd like to give the dog to him, but his mother needs to agree to it."

"Have you talked to her? Has she said no?"

"It's awkward for me to call her; she doesn't want to talk to any of us from the town council. She thinks we're all to blame for the mess her husband got into. I think she'll go along with it if you tell her it's a good idea."

Glenn gazed into the distance.

"You may be right," he finally said, turning back to the car. "I'll see her Saturday morning when I pick David up to go fishing. I'll talk to her then. Don't let that dog get adopted by anyone else."

Haynes reached out and shook Glenn's hand. "You get her okay, and I'll have the dog ready and waiting. Why don't you bring David around on Saturday afternoon when you're done, and together we'll send him home with a dog."

Glenn waved as Frank Haynes pulled away.

R

Glenn and Gloria hurried home from church that Sunday to put the finishing touches on the decorations for the inaugural dance of the Westbury West Coast Swing Society at Fairview Terraces. Crepe paper streamers crisscrossed the entrance to the Great Hall and the new disco ball was in place. Glenn dimmed the lights and flipped a switch, and he and Gloria watched as sparks of light swept the room.

Gloria took his hand. "You've done it! This looks fantastic. Everyone around here is more excited than they've been in years. I wonder if we'll have enough refreshments," she said, nervously glancing toward the boxes of cookies and cupcakes lined up on the food tables.

"You've got enough to feed an army, honey," Glenn reassured. "I hope we pack this place. We need this to be a success. I want to pay back Councilman Haynes."

"Stop worrying and come out here and dance with me, you old fool," she replied.

"There's no music," he said, hoping she wasn't serious. Even *with* music, he couldn't keep a beat.

"There will be." She took his hand and led him to the center of the floor. She positioned their arms and leaned close, pressing her lips to his ear. In her still-clear soprano, she softly sang the lyrics from the old classic "Let Me Call You Sweetheart."

Glenn closed his eyes as they swayed gently and basked in anticipation of the words *I'm in love with you.* He might have two left feet, but it didn't matter.

R

John Allen reluctantly pulled himself away from the television to shower, shave, and put on a suit for tonight's date with Maggie. When she phoned to invite him to the Westbury West Coast Swing Society's inaugural dance, he had readily accepted because he wanted to be with her any chance he got, but he hadn't thought this through. He was a horrible dancer. Embarrassing, truly. And some of these oldsters were really good. He'd look even more inept by comparison. Plus the football game he had been watching was a good one. In addition, he wasn't particularly looking forward to getting all dressed up on a Sunday night. He was feeling thoroughly dyspeptic by the time he rang the bell at Rosemont to pick her up.

His mood changed instantly as she opened the door. She looked glamorous and sexy in a shiny copper-colored halter-neck dress, her mane of chestnut hair caressing her shoulders. She had evidently enjoyed her afternoon of prepping and primping. Her high spirits were infectious.

"Whoa! Don't you look amazing? You're going to have to beat the guys away with a stick! Where's your dance card? I want to sign up for every dance right now."

Maggie beamed and then twirled. "Why thank you, kind sir," she said in a mock Southern drawl. "This old thing?"

"Is it new? You look spectacular!"

"It most certainly is. Buying a new dress for a dance is one of the not-to-be-missed joys of a girl's life."

John offered his arm. "Madam, may I have the pleasure of escorting you to the dance?"

R

Across town, Frank Haynes struggled into his tuxedo jacket and checked his reflection in the mirror. It still fit his trim frame, and he had to admit he looked good. Maybe going in formalwear was a bit overboard, but he was delivering the opening remarks and he knew that clothes set the right tone. He was dressing to impress. Whether that was for Maggie Martin or his constituents, he wasn't sure.

R

By three forty-five, a nice-sized crowd had gathered in the hallway outside of the Great Hall at Fairview Terraces. Women were perched in chairs along the walls, changing into their dancing shoes. An expectant buzz hung in the air.

"You see?" Gloria told Glenn. "Lots of people turned out."

"You're right. And most of them are from the Westbury West Coast Swing Society. I was afraid we'd have mostly Fairview Terraces folks for this first dance, and then attendance would dwindle. It looks like this facility-rental idea will be a success after all," he said, sounding pleased with himself.

"Showtime," Gloria observed as the doors swung open.

The dancers were lining up for their first lesson when Mayor Martin, accompanied by a distinguished-looking man, entered the room and hastily took her place, followed by Councilwoman Tonya Holmes and her husband, George. At six feet and six-six, respectively, the Holmeses towered over the crowd. George shook John's hand, remarking under his breath that misery loves company. John chuckled in agreement.

A moment later, the crowd began applauding to welcome their instructors. Sam Torres led his wife Joan onto the dance floor with some quick footwork and a fancy spin. Maggie leaned over and caught Tonya's eye with an arched look. Both women giggled.

"Did you know the Torreses were dancing stars?" Maggie whispered to John as Sam and Joan began their instruction by separating the dancers into female and male groups.

After fifty minutes of instruction, even the most wrong-footed would-be dancer was feeling confident. Sam and Joan exchanged a satisfied glance; everybody had mastered the basics.

"Maybe we'll even get John and Maggie to join the group," Joan said in an aside to Sam.

Maggie rejoined John and was about to comment that she hoped Frank Haynes would show up—he was supposed to make the opening remarks to the crowd—when the double doors opened and the very dapper-looking councilman made his entrance.

The hum of conversation slowly stopped as all eyes followed his progress to the center of the room. He stood for a moment and surveyed the crowd. *He's letting them admire him,* Maggie thought.

Haynes made his way to the stage and turned to the crowd. "Ladies and gentlemen, members of the Westbury West Coast Swing Society and residents of Fairview Terraces, welcome to this auspicious occasion— the first dance of the society in its new home here in this beautiful Great Hall. As you know, Fairview Terraces recently faced high financial hurdles. With the help of the resourceful residents here—and I want to particularly single out Glenn Vaughn standing right over there—we've been able to get over those hurdles. The use of this Great Hall for wonderful activities, like the dance we're enjoying tonight, is his doing. Let's show our appreciation, shall we? Put your hands together for Mr. Glenn Vaughn, ladies and gentlemen."

The crowd clapped enthusiastically and Glenn shrunk back. "If I didn't have you firmly by the hand," Gloria noted, "I think you'd hightail it out of here. Just nod and wave and accept the compliment."

She knows me pretty well for being together such a short time, Glenn thought, moving forward and slipping his hand over hers.

"And now, enough talking. Let me get out of the way and let the dancing begin!" Haynes was stepping off the stage when the newspaper reporter who had covered the Easter carnival at Rosemont caught his arm. She had Maggie in tow, as well. "You both look so nice. Let's get a photo of you dancing for tomorrow's paper. I think I'll be able to get this story on the front page if I've got the two of you."

Haynes shifted uncomfortably. *For heaven's sake,* Maggie thought. *It's only one dance and front-page publicity will help Fairview Terraces advertise their new availability for events and parties.* She smiled at Haynes and nodded to the dance floor. "Shall we?"

"You look very handsome in your tuxedo, Frank," she murmured as they proceeded to the center of the floor and the photographer took her position.

To Maggie's relief, the disc jockey selected an upbeat number; she didn't want to slow dance with Haynes while John waited on the sidelines. The councilman took her hand and steered her through some basic steps. To her surprise, he was an accomplished dancer and, most importantly, knew how to lead. Maggie was enjoying herself, and Haynes knew it. Having Maggie in his arms stirred feelings that he'd suppressed for years. The photographer circled them, clicking away with her camera. Maggie threw her head back and laughed.

"We're quite the celebrity couple, aren't we, Frank?"

Maybe she did feel something for him, he thought.

"That was a very generous speech you gave, Frank. Glenn Vaughn was so flattered. Giving other people their due is a good thing, isn't it?" she asked innocently.

He didn't know if she was trying to make a point or not.

The music trailed away. Haynes was about to suggest that Maggie remain right where she was for the next dance when Dr. John Allen appeared at her side so quickly it was obvious he had been waiting for his opportunity.

"Hello, Frank," John said, extending his hand. "Mind if I steal my date back from you?"

Haynes returned the warm handshake, but his eyes had grown steely. So that's the way it was? Maggie was with John again? He cocked an eyebrow at Maggie.

"John and I re-met on DogLovers.com. That'd be the perfect site for you to meet someone, Frank.

"You ought to give it a try," she tossed over her shoulder as John led her onto the dance floor.

I've tried it, Haynes thought, as he watched John sweep her into his arms. *And the one woman who looked interesting cancelled on me.*

The disc jockey started a slow ballad, and Haynes turned abruptly on his heel and wove his way through the sea of dancing couples. Ignoring the inviting glances of women lining the wall by the door, he strode out of the room.

Chapter 32

Glenn shifted the small velvet box from his jacket to his pants pocket. His grandmother's emerald, now flanked by two clusters of tiny diamonds, was elegant and dignified. The jeweler in town had done a wonderful job of refurbishing the ring. He chuckled as he remembered the astonished look on the young clerk's face when he requested a fancy ring box because he was going to propose. *Ha!* Kids hadn't cornered the market on love. He felt it more strongly now than ever.

The emerald had lain hidden in his safety deposit box for decades. Nancy had never liked the large square-cut stone—or maybe it was just that Nancy and his grandmother had never gotten along. He fervently hoped Gloria would love the ring. He felt certain she would; the stone complemented her deep green eyes.

He paced up and down the living room, rehearsing his speech. He would propose when he walked her home from the next dance. And did that woman love to dance! She was always happiest during their Sunday night sessions with the Westbury West Coast Swing Society. She praised him constantly, telling him he was catching on fast and soon she'd be battling other women for partner privileges. He was self-aware enough to know that she was being kind. If left to his own devices, he'd have thrown in the towel weeks ago. Still, he was beginning to enjoy himself, and if dancing made her happy, he was willing to go along.

He checked his watch and decided to head over to her place. *It's showtime,* he thought wryly. He checked his pocket for the ring for the thousandth time and set off.

R

Gloria was in particularly high spirits that night. Her life had taken on such unexpected richness in the past few months. Finding a wonderful beau at her age had been unthinkable. Now here was Glenn Vaughn, knocking at her door, collecting her to go to a dance. Her heart soared every time she saw him.

Gloria opened the door quickly.

"You're early," she said and stopped short. "Are you feeling all right, Glenn?" she asked, peering up at him. "You're flushed. Are you getting sick? We don't have to go tonight, you know. Maybe you should go home and go back to bed."

Glenn held up a hand.

"Stop. I'm fine. Fit as a fiddle; right as rain. Nothing wrong with me that dancing with my best gal won't cure. Now come on. I want to be there for the first dance."

Moving to the music with the familiar steps helped calm Glenn's jittery nerves. Other than an odd tendency to put his hand in his pocket, Gloria felt Glenn was doing really well. She was sorry to leave when the last dance was over.

"Let's see if the DJ will keep the music going," she said as they stepped off the floor. "Sometimes he does that, you know. If enough of us want to keep on dancing."

"I'd like to get going," Glenn replied quickly. "I've got something else I want to do tonight."

Gloria turned to him in surprise. "Oh, all right. I had no idea. You should have said something. We could have left earlier, you know."

"I didn't want to go earlier, but I do now," he replied cryptically.

He took her hand and placed it in the crook of his elbow. They left the hall and strolled through the still night air in companionable silence.

When they reached her door, Gloria quickly unlocked it and stepped over the threshold.

"I won't keep you," she said, turning to him. "I know you have other things to do. Talk to you tomorrow," she said, leaning over to kiss him.

"May I come inside?" he asked simply.

"Of course," she said, stepping aside and turning on a lamp in the living room. Looking perplexed, she asked, "Can I get you something?"

"No," he replied firmly. "Come. Sit down." He steered her to a chair by the lamp. "I have something to ask you."

Gloria settled herself into the chair and looked expectantly at Glenn. She was first confused and then astonished when he, with some effort, knelt down on one knee and took her hand.

"Gloria, I love you with all my heart. Much is written about the joys of first love, but I believe the greatest joy of life may be last love. The one you're going to love until you die. For me, Gloria, that one is you."

A tear rolled down her cheek, and Glenn gently wiped it away.

"You've brought so much light and energy back into my life, my dear. So much fun. And you've inspired me to take on challenges that I wouldn't have had the courage to tackle if you didn't believe in me so completely. I'm *more* with you. I cannot imagine living without you. I hope you feel the same way."

He shifted from one knee to the other. "I know we haven't been a couple for long, but at our ages, we don't have the luxury of time."

He retrieved the box from his pocket and flipped it open. "Gloria—my beloved Gloria—will you do me the honor of marrying me?"

Gloria, who had been keeping her tears at bay, now let them loose.

"Oh, Glenn. Why are you doing this? I love you; I truly do. I'm happier than I've ever been in my entire life. But I can't marry you. I'm so much older than you, and at our ages that accounts for a lot. I watched how wonderfully you cared for Nancy in her final days. I don't want you to have to do that again. That wouldn't be fair. It's very likely that I'll be the first to go. I couldn't bear being a burden to you. I simply won't do that to you."

Glenn rocked back on his heels in shock. He stiffly got to his feet and snapped the box shut. Gloria leaned forward and took his hand.

"I'm so very sorry. You are a wonderful, dear man. I wouldn't hurt you for the world."

Glenn nodded slowly. He hadn't considered that she would refuse him. He cleared his throat.

"I'd better be going," he said slowly.

Gloria began to rise to walk Glenn to the door.

"No. Don't get up," he stated firmly. "I'll see myself out."

R

Gloria didn't sleep that night and neither did Glenn. He scribbled a quick note and stuck it in her door sometime before six o'clock the following morning, saying he knew she would understand that he needed a day or two to sort out his feelings. Understand she did, but the hours dragged with a heaviness she had never known. Had she done the right thing? She knew she had. Her decision had been strong and loving; she was putting him first. She'd been a front row spectator to his agony and despair as he cared for Nancy. Once in a lifetime was enough for anyone. She prayed earnestly that they could get past this and resume their relationship as if nothing had happened.

Gloria occupied herself with housekeeping and correspondence, but she felt like she was holding her breath under water. She needed to hear from Glenn.

R

When Glenn got over the initial shock and embarrassment of being turned down—on his knees, proffering an emerald-and-diamond ring, no less—his thoughts turned to Nancy and all they had gone through. Was Gloria right? She was older and more likely to need care. Should he spare himself a replay of the wrenching experience of watching a loved one die? As he considered this, he knew with absolute certainty that if Gloria were sick, he would care for her as he had for Nancy. Whether

135

they were married or not. Whether she wanted him to or not. Gloria's objections were groundless. He knew what he had to do.

R

On the morning of the third day, Gloria found a vase filled with white roses on her doorstep, a note tucked by its side. Her heart skipped a beat as she brought them to the table and sat down to read his message:

My dearest Gloria,

Your objections are without foundation. You are my true love, for the rest of our lives. Whatever might befall you, I will be there for you, to care for and comfort you whether we are married or not. You must know that. I'm an old-fashioned man and believe in the sanctity of marriage.

Consider this from Ecclesiastes 4:9–12:

Two are better than one, because they have a good return for their labor; If either of them falls down, one can help the other up. But pity anyone who falls and has no one to help them up. Also, if two lie down together, they will keep each other warm. But how can one keep warm alone? Though one may be overpowered, two can defend themselves. A cord of three strands is not quickly broken.

I believe with every fiber of my being that we should bind our strands together and finish this journey as husband and wife. If you will, if I am the man for you, you only have to let me know. I'm not going to pressure you or bring this up again. I'll pick you up for dinner tomorrow night. Pray on this. I'll abide by your decision.

Yours faithfully and forever,
Glenn

Gloria reached for a tissue to dab at her eyes and re-read the note. What a complete fool she had been. If God had seen fit to send this wonderful man to her, then she was going to accept him and be as kind and good to him as humanly possible for as long as possible. Only He knew what was in store for them. She'd have to trust in that, as she always had.

Gloria reached for her Bible and found the verse she was looking for.

R

When Glenn stepped out of his door the following morning, he was greeted with a homemade apple pie and a simple one-line note from Gloria that read:

136

2 Samuel 12:7
Thou art the man.

Glenn flew back into his living room and snatched the ring box from the end table where he had tossed it the other night. He was heading straight to Gloria's. What was that lyric to the song that was so popular with the kids? "If you want it, better put a ring on it?" Well … he was going to put a ring on it!

Chapter 33

Glenn and Gloria were finishing up lunch at Pete's Bistro in celebration of their engagement. His grandmother's emerald had delighted Gloria, but the ring was far too big. They had dropped it at the jeweler the day before, Gloria telling them to "put a rush on it, like never before." The jeweler called first thing in the morning to tell them it was ready and Gloria insisted that they set out straight away to pick it up. *No matter what age, you don't want to get between a woman and her rock,* Glenn realized.

He was helping Gloria with her coat when Laura appeared in the archway that joined her bakery to her husband's restaurant. She made a beeline to their table.

"What's this good news I'm hearing about the two of you?" she said excitedly.

Glenn and Gloria exchanged a bemused glance. "Why, whatever do you mean, dear?" Gloria asked sweetly.

"Your engagement, of course! Valerie from the jewelers just called and said that you're engaged and have the most amazing vintage ring," she announced gleefully. "Congratulations, you two. I'm so happy for you. We all are. Now let me see that ring!"

Gloria held out her hand proudly. "Thank you. Very kind of everyone to be so interested in what two oldsters like us are doing."

"Not at all. Are you kidding? You're the town's main topic of conversation. This ring is simply gorgeous. Did he surprise you with it? Down on one knee and everything?" Laura glanced over at Glenn. "Sorry. None of my business. I just love weddings. I do beautiful wedding cakes, you know. They're my favorite things to make."

"That's all right, dear. We're flattered by your interest. Yes, the ring was a complete surprise and I adore it. And he made a traditional proposal."

Laura sighed dreamily. "That's so romantic. When's the big day? Will you have a ceremony and reception?"

Glenn laughed. "We haven't gotten that far yet. I've just managed to get the ring on her finger."

"Do let me know. I'd love to bake a cake for you. Again, congratulations," Laura said as Gloria took Glenn's arm and pressed him toward the door.

"Sweet girl," Gloria remarked when they were outside on the sidewalk. "But how silly. Can you imagine having a wedding at our ages? Who'd want to come, anyway?"

"I can imagine it perfectly well," Glenn stated emphatically. "Why not? We may be past throwing the garter and the bouquet, but I think a ceremony to mark the occasion is in order. Something dignified and joyful."

"You've thought this through, haven't you?" Gloria remarked, looking up at Glenn.

"Yes, I have. I'd rather not rush off to the justice of the peace."

"Well, no," Gloria replied slowly. "In our day, people always thought the bride was pregnant. We can't have that, now can we?"

They both laughed.

"Seriously, Gloria, why don't we get married when your son comes for Thanksgiving? I don't want a big, fancy wedding, but I want our marriage to be sanctified in a religious ceremony with our family and friends present."

Gloria looked into Glenn's earnest blue eyes and knew he was right. "In that case," she said, "why don't we walk over to Town Hall to get our marriage license? We've got a lot to do. We've got a wedding to plan."

R

By the time they left the clerk's office, license in hand, the solid outline of their wedding had been formed. When they ran into Mayor Martin on their way out, the couple exchanged a conspiratorial glance. Glenn was the first to speak.

"Mayor Martin," he said, extending his hand. "Glenn Vaughn from Fairview Terraces."

"Yes, of course I remember you, Mr. Vaughn," she said, shaking hands.

"This is my fiancée, Gloria Harper," he said proudly, turning to Gloria. "We're wondering if you'll be attending the Thanksgiving Prayer Breakfast at Fairview Terraces. It's going to be especially meaningful, and we'd be honored if you'd be there."

Maggie smiled. "I'd be delighted to, wouldn't miss it for the world," she answered, all the while thinking that her family would be in town for Thanksgiving and she would need to be at home, in her kitchen, cooking. Did being a politician mean that she was always on call? Was she letting this job take precedence over her personal life again? Maggie stifled a heavy sigh and turned her attention back to this sweet couple. "I've got my kids coming to town for Thanksgiving, so I'll do my best to be there," she said, feeling slightly better about herself having amended her answer.

"Bring them along," Gloria stated. "We're counting on you to be there."

Maggie nodded her agreement and returned to her office as Glenn and Gloria headed toward the exit.

R

Maggie was still thinking about the prayer breakfast as she pulled into the supermarket parking lot on her way home from Town Hall. She would pick up groceries and something from the delicatessen for dinner.

She was waiting in line at the register when a neatly dressed man in his mid-fifties approached her.

"Mayor Martin? I'm Tom Barton," he said, extending his hand. "I teach math at the high school. I need to know what's happening with my pension. I've only got another ten years to work. If the pension fund goes belly up, I have to find a new job. Move away from Westbury and teach somewhere else."

"We're working through this as fast as we can. We have to be deliberate in our approach and not make any snap decisions. The pension fund hasn't gone belly up, but it's suffered significant losses."

Maggie sighed. At the end of a long day, this was the last conversation she wanted to have. Couldn't she even buy groceries in peace?

"How long have you been at the high school?"

"Since I graduated from college—over thirty years. I've got everything tied up in the pension fund." Tom waved at a slightly younger man dressed in overalls and work boots. "That's my neighbor. He works at the water department. Been there for twenty-five years. We've been talking about this mess and our wives are worried sick."

Tom's neighbor joined them. "Where the hell's my money?" he asked, his voice projecting to the produce section. "You can't get away with this! We're going to throw all you crooks out of office and into jail if we don't get what's coming to us."

Maggie pulled her shopping cart out of line and turned to the two men. "We're working very hard to identify the scope of the problem and to implement solutions. It's going to take time. I appreciate how distressing this is for you. Transparency is important, and we're doing our best to give you information as soon as it's available."

The man pulled a rumpled paper out of the pocket of his overalls. "This is a petition, signed by people who want you removed from office. I've already collected six pages of signatures. We don't want information; we want our money back in the pension fund. And you don't have much time," he said, shaking the paper in her face.

A crowd had gathered around them, trapping Maggie. She clutched the handles of the shopping cart and searched for words that would diffuse the situation. "I understand your concerns," she stammered, as the store manager broke into the circle.

"What's the problem here?" he asked. His eyes locked on Maggie. "Let's give the mayor some space, will you? She was just leaving," he said as he took her elbow and steered her toward the exit.

Maggie made her way quickly to her car. To hell with her groceries, she thought. And to hell with this store; she'd take her business elsewhere. She'd just been thrown out of a supermarket. What was her life coming to?

Chapter 34

Maggie swept her eyes from her computer screen to her office door. "Come in," she called, as Chief Thomas entered her office.

"Hello, Chief," she said, rising from her seat.

"Please, don't get up. I'm here to deliver the result of the coroner's report on William Wheeler's death."

Maggie waited expectantly.

"Natural causes. As I said at the time, he was alone in his cell when he died and there was no evidence of foul play. The toxicology reports found no opiates or cocaine. He was a lifelong smoker and drinker. Couple that with all the stress he was under and it evidently proved too much for him."

Maggie shook her head. "I don't know, Chief. He seemed pretty hardy to me. Have you told Alex yet?"

"Yes. I just came from his office; I actually walked into the building with him. He figured I was here to deliver the results."

Maggie pursed her lips. "Is he satisfied with this explanation? Are there further tests that can be run?"

Chief Thomas shifted uncomfortably. "There are other tests, but they cost a lot of money. We've followed protocol to the letter, here," he stated defensively. "Alex is satisfied and so am I. Wheeler had a heart attack."

Maggie rose from her chair. "Is Alex in his office? I'd like to discuss this with both of you." She preceded him out the door, not waiting to see if he would follow her.

"Alex," Maggie said, rapping lightly on his door.

She motioned Chief Thomas into the room and closed the door. Alex raised a brow at them both.

"Maggie isn't happy about the cause of death being natural causes," Chief Thomas stated.

"It's not that I'm unhappy about it," Maggie snapped. "That's the result we all wanted. It just strikes me as extremely unlikely. What's the harm in doing some additional investigation?"

Alex rose from his chair and came around his desk to face them. "The harm is that it isn't necessary. We've done everything by the book and we've received the most likely answer. Wasting taxpayer money digging for something else makes us look like conspiracy theorists searching for the sinister answer we want rather than the simple truth that we've found."

Maggie sighed and leaned back against his desk.

"Wheeler's death is a terrible impediment to your investigation. Maybe it's time to call in the feds; let them use their expanded resources to investigate this whole thing—including running additional tests on Wheeler's body."

Both men rounded on her in unison.

"If you think I'm not competent to run this investigation, just say so," Chief Thomas spat. "Maggie, you're out of line," Alex stated coldly. "I've worked with Chief Thomas for almost twenty years. He's the best in the business. We're working night and day to develop this case carefully and thoroughly, so we can convict anyone involved. And we don't need a newcomer second-guessing us."

Maggie felt her cheeks flush, and she fought the urge to say something she would regret. She stood and steadied herself. When she spoke, it was slowly and with emphasis. If they were no longer her friends and supporters, so be it. She had a job to do, and she wouldn't let anyone deter her.

"I'm not questioning your competence or diligence. But the scope of this investigation may be beyond our resources."

Both men shook their heads and she held up her hand to silence them. "Make no mistake about this. If I decide that we need to turn this over to federal officials, I'll do so. With or without your consultation or support. Until that time, I expect you to continue to the best of your abilities."

Maggie fixed each of them with an icy stare, and re-treated to her office.

R

Later that evening, Frank Haynes received a call from his old friend, Professor Upton. "It's almost ten o'clock, Don," Haynes observed. "Something must be troubling you."

"It is, Frank. You've got a mess going on down there in Westbury, don't you?"

"Why do you say that?"

"I've just had a call from Mayor Martin. She doesn't believe the coroner's report that William Wheeler died in jail from natural causes. She suggested to Special Counsel Scanlon and Chief Thomas that they turn the investigation over to the feds; a suggestion they took great umbrage to. I gather that her exchange with them got quite heated. She's feeling no support from them—or anyone. Did you know that she's been getting hate emails? She's even being accosted in restaurants and the supermarket."

"The press has been having a field day with her, but I didn't know about the rest of this."

"She's having a real crisis of confidence, Frank. She's putting up a good front, but she's scared and miserable. Feeling like she's not competent to do the job. I wanted you to know. Maybe you can weigh in on her side; help her out."

Haynes leaned back in his chair as he hung up the phone. Just six weeks ago, he would have found the news of Maggie's despair absolutely delightful. Strangely enough, he found himself feeling sad. Maybe he should do something to assist her after all.

Chapter 35

Frank Haynes stretched and looked at his watch. It was almost noon, and he had been hard at work on next year's forecast since before six that morning. His spirits were high; his new restaurants were ahead of projections. Next year would be a banner year for Haynes Enterprises.

He leaned forward in his chair to watch his new financial analyst hard at work in the reception area. Loretta Nash was nice enough—pleasant looking to be sure—and maybe even quite capable. Not that he'd ever let her near his real books. Some things, like the financial statements of his business, were best kept private.

Haynes steepled his fingers and rested his elbows on his desk. Ms. Nash's principal attraction was that she had been the mistress of Paul Martin, the late husband of their mayor. Maggie seemed determined to get to the bottom of Westbury's financial crisis, including prosecuting everyone involved. Getting to the bottom of things wasn't good for Frank Haynes. And it might not be good for her, either—he wasn't convinced that Wheeler's death had been from natural causes. If she kept digging, she might meet the same fate. If he had some dirt on Maggie, he'd be able to force her out—if only to protect her. And himself, of course.

Loretta Nash might just hold the key. Did Maggie know about her husband's affair? Was Loretta's youngest child Paul Martin's daughter? Based upon the timing unearthed by his private investigator, Haynes knew that was a distinct possibility. But with women like Nash, you never knew. He wouldn't bet a nickel on her fidelity. But that was neither here nor there. In all likelihood, she had information he would find very useful. He was sure of it.

The time had come to start assembling ammunition. Haynes rose from his desk and approached Loretta. "It's a beautiful day; shame to spend it all in here. How about we drive out to The Mill for lunch?"

Loretta stared at him, puzzled by his sudden friendliness.

"Leave all that. You can pick it up later. You've been working very hard since you started here, and I'd like to show my appreciation."

Haynes' shifting moods—from easygoing one minute to overbearing the next—made Loretta uneasy, but she could hardly refuse. She retrieved her purse from her desk drawer, slung her sweater over her shoulders, and they set off.

The drive to The Mill on this bright afternoon was glorious. Haynes was an expert driver and his Mercedes hugged every corner and dip as they sped through the mid-day sunshine. She vaguely worried that he might make a pass at her, but his every move was professional and courteous. Maybe he was just being a thoughtful employer after all.

Loretta relaxed as they placed their orders. She answered all of his questions about her children and about living in the desert, but she sensed he was only barely listening to her answers. His mind was elsewhere, she was sure of it.

"You once told me that you knew of Rosemont—that you knew Paul Martin," he said, his eyes locked on hers.

Loretta nodded and waited for him to continue.

"I'm sorry that I never met him; he must have been quite the man. Very accomplished. How did you know him?"

"He gave a talk at my college."

Haynes waited, but she didn't supply any further details. "He must have made quite an impression on you if you remember him from a talk."

Loretta concentrated on her salad and didn't respond.

"Did you see him after the talk?"

"Yes, I believe so. I attended a conference that he participated in."

Haynes fumed. This was like cross-examining a witness. Clearly, Loretta Nash was holding her cards close to her vest—whether out of loyalty to Paul Martin or to protect herself, he wasn't sure. He'd change tactics and approach her from a different angle.

"Shame that he didn't spend any time here, what with owning Rosemont and all. Quite a place to inherit, don't you think?"

She looked up and nodded. "Yes. It's spectacular. Like something from the English countryside."

Haynes smiled inwardly; he had her now. "Worth a fortune. Anyone would be thrilled to live there. I wonder why he never brought his family to see it. Or if he wasn't going to use it, why he didn't sell it. He would've gotten a pretty penny for it."

Loretta looked thoughtful. "It's odd; I agree."

Haynes continued. "They say that his wife—our Mayor Martin—didn't even know he owned it until she inherited it at his death. Now that's really strange don't you think?"

Loretta had a wistful look on her face as she answered, "I couldn't say."

Haynes felt his frustration rise; this conversation was going nowhere. "Did Paul Martin ever mention Rosemont to you?" he asked boldly.

"He may have mentioned it in passing."

"What did he say about it?" Haynes pressed.

Loretta gave him a quizzical look. "I don't remember. I didn't know him very well," she lied.

So that's how she wants to play it, Haynes thought. *All right, Ms. Nash. Round one to you. But I'm not done digging yet. I'm a patient man; you'll tell me what I want to know eventually.*

Haynes abruptly signaled to the waiter for the check. "We've been gone too long—time to get back to work."

Chapter 36

John sped up the driveway of Rosemont at seven fifteen Thanksgiving morning, about to meet Mike Martin and his wife and kids for the first time. Before stepping out of the car, he straightened his tie and checked his reflection in the rearview mirror. Maggie had assured him that this Thanksgiving Prayer Breakfast would not be anything fancy, but he wanted to make a good impression on her family.

As he mounted the stone steps, Maggie's daughter, Susan, flung open the massive door before he had even reached the bell.

"Saw you coming up the driveway," she said, pulling him into a hug before ushering him into the living room. "How are you? You look terrific! Very official. I'll need to go change. But first, let me introduce you to my brother."

Mike Martin rose and appraised John, a grin lighting his face as he extended his hand.

"So this is the incomparable John Allen I've heard so much about from my sister," he said. "Pleased to meet you."

John relaxed. "I could say the same about you, Mike. You should hear how your mother talks about you. Nice to finally meet you."

Mike introduced his wife, Amy, and the twins, Sophie and Sarah.

"I hear you have a really friendly dog," Sophie said.

"Where is he?" Sarah asked. "Did you bring him?"

John shook his head.

"It's not nice to leave a dog home alone on Thanksgiving. And Eve needs someone to play with. Can we stop on the way back and pick him up?" Sophie asked.

"Of course we can," Maggie interjected as she entered the room, taking off her apron and retrieving her coat from the closet. "Why didn't I think of that, Sophie? Good idea."

She gave John a wink.

"We'd better get going," Maggie said. "Susan," she called up the stairs. "We need to leave. I thought you were ready."

"Changing into something nicer. Be right there."

Maggie tossed her keys to Mike. "You guys take my car and follow us. Susan and I will ride with John since he's generously offered his chauffeur services. Let's roll."

R

The lot was full when they pulled into Fairview Terraces that morning. To her embarrassment, a sign marked "Mayor" had been set out to save her a parking spot. She motioned for Mike to take the spot and John squeezed his SUV into an opening at the loading dock by the kitchen.

"Reserved parking, Mom?" Susan chided. "You sure are a bigwig."

Maggie rolled her eyes. "Come on, let's catch up with the others."

As they hurried across the campus toward the open-air area set up for the Thanksgiving Prayer Breakfast, Maggie was gratified to see the large turnout. This wasn't just a gathering of a handful of the religious faithful from Fairview Terraces; citizens from all over town were there. She smiled and waved at Sam and Joan Torres; she should have expected them to be here. And Tonya Holmes had told her yesterday that her family would attend. Alex Scanlon was seated toward the back. His partner, Marc Benson, was playing the keyboard for the service. She didn't recognize the man sitting with Alex.

She spotted Mike, Amy, and the kids milling around the food tables and motioned them to join her in the front row. As they made their way to their seats, she was amazed to see Chuck Delgado and Frank Haynes seated at the end of the same row.

Maggie leaned across John, smiled, and mouthed "Good morning. Happy Thanksgiving" to them as Glenn Vaughn, dressed smartly in a black suit with a white rose pinned to his lapel, quietly approached Haynes.

She watched the unfolding scene with rapt attention, leaning further over John in an unsuccessful attempt to eavesdrop. Glenn handed Haynes an envelope, which the councilman promptly opened. Delgado leaned out of his seat, straining to read the amount of what looked like a check. Delgado's satisfied grin was shattered when Haynes ceremoniously tore the check in two and handed both halves to Glenn, clapping him on the back as Glenn pumped Haynes' hand, thanking him profusely.

John turned to Maggie. "Looks like Glenn tried to pay Frank back, and Frank did the generous thing and refused the money. Will wonders never cease?"

"He's probably hoping that everyone will notice and he'll get good press for it," she said. "Maybe he thinks that they'll mention him during the prayer service. You know Frank. But if he's done a good thing, why not?"

"Did you see Delgado's face? He wouldn't have given the money back."

Maggie snorted. "That's for sure. Still, didn't his reaction seem strange to you? Why did he care? It wasn't his money. If I didn't know better, I'd think something fishy was going on."

"With those two, something fishy is always going on," John agreed. Their discussion was cut short as three men and a woman rose in unison and stood by the podium.

"Good morning," began the woman, whom Maggie recognized as the senior pastor from the Methodist church. "Rabbi Goldstein, Fathers Harper and Chavez, and I want to welcome you here on this fine morning to our inaugural Thanksgiving Prayer Breakfast. Thank you all for tearing yourselves away from your kitchens and television sets to come together, as a community, to worship together. Father Harper is an Episcopal priest from Charleston, South Carolina. He's with us today to visit his mother, Gloria Harper. Gloria is a longtime resident of Fairview Terraces, and we're honored to have Father Harper with us today."

"That's nice," Maggie whispered to John.

Rabbi Goldstein stepped to the microphone and began the invocation. The brief but meaningful service concluded as the sun cleared the trees, bathing the area in brilliant sunshine that seemed to intensify the clear blue sky.

At the end of the service, Father Harper rose from his seat and walked around the podium to stand at the end of the center aisle. His booming voice needed no microphone.

"Dearly beloved, we have gathered today to give thanks as a community for our many blessings. Two among you would like to give thanks to God for bringing them together in a special part of their journey through life by joining together in Holy Matrimony." The Father paused as the surprise rippled through the crowd.

"My mother, Ms. Gloria Harper, and Mr. Glenn Vaughn invite all of you to rejoice with them as they take their vows. If any of you need to leave, we wish you Godspeed and will await your departure." With that he stepped back and regarded the crowd. Not a soul stirred. He signaled Marc with a slight nod and the gathering was bathed in the majestic chords of Pachelbel's Canon in D Major.

Father Harper raised his chin and smiled, and all eyes turned to the back row. Gloria Harper, looking radiant in a jacketed tea-length lavender dress with a crown of white roses in her generous, upswept hair, was proceeding down the aisle on the arm of a very dapper-looking Glenn Vaughn. Unaccustomed to all the attention and slightly embarrassed, they both kept their eyes locked on Father Harper. As handkerchiefs and tissues were pulled from pockets and purses throughout the crowd, Glenn's granddaughter Cindy Larsen handed their six-week-old baby to her husband and furiously began snapping photos with her cell phone.

By the time the simple, traditional vows had been exchanged and Father Harper had declared the couple husband and wife, there wasn't a dry eye in the crowd. Father Harper signaled Marc once more and the strains of "Ode to Joy" rang out as the newlyweds made their way back down the aisle, pausing to accept hugs and handshakes from friends who surged to congratulate them.

"So that's what they were hinting at a couple of weeks ago," Maggie said, leaning in to John to be heard over the boisterous crowd. "I ran into them at Town Hall, and they insisted I be here. How sweet they are."

"Mom," Susan called.

Maggie turned to her daughter.

"This was a surprise to everybody, wasn't it? What a lovely, romantic thing," she said, dabbing her eyes.

"They just brought out the biggest cake I've ever seen, Gramma," Sophie shouted. "Can we go have some?"

Maggie glanced at Amy, who threw her hands up in mock exasperation and laughed.

"How often do you attend a surprise wedding?" she asked, grabbing her daughters' hands. "Let's go get in the queue."

"What are you crying about, Sis? You don't even know these people," Mike chided.

"I know," she said, still wiping at her eyes with the damp tissue in hand. "But it was just so beautiful. And they look incredibly happy. And comfortable together."

"Does anyone else want cake?" John asked. "Laura is handing out slices, so it must be one of hers. It'll be good."

Susan shook her head.

"Not me," Maggie answered. "I'm going to congratulate the happy couple, and I'd like to introduce Mike to Alex and Marc." Thankfully, she and Alex had managed to retain their personal closeness despite the recent professional showdown.

Susan nodded. "I'd like to say hi, too. I had so much fun hiding eggs with them at the carnival last Easter."

John spotted them on the far side of the lawn, talking to Sam and Joan Torres.

"Over there. Follow me," he ordered, taking Maggie's hand and leading the small caravan through the crowd.

Sam gave an exaggerated wave. "So glad that you were here for this," he said.

"Wasn't it just wonderful?" Joan said with a sigh. "A Thanksgiving to remember, for sure."

"You all know my daughter, Susan? She was here last year at Easter?" Everyone nodded. "And this is my son, Mike. He and his wife, Amy, and my twin granddaughters are here for Thanksgiving." She turned in the direction of the food tables. "Those girls are out there somewhere, snagging a piece of wedding cake."

Alex smiled warmly at Susan. "I *thought* I saw you with your mom," he said, giving her a quick hug. "You remember Marc?"

"Yes, of course. How are you? Loved your playing during the prayer service and the wedding," she said, eyeing the handsome stranger standing next to Alex.

"And I'd like to introduce you to my brother Aaron. He's an orthopedic surgeon. Just finished his residency and has a job offer with a practice here in Westbury," Alex concluded proudly.

"Really?" Maggie replied, shaking Aaron's hand. "That's wonderful. Congratulations. Moving to Westbury has a lot of benefits, besides being near your brother. I'm sure he's told you. Our schools are first rate and housing is reasonable. Do you have a family?" she asked, looking about.

"No. I'm not married," he responded politely to Maggie, but his gaze was locked on Susan.

"Do you live in Westbury, Susan?" Aaron asked, extending his hand to her. The two stared at each other for an awkward moment as they shook hands.

"No. I'm from Southern California. Just visiting Mom for Thanksgiving."

"Do you get here often?" he pressed, holding onto her hand for a split second longer than necessary.

"From time to time," she said, deciding on the spot to turn the lie into a truth.

Maggie and Alex exchanged surprised glances. *Those two are really hitting it off.*

Maggie improvised.

"Do you all have plans for dinner today?"

What a ridiculous question, she realized. *Who didn't have dinner plans by eleven o'clock on Thanksgiving morning?*

Alex was as pleased about the sparks flying between Susan and Aaron as Maggie was.

"Nothing definite," he replied.

"The three of you must join us at Rosemont. We have plenty of room, and that will give us all a chance to catch up," she declared matter-of-factly. She turned to the Torreses. "How about you and Sam, Joan? What are you doing?"

"I have to work the three-to-eleven shift," she replied. "So we aren't doing anything. I made a turkey when I was off yesterday and Sam has leftovers."

"Then it's settled. You'll come too, Sam," she stated, putting an end to the discussion. She turned to John and Susan. "We'd better get back to the kitchen at Rosemont. See you all at four; dinner will be at five."

With the new Thanksgiving plans locked in, she headed off to congratulate the newlyweds and collect the rest of her brood.

Chapter 37

Maggie turned to Susan in the backseat as they were pulling away from Fairview Terraces. "So, Aaron seemed nice, didn't he?"

"Yes, of course he did," she replied nonchalantly.

"And he's single." Maggie had to restrain her glee.

"For heaven's sake, Mom." Susan could barely control her frustration. "Is that why you invited them? When we were planning on a family dinner?"

"You liked him. You can't tell me there weren't sparks," Maggie retorted, stung by Susan's tone.

John glanced at Susan in the rearview mirror. "Your mom's got a point. We all felt it."

Susan turned to stare out the window. "Well, okay. Maybe there were some sparks," she admitted. "But what good are sparks when I'm in California, and he's here? Why don't I ever meet someone I might have a chance with?"

"You don't know how this is going to turn out. Don't go discounting things before you have the whole story," Maggie said, turning to smile at John. "You don't want to miss something that might be wonderful for you both."

R

The afternoon passed in a blur of activity. Susan, Maggie, and Amy settled into an amiable routine in the kitchen, with Sophie and Sarah racing in and out, chasing the dogs, and generally making a nuisance of themselves.

By midafternoon, Amy had had enough. She corralled both girls and told them to get their coats. She marched into the library where John and Mike, comfortably sunk into the leather chairs flanking the fireplace, were watching football on television.

"Okay, you two," Amy ordered. "It's time to make yourselves useful. Why don't you take the girls to the park? They're driving us crazy."

"No, Mom. We don't want to go out. We'll be good," came the united cry.

John stood. "That's a great idea. Let's take Eve and Roman, and we can all go to the dog park."

Enthusiastic squeals told him that he'd hit the mark.

Mike glanced up from the television to look at his wife and knew he wouldn't be able to weasel out of this mission. He checked the score one last time and headed out the door with the others.

R

By three thirty, the cooking was in full swing and dinner was on schedule. Maggie declared that she was going to her room to put her feet up for fifteen minutes, and they were welcome to join her. Based on her daughter's incessant clock-watching during the last hour, she suspected Susan would want to touch up her makeup. Amy volunteered to stay downstairs to keep an eye on things.

Maggie stuck her head inside Susan's door shortly before four. "I'm going down now. Ready?" she asked.

"Almost," Susan called from behind her closed bathroom door.

"Don't worry about being downstairs when they arrive. You can always make a grand entrance."

"Mom, you're being ridiculous," she said as she opened the door and stepped out wrapped in a towel. "I just wanted to freshen up."

"You've showered and washed your hair," Maggie observed. "That's a bit more than freshening up. Will you be ready in time for dinner?"

"Of course I will," she replied. "Now go downstairs and let me finish. I'll be there in fifteen."

R

Alex, Marc, and Aaron arrived promptly at four o'clock, with Sam Torres on their heels. They were milling around the fireplace, Mike taking coats, and John handing out glasses of wine when Susan descended into the living room. Maggie thought how lovely and natural her daughter looked; her shiny blond hair cascading over the back of her slender black dress. She snuck a surreptitious glance at Aaron and was gratified to see him zeroed in on Susan. Marc caught Maggie's eye and winked conspiratorially.

Mike turned to his sister. "Actually, Susan is the family expert on wine. She goes up to Napa a couple times a year, don't you?" Susan nodded and joined in a lively discussion of the merits of domestic wine.

Maggie intercepted John as he tried to slide into position to watch the football game. "A word, please," she whispered earnestly in his ear. "Did you see how she gussied herself up for dinner? That's because Aaron is here. This isn't like her. I want to make sure they have the chance to get to know each other."

John nodded absentmindedly, one eye on the television.

155

"You can get back to your silly game in a minute," Maggie said, gently pulling his face to hers. "I didn't make place cards, so I want you to help me make sure that Susan sits with Aaron at dinner. Okay?"

"Don't you think you should let things take their course?"

"No, I most certainly don't. That's why I'm putting you in charge."

Knowing when it was wise to retreat, John shook his head emphatically. "I've got it, loud and clear. If I have to pull a chair out from under someone, if I have to use an old football tackling move, I'll make sure they sit together." He brushed the top of her head with a kiss. "Now relax, and enjoy your party. Everything'll be fine."

R

John was right. Everything was better than fine. The food was delicious and her only oversight was leaving the second pan of rolls in the oven until they resembled hockey pucks. For as frustratingly ill-conceived a meal as Thanksgiving, where there were far too many last-minute, labor-intensive dishes on the menu, it had turned out well. Best of all, Aaron sat next to Susan without any intervention from John or Maggie.

When the meal ended, everyone helped clear the table and clean up the kitchen. Even Sophie and Sarah helped, while Roman and Eve curled up together, snoozing on the hearth rug. They finished in record time.

Maggie was bringing coffee into the living room when Amy looked at her watch and reluctantly announced that it was bedtime for the twins.

"Aw, Mom," Sarah whined. "Can't we stay up? We're being good."

Susan broke in, "Do let them, Amy. Let's all play a game! What've you got, Mom?"

Maggie paused, not sure she had any games at all. She suddenly remembered the old set of dominos she'd run across during her day in the attic. "I don't know exactly where it is—or even if it's complete—but there's a set of dominos in the attic."

"Fabulous!" Susan leapt up. "I've been itching to get up there all week." Aaron smiled at her and got to his feet. "You're a little overdressed for attic rummaging. How about I go with you? You direct me and I'll retrieve them."

Maggie struggled to stop herself from beaming ear to ear.

"Back in a flash," Susan said as they tore up the stairs with Sophie and Sarah bringing up the rear.

R

The group downstairs relaxed comfortably by the fire, sipping coffee and trading observations about the surprise wedding and plans for the upcoming holidays. Maggie finally put down her coffee cup and announced that she was going upstairs to check on the domino seekers. She added, half-kidding, "I hope they didn't get locked in."

She made the turn at the landing as Susan and Aaron were slowly descending the attic stairs in single file carrying a dusty old trunk between them.

"Mom," Susan gasped before Maggie could speak. "You won't believe what we found up there."

"Dominos?" Maggie asked lamely.

"No. Gosh. We forgot about those," she said with a chagrined sigh. "We found tons of the most glorious antique Christmas decorations."

Maggie moved to let them pass as Susan said excitedly, "This is full of ornaments. Wait until you see them."

Hearing their labored progress, John joined them on the stairs. "What in the world? Here, let me take this end," he said to Susan. She backed away, and Aaron and John muscled the trunk down the remainder of the stairway. Maggie pounced on it as soon as they set it down, throwing open the lid with Susan at her side.

Susan was right; nestled in tissue paper were brightly hued blown-glass ornaments of intricate design. Maggie had never seen anything like them.

"Didn't you find these when you were up there, Mom?"

Maggie could only shake her head.

"There's tons of this stuff. It was all in the far corner. Behind the hotel silver. I guess that stopped you in your tracks," Susan said, giving her mother a knowing glance.

"Aaron and I decided we're going out to buy the biggest Christmas tree in Westbury tomorrow and we're going to bring all of this stuff downstairs and decorate Rosemont like it hasn't been in years. Sophie and Sarah are coming, too," she said, smiling at her nieces. "Anybody else up for this?"

"I'm off tomorrow," Sam finally answered. "I could help set up the tree. But I don't want to intrude on family time."

"Nonsense," Maggie and Susan said in unison. "You're family," Maggie smiled at him. "You, too, Alex and Marc. John? Are you working tomorrow?"

"Half day," John replied. "I can come over after that."

"It's settled then," Susan said, beaming at the others. "We'll get started early. Let's gather here at eight thirty."

Maggie regarded her daughter with admiration; what an organizer she was.

"Should we bring breakfast?" Alex asked.

"Don't worry about food; we've got enough leftovers for an army," Maggie assured him.

"Dad," Sophie said from the stairway, "we're going to bed. We've got a big day tomorrow."

"Good point. See you all tomorrow," Alex said, giving Maggie a hug. "Today was wonderful. Thank you."

Maggie raised an eyebrow and slanted her gaze to Aaron and Susan, huddled in conversation in the corner.

"Remarkable, actually," Alex continued. "He's normally so shy. Susan's having quite an effect on him. Who could blame him?" he said with a smile, then looked to the corner. "Break it up, you two. You can continue plotting tomorrow. Right now, we need to get out of here, and let the Martins get to bed."

Aaron turned reluctantly and followed Alex and Marc to their car. Mike stretched and turned off the TV. He extended a hand to Amy and pulled her to her feet. "Let's see what our girls are up to. Good night, John," he said, shaking his hand.

R

Maggie sighed and moved into the warmth of John's arms and rested her head on his shoulder. "It's been a wonderful day," she said, her voice dreamlike. "Could you believe that wedding? It really affected me."

John nodded.

"Me, too. What a hopeful, courageous thing to make that commitment at their ages. Makes one think, doesn't it?" he said, pulling back to look into her eyes.

He kissed her slowly.

"Big day tomorrow. I'd better go. Will you be all right here? Need any more help?" he asked, glancing around the room.

"Nope. I've got it. I'm not working tomorrow. Just go home and get a good night's sleep."

She turned him toward the door and gently ushered him out.

Chapter 38

Sophie and Sarah were up early, excited about the day ahead. It was not yet seven, and Maggie couldn't hear any signs of life stirring from Susan's room. Mike had pledged Maggie a lifetime of gratitude if she would let them sleep in. She remembered the fatigue of parenting all too well; she didn't miss those days. Especially since Paul had rarely pitched in to help.

Maggie put her fingers to her lips, motioning the girls to keep quiet. "Let's have hot chocolate in my bed," she whispered. "You two go get yourselves propped up with pillows. I'll feed Eve and bring a tray back upstairs with me. We'll make secret plans for the day."

They both looked intrigued at the prospect.

"Keep quiet. We don't want the others to hear," she said softly as she and Eve trailed off to the kitchen.

By the time she returned with three steaming mugs and a bowl heaped with mini-marshmallows, the girls had rounded up a pen and paper.

"Here," Sophie said earnestly, thrusting them at Maggie. "We'd better make a list."

Maggie smiled. The apple hadn't fallen far from the tree. She and Mike were both consummate list makers.

"Okay. That's what I like to see," she said, carefully placing the hot mugs on her nightstand. "Where shall we start?"

When Susan drifted in an hour later, they had made lists of things to do, things to buy, and assigned names to tasks.

"Very organized," she said, turning to the twins. "Did you help Gramma with this?"

They nodded in unison.

"I don't see your names down here. You're going to help, aren't you?"

Sarah couldn't contain herself any longer.

"We want to go with you and Aaron to pick out the tree. See, we wrote our names there. But Gramma made us erase them."

She shot a resentful look in Maggie's direction.

"She said that two's company and three's a crowd."

"Whatever that means," Sophie chimed in. "Besides, we'd be four, not three."

She joined her sister in giving Maggie the stink eye.

Susan laughed. "Of course you can come. Just promise me that you'll stay with me; no wandering off."

"We know," both girls cried in unison.

"We never wander off," Sarah said reproachfully.

"Aaron will be here soon; you'd better get ready. And wake up those lazy parents of yours," she said with a wink.

"Are you sure you want to take them with you and Aaron?" Maggie asked as the girls bounded down the hall, calling to their parents.

"Quit matchmaking, Mom. For heaven's sake, he's a nice guy, but nothing's going to happen between us. We're geographically incompatible."

Maggie studied her daughter. "You can't fool me, young lady. You've styled your hair and put on your full makeup. You wouldn't do that if you weren't interested."

Susan rolled her eyes but didn't attempt to contradict her mother. "We've all got to get cracking around here. You too, Mom," she said, eyeing Maggie's pajamas and slippers. "People will be here soon."

"Okay, Sarge. I'll be right down. Go figure out where you're going to put the tree. I'll have Sam and Mike move furniture around, and we'll bring down the other Christmas decorations from the attic. When you get back with the tree, we can start decorating."

"Perfect. We'll need lights. There weren't any that I saw."

"Even if there were, they'd be too old to use. I'll give you money to buy new ones."

"Will do, but I don't want your money. Alex told me last night that he and Marc will buy the tree as a thank-you gift, and I'll spring for the lights."

Maggie smiled. She was unaccustomed to being the recipient of such thoughtfulness. It felt good.

"We should be back by noon," Susan said, tapping her fingertip on her teeth. "With everyone helping, I think we'll get the tree up and the inside decorated by suppertime."

"That'd be incredible. I never thought about getting this place all decked out," Maggie said thoughtfully. "Since I'll be in California for Christmas, I planned to put a wreath on the front door and leave it at that."

"That's just crazy, Mom. You and Rosemont deserve better than that," Susan scolded gently as she turned toward the door.

R

Maggie was setting out bowls of Greek yogurt, granola, and bananas for breakfast. That, plus coffee and orange juice, was the best she could muster this morning. The twins were finishing up their Fruit Loops as Mike and Aaron came through the kitchen door, Eve yapping at their heels.

"Good morning," Maggie said. "I didn't hear the doorbell."

"I saw him pull up and let him in. Amy's still asleep, and I didn't want the bell to wake her," Mike replied.

"Would you like some breakfast?" Maggie asked, motioning to the counter where everything was laid out.

"Just coffee for me, thanks," Aaron answered. "Ready to go?" he asked the girls. They nodded in unison. "Where's your aunt?" he asked, scanning the kitchen for Susan.

"Probably upstairs making herself beautiful for you," Sophie answered, rolling her eyes.

Maggie cut her off. "Sophie, run upstairs and tell Susan that Aaron's here. Sarah, bring me your cereal bowls, then go get your coats. You'll need your hats and gloves, too."

Maggie turned to Aaron and smiled. "We didn't get a chance to talk much yesterday. Will you be joining another practice or starting your own?"

"I'd like to join an established practice. I like being a doctor, not an office manager. I don't want to deal with the business end of it all."

"John Allen would agree with you on that score. He's the vet you met yesterday. He's had challenges with running the animal hospital, including an embezzling office manager. Setting up your own practice is like starting a small business. It takes tremendous time."

"Alex told me you were a forensic accountant before you became mayor. You've had an interesting career."

Maggie smiled. "My life has taken some unexpected turns, that's for sure," she replied simply.

Aaron set his coffee cup on the counter. "You know, ever since Alex's accident, I've been wanting to thank you for taking such good care of him and Marc. Letting them move in while their house was being rebuilt after the arson fires, and allowing them to stay on while Alex recuperated. I was in residency and put in for a leave to come lend a hand, but Alex assured me it wasn't necessary. Leaving my residency then would have been very difficult. I was prepared to come," he added hastily, "but I'm grateful that I didn't have to. Your kindness helped both of us. So thank you," he concluded, holding her gaze.

Maggie smiled and patted his arm. "It wasn't that big of a deal; I was happy to have them here," she said.

Just then, Susan burst into the room. She stopped short, glancing from her mother to Aaron. "I'm sorry. Am I interrupting something? You two look pretty serious," she said, starting to back toward the door.

"Nonsense," Maggie replied.

"I was just thanking your mother for all she's done for Alex and Marc. And me."

"That's my mom for you," Susan said proudly. "We need to get rolling. The girls are waiting outside, and it's chilly! Mom, better put Sam and Mike to work getting this place ready, because we plan to bring back the biggest Christmas tree in the county."

R

Aaron and Susan pursued the perfect tree with relentless determination. Alex had equipped Aaron with a list of four lots to visit. They combed through each one, with Susan taking pictures and keeping notes on her phone. True to their word, the twins remained cooperative and patient, thrilled to be tagging along with their aunt and the man that they referred to between themselves as "her boyfriend."

When they all got back into the car after completing their inspection of likely trees on the fourth lot they had visited, Susan dug her cell phone out of her purse. "Let's look through the photos of the candidates and pick the winner."

Aaron checked his watch. "Good plan. It's almost eleven. We can get the tree, stop at Westbury Hardware on the way home for lights, and be back to Rosemont by noon."

Susan leaned close to Aaron and the girls hung over the seatback as she scrolled through the pictures. "We've got the classic debate. Taller or fuller. Let's take a vote."

With a tally of three-to-one for a tree they had seen at the second lot, they set out. By twelve twenty they were pulling slowly up the drive to Rosemont with the fourteen-foot spruce tied securely to the top of Alex's SUV and one hundred strings of lights in the cargo hold.

"Remember," Susan turned to Sophie and Sarah in the backseat, "Gramma doesn't know about the other lights. She's only going to see the twenty boxes of lights for the tree. We'll be decorating the inside and your dad, Sam, and John will be outside putting up lights. When it gets dark we'll take her outside and surprise her."

Sophie and Sarah squirmed in excitement. "We know," they whispered in unison. "We won't tell."

Aaron smiled at Susan. "They look trustworthy to me," he said, winking at them. "Let's get started."

R

By noon, the peace and orderliness of Rosemont were a mere memory. Maggie and Amy diligently sorted through all the boxes Mike and Sam brought down from the attic, laying out ornaments and decorations on every tabletop and chair.

Amy finally collapsed on the bottom stair and leaned against the railing. "I'm exhausted." She pulled out a tissue and blew her nose loudly.

Maggie abandoned the box she was working on and joined her daughter-in-law. "Are you feeling all right? Coming down with a cold?"

Amy smiled. "No. Just the dust from all this stuff. You've got some wonderful things here," she said, gesturing to the chaos surrounding them.

"I know," Maggie replied. "More than I'll ever use. If there's anything you'd like, we can box it up and send it to you."

Amy smiled and shut her eyes. Maggie regarded her carefully. She wasn't acting like the dynamo she knew. "Why don't you go upstairs and lie down? I can finish here. The others will be back soon. You'll lose your chance for a nap if you delay much longer."

Amy nodded and opened her eyes. "I think I will, just for a bit. I'll be down before they get back."

Maggie watched her slow ascent to the second floor, making a mental note to share her concerns with Mike.

R

Maggie cleared away the now-empty packing boxes and headed for the kitchen. She was overwhelmed by the mass of decorations in the living room that had to be dealt with. Why had she allowed Susan to open this can of worms? She didn't feel like hauling the Thanksgiving leftovers out of the fridge. Instead, she reached for her phone and placed an order at Tomascino's for enough pizza to feed the lot of them. With that accomplished, she summoned Eve and they both headed into the back garden to enjoy a few moments in the chilly sunshine, away from the musty smell that clung to everything from the attic.

As Maggie and Eve toured the mulched beds in the bottom garden, Susan and the twins crept through the front door, hoping that Maggie was busy elsewhere. Sam and Mike came around the side of the house to help Aaron unload the tree.

"Holy cow," Sam said. "This is huge. Looks like it should be the White House tree."

"I'm afraid we got carried away," Aaron apologized. "We can cut a couple of feet off the bottom."

"No way. If we can get it through the door, we can put it by the stairway. The ceiling there is two stories," Sam insisted. "We can stand on the stairway to decorate the top."

"How in the heck are we going to set it up?" Mike asked.

"Leave that to me," Sam replied. "I've seen them install the big trees at the mall. The three of us can do this." He motioned toward the back of the car.

After twenty minutes of careful maneuvering, the tree stood majestically in its spot, filling Rosemont with the unmistakable aroma of Christmas.

R

Rosemont buzzed with activity and laughter all afternoon. Maggie thought they had far too many lights, but Sam and Mike managed to get them all strung around the tree in no time. Amy rose from her nap when the pizza arrived, seemingly restored. Maybe Maggie had been worried about nothing after all.

John arrived shortly before two o'clock and disappeared after grabbing a couple slices of cold pizza. Maggie intended to search him out, but every time she tried to slip away, Susan or Amy asked her opinion about a decoration or the twins called her to help them hang ornaments on the tree. She noted that Sam, Aaron, and Mike were also missing in action. Wasn't that just like men to leave all the decorating to women? Nobody was watching football, so she couldn't imagine where they might be.

As the afternoon shadows grew long and everyone's enthusiasm turned to exhaustion, the midday chaos was replaced by the glorious beauty of Rosemont, her halls decked in splendid abandon. At a quarter to five, Maggie climbed to the bottom landing and summoned everyone's attention.

"Okay, everybody. I hereby declare that we are done! Rosemont looks perfect. We don't need to put up another thing. Let's get this mess cleaned up. Girls, you take the boxes to the garage. Susan, will you please run the vacuum? Amy can help me in the kitchen. I'm going to run out front to pick up the mail; I'll be right back."

"No!" Susan said, intercepting her mom at the door. "It's cold out there and you don't have your jacket. I've got a sweater on. I'll go get the mail and bring it to you in the kitchen. It won't take long to run the vacuum, and then I'll come help you guys in the kitchen. I'm starved, so let's get some food going."

"Fine," Maggie said, eyeing Susan curiously.

Within the hour, all three women chatted amiably in the kitchen as they warmed up leftovers. Sophie and Sarah were setting the generous farmhouse table when Maggie's phone rang.

"Sweetie," she called to Susan. "Could you please answer that? I'm dealing with this turkey carcass, and my hands are a mess."

Susan snatched the phone and stepped out of the kitchen. "Joan's on her way over with a salad," she said when she returned.

"Really?" Maggie replied. "Is Sam still here? I haven't seen any of the men for hours."

"Yes you have," Susan lied. "They've been in and out all afternoon."

"Sam and Joan are more than welcome to stay for dinner." Maggie turned to Sophie; "Make sure you set enough places for everybody.

"Susan," she said distractedly, "help the girls with that, will you?"

"Hello," Joan said as she entered the kitchen.

"Hi, Joan," Maggie said over her shoulder while she and Amy were removing pans from the oven and placing everything on the kitchen island.

"Bring the plates to the end, here," Maggie told Susan, wiping her brow. "We'll serve buffet style. Girls, go find your father and the others and tell them dinner is ready."

"They're right behind me," Joan said as Mike, Sam, and John entered the kitchen.

"What have you been doing all day?" But her question went unheard as the hubbub of greetings and chatter filled the kitchen.

"Everybody grab a plate and dig in!" she said, raising her voice and managing to make herself heard. "We're eating in the kitchen tonight."

R

Maggie was pleased to see that everyone enjoyed generous helpings. *Thanksgiving food is always better the next day,* she thought as she rose from the table, picking up her plate and reaching for Mike's when Marc stepped in.

"You've been working like maniacs around here today. You sit. Alex and I are going to clean up," he stated firmly. "It's not up for discussion."

"I should at least get the coffee started and set out the pies," Maggie said, attempting to get up once again.

John gently pulled her back down. "In a minute. Let's wait a bit. Everyone agree?"

She scanned the group assembled at her table. Clearly no one was in a hurry. Maggie relaxed back into her seat.

"So what did you guys do today?" she asked, turning to John.

"We did a bit of outside work," Sam said jumping in. "As soon as they're done cleaning up, we'll show you."

"Won't it be too dark if we wait? It's almost too dark now," she said, looking at Sam with a quizzical expression.

"No. You'll be able to see," he replied nonchalantly.

"You've done an incredible job in here," Joan interjected, diverting Maggie's attention. "Amy told me you found all the decorations in the attic. They must have been there for decades. I don't ever remember Rosemont being decked out for the holidays."

Joan discussed the attic finds with Maggie until Alex returned to the table, declaring that they'd completed KP duty.

John jumped up, rubbing his hands together. "Okay, everyone. Get your coats on. We're heading outside."

"Really?" Maggie asked, eyeing him suspiciously. "What have you been up to?"

"You're about to find out," Sam replied, barely controlling his glee. "Don't stand around here dawdling. Everybody, get your coats and get crackin'."

John took Maggie's hand and held her back. "We go last," he said softly.

"You've been decorating the outside all day, haven't you? I wondered what you were up to. I was getting suspicious, but didn't want to risk spoiling your surprise."

"Well done," John replied. "That's one of the things I love about you; your generous spirit."

Maggie's head snapped up as she regarded him with surprise and delight. He'd said the "L" word!

He kissed her lightly on the lips. "They're so excited out there they can hardly contain themselves. Let's go. And act surprised."

Maggie smiled. "You think you need to tell me that?"

Arm-in-arm, they stepped across the threshold. John walked her to the center of the group, huddled in the dark night on the far side of the driveway.

"One, two, three—Merry Christmas!" Sam yelled as he, Mike, Alex, and Marc connected the strings of lights. The façade of Rosemont burst into illumination, with white lights tracing every dormer, peak, and gable. Lighted wreaths hung in every window.

The assembled group gasped, then broke into a boisterous round of applause.

"Say something," John whispered in Maggie's ear before he realized she was crying. "It appears the unflappable Maggie Martin is completely undone; reduced to tears," he told the crowd.

Sophie and Sarah rushed to their grandmother for a hug.

"Isn't is wonderful, Gramma?" Sophie gushed.

"We knew about it all day long, and we didn't say a word, did we?" Sarah said proudly.

"You are the best secret keepers ever," Maggie said, finding her voice. "And you are the most caring, remarkable group of friends and family a person could ever have," she said, moving to the front steps. "Rosemont looks spectacular. I don't know how to thank you all."

She turned to Joan and Alex. "Since I'm going to be in California for Christmas, why don't you use the house? Come here as much as you want; have your families over."

"Actually, Mom," Mike said stepping in. "We've been talking." He pointed to Amy and Susan. "With your permission, we're all planning to come to Rosemont for Christmas. And everybody here is invited to Christmas dinner."

Maggie's heart swelled with joy. No two ways about it—she loved having her children in her home for Christmas. "What about the girls?" she asked. "I thought they wanted to be home for Christmas?"

"It was their idea," Amy supplied, giving Maggie a hug. "We all want to be at Rosemont."

R

Later, after Amy herded the girls upstairs to get ready for bed and the others lingered over a last bite of pie in the kitchen, Aaron caught Susan's eye. Raising his coffee cup slightly, he nodded in the direction of the front of the house. She gathered her sweater around her shoulders and followed him outside. They turned and looked at Rosemont, resplendent in her holiday décor.

"I was awfully glad to hear that you'll be back at Christmas," he said, turning to face her, the lights bathing her upturned face in a soft glow.

Susan smiled at him and his heart skipped a beat. "Will you be with Alex for the holidays?"

"Now that you're going to be here, I will be," he replied happily. Susan shivered and Aaron put his arm around her, drawing her close. "You're very special. You know that, don't you?" he whispered against her hair.

Susan tried to read his expression but he had his back to the house and darkness shielded his face. "I'm so glad you'll be in Westbury. I was hoping."

167

Aaron kissed her then, a slow, leisurely kiss. "I've never met anyone like you. I want to know more about you."

Susan drew back to tell him she felt the same way, and sneezed instead.

"I'd better get you back inside," Aaron said, pushing her gently toward the door. "I don't want you being sick for Christmas."

Chapter 39

Loretta Nash looked up from her computer screen when the front door of Haynes Enterprises opened late in the afternoon on the Friday after Thanksgiving. She quickly closed out of Pinterest, where she had been researching DIY Christmas gifts, and opened up an accounts receivable report as the balding, stocky man approached her desk.

"May I help you?" she asked pleasantly, walking around her desk to intercept him as he made his way to Mr. Haynes' office. *Who did he think he was barging in here?* she thought.

Chuck Delgado paused, allowing himself a lascivious glance along the shapely body of this tall, curvy blonde. He was too self-absorbed to notice the look of revulsion on her face.

"I'm here to see Frankie," he answered. "But first, I'd like to meet you," he said, offering his hand. "Charles Delgado. People call me Chuck."

Loretta half-turned, pretending not to have seen his outstretched hand, and replied, "Let me see if he's expecting you. Do you have an appointment, Mr. Delgado? I don't see you on his calendar."

Cheeky broad, Delgado thought. "I don't need no appointment. We're old friends. And we're both councilmen," he stated, proudly throwing his shoulders back. He resumed his progress toward Haynes' office.

"Would you have a seat while I check with Mr. Haynes?" she stated firmly, gesturing to the sofa along the wall by the entrance.

"I told you, I don't need no appointment," Delgado growled as he continued to walk.

"Sir, please wait," Loretta raised her voice slightly. Haynes came to his door.

"It's all right, Loretta. Thank you," he said in the calm, slow manner he used when he was coiling and about to strike. "What brings you here today, Charles? Come in."

He motioned Delgado to a chair in front of his desk then turned to Loretta, who was unsure of what she should do next. "I'm sorry, I tried to stop him," she mouthed.

Haynes' expression relaxed for a nanosecond.

"Can I get you some coffee?" she asked.

"No. We're fine." He turned and then looked back. "Why don't you go on home? The phones have been quiet all afternoon; everyone's out Christmas shopping."

"Thank you, Mr. Haynes. My kids would love that. I appreciate it very much," she said, even though she knew instinctively that he wasn't being kind but simply wanted to get rid of her. He was hiding something that had to do with this creep Delgado, she was sure of it.

"Get your purse, and I'll lock the door behind you," he said, as he retrieved her coat from the rack by the door and held it for her in gentlemanly fashion.

Loretta stepped through the door he opened for her, resolved to find out what the two men were up to.

R

"Quite a looker, Frankie," Delgado said as Haynes returned to his chair behind his desk. "I didn't know you'd hired somebody new."

"I have over 500 employees, Charles. I'm not in the habit of consulting you about my staffing."

"She's not some burger flipper now is she, Frankie?" he answered, ignoring Haynes' sarcasm. "What's she do?"

"She's my office gal. Not that it's any of your business."

Delgado raised an eyebrow. "You haven't needed an office gal before. Why now?"

Haynes stared icily at Delgado.

"She from around here?" he pressed. Haynes didn't do anything without an ulterior motive.

"No, she's just moved here."

"Huh. Well, you lucked out, Frankie boy. She's a hot broad. If she doesn't work out for you, I'm sure she could work under me." He grinned at his crude pun.

"I'm busy, Charles," Haynes replied curtly. "Why are you here?"

"You know why, don't you, Frankie," Delgado snarled. "Tearing up the check from that old geezer at Fairview yesterday? Made quite a stir for yourself, didn't you? Good publicity. But the boys didn't like it. Didn't like it at all," he glared at Haynes.

"Is that what this is about?" Haynes sighed in disgust. "I was going to give the money to you anyway." He reached into his side drawer and pulled out an envelope with cash. He slid it across the desk to Delgado. "Here. Don't trust me. Count it."

Delgado's eyes darted from the envelope to Haynes. He hesitated, then put the envelope in the breast pocket of his jacket.

"Okay, Frankie. We trust you," he said, trying to regain favor with Haynes.

"No, you don't. We don't trust each other."

"Don't talk like that, Frankie. You know how the boys is. We don't want any more of us dying of natural causes now do we?"

Haynes swung on Delgado.

"What are you saying, Charles?"

"Let's just say that guys who cross us don't live as long as people who don't. The boys saw all that stuff in this morning's paper about what a great humanitarian you are, and they got a little miffed. I'll straighten them out."

"You do that," Haynes said.

He rose from his chair and headed to the door, motioning Delgado to follow him. With little choice, Delgado heaved himself to his feet. He paused, halfway to the door.

"You having some extracurricular fun with your new office gal? What was her name?"

"We don't all have sex with our employees, Charles," Haynes replied with a sneer as he unlocked the door and ushered Delgado into the growing dusk.

"Word to the wise, Frankie boy. Get yourself a piece of her. Gotta have some fun in life," Delgado advised as Haynes shut the door.

He shook his head as he heard the lock click. If that idiot Haynes didn't want to have fun with her, he sure did. He'd have to find out more about Haynes' new assistant.

Chapter 40

Maggie sat at her desk at Town Hall in the early afternoon the Wednesday after Thanksgiving, unable to concentrate on any of the urgent matters before her. The kids had all departed for California early Monday morning, and she had rushed straight to her office after dropping them at the airport. She was exhausted and her energy level and enthusiasm were going downhill, fast.

Maggie pushed back her chair and picked up her coffee cup, then replaced it on her desk. What she needed wasn't more caffeine; she needed something to cheer her up. She was an empty nester again and life seemed dreary after the excitement of getting ready for Thanksgiving and the visit from her family.

Her cell phone began to ring, and she retrieved it from its perch on the corner of her desk. She was delighted to hear the deep, masculine rumble of John on the other end.

"Hey, you; how's it going?" he asked.

"Fine, I guess," she replied.

"Anytime someone qualifies 'fine' with 'I guess,' things aren't going fine. What's up? More murder and mayhem at Town Hall?"

"No. Nothing like that. Just the same old stuff," Maggie said with a small smile. "I'm exhausted and it's not from lack of sleep. I got eight hours the last two nights. I'm feeling blue after the family visit, after all the hustle and bustle."

"I'm not surprised. You put so much time and energy into making everything perfect—you succeeded, by the way—you were bound to experience a letdown."

"Thanks for understanding," she replied.

"I've got an idea to cheer you up. Can you get away? Now?"

"I guess so." She checked her watch. "I think I can leave early for once. But what about you? I've never known you to close the animal hospital early."

"I don't have any appointments booked for the rest of the afternoon. My staff can close up. And they can call me if they get any emergencies. I haven't played hooky for years, and I think today's the day. You with me on this?"

Maggie laughed. "All right, Ferris Bueller. I'm in."

"Perfect. What are you wearing right now?"

"Why on earth is that important?"

"Need-to-know basis. What is our distinguished mayor's current attire?"

"I'm pretty casual, if you must know. Slacks and a sweater."

"Perfect. Warm coat?"

"Yes. What are you up to?"

"You'll find out soon enough. I'm on my way. Meet you at Rosemont in twenty minutes." He hung up without waiting for her response.

R

Maggie was sitting on the front steps of Rosemont when John pulled up. She had exchanged her Burberry trench coat for a warm jacket and retrieved gloves and a scarf from the hall closet. She didn't know what he had in mind, but she guessed it involved being outside.

John pulled to a stop and intercepted her as she made her way directly to the passenger side of his car. He swept her into his arms and kissed her slowly.

Maybe they should skip whatever activity he had planned and just go inside now, she thought fleetingly.

John opened her car door and waited for her to sit. She watched as he crossed in front of the car and slipped behind the wheel, thinking what a fine-looking man he was—agile and strong.

"So, where are we headed?" she asked casually.

John shot her a sidelong glance. "Patience, Prudence."

Maggie laughed and the gray cloud that clung to her began to dissipate. "Have it your way, then, mystery man."

She relaxed into her seat and enjoyed the warm sunshine on her face through the car window and the stark beauty of the leafless trees outside. Westbury's first snowstorm was predicted for the weekend and she thought how pretty this drive would be with a fresh dusting of snow.

They made small talk, recapping the events of the long Thanksgiving weekend. Maggie finally leaned forward and tapped the dashboard.

"That's it! We're headed to The Mill, aren't we?"

John smiled broadly.

"How wonderful! I'm starved; I'd love to have an early dinner there."

John looked worried. "Are you really that hungry?"

"I'm famished. But if we're not going there for dinner, that's fine. I shouldn't have assumed. It's my own fault for not eating lunch today. I can wait."

"We'll eat there, but the dining room doesn't open until five thirty."

"That's fine. Where are we going until then?" she asked as John turned into the long, winding driveway along the Shawnee River.

John pulled into the deserted parking lot and turned to face her. "One of the maintenance men was in my clinic with his dog on Monday and said they were setting up the skating rink on Tuesday. Said it would be open for public skating this weekend."

He paused and was gratified to see the smile sweep across her face.

"You didn't!" she squealed.

"I did. Came out here yesterday afternoon and spoke to the same young woman I dealt with last spring. She remembered me and thought it would be fitting for us to open up the rink, since we closed it down last season. Talked her manager into it; she told him it would be good karma."

Maggie laughed. "I think she's absolutely right. And what an inspired thing for you to do. You never cease to amaze me," she cried, placing her hand on his cheek and smiling into his eyes before kissing him warmly.

"I'm sure we can rustle up some food from the bar to tide you over until dinner. Let's do that first."

"Who's hungry? Not me," she scoffed. "I want to go skating. Race you," she cried as she leapt out of the car and bounded up the steps.

R

They stepped onto the pristine surface, their skates making the initial tracks. And soon they were gliding effortlessly, hand in hand, letting the breeze whip through their hair as the sun made its trek to the horizon; the only sound, the swoosh of their skates. By the time the young man signaled that it was time to get off the ice, their ears and noses stung. Still, neither of them wanted to quit. Reluctantly, they complied and turned in their skates.

Among the first to arrive for dinner, they chose a table along the bank of windows overlooking the river and the now deserted rink. Maggie smiled lovingly at John.

"This is even more romantic than last time," she said. "I wouldn't have thought it was possible to top the best first date ever!"

John beamed. "I guess I've still got a few tricks up my sleeve. Who would have thought?"

"Anyone who knows you, that's who. You are the kindest, most generous soul I've ever met." She gazed at him seriously. "I love you, John. I'm so very grateful that you gave us a second chance."

John flushed. "I wanted to be the first to say it," he sputtered. "I had it all planned. I wasn't sure if you were ready to love someone again. I'm so glad you are, because—"

Maggie leaned over and touched his arm. "Wait. Let's wait. I want to hear it however you planned it. There's something special for both the bearer and recipient of the statement 'I love you.' It's as important to say as it is to hear. One of the great joys of life, don't you think?"

John nodded and brought his hand over hers. "The three best words will wait in any language," he replied and smiled. "Your wish is my command. Proceeding as planned."

They finished the meal in leisurely fashion, even though both were anxious to return to Rosemont and spend time alone in each other's arms. John was visibly relieved when Maggie declined the dessert menu; he followed suit. They made the drive to Rosemont in companionable silence, their hands clasped on the console between them.

"Will you come in?" Maggie asked as they climbed the steps to the massive front door.

"I'd like nothing better." John turned Maggie toward him and gazed at her upturned face. "You are the most remarkable woman I've ever met. You have completely captured my heart. When we were apart, you occupied my every thought. I love you, Maggie. I admire you and am so proud of everything you've accomplished. I'm here to support you in any way I can; in any way you need. You can always count on me."

Maggie brought her lips to his. After a delicious eternity, she unlocked her front door and the lovers entered into the protective embrace of Rosemont.

R

Much later that night, John carefully withdrew his arm from under Maggie's head. She stirred and brushed her hair back from her face. Rising on one elbow, she turned to him.

"Are you awake?" she whispered.

"Just woke up. I have to be at the hospital at five thirty for surgery. I should probably get going; I don't want to disturb you at that ungodly hour," he said, pulling the cover over her bare shoulders when she shivered.

"Don't go. Stay with me. I'm an early riser; you won't bother me. Unless you don't think you'll get a good night's sleep here. I know you have to be well-rested in the morning."

John pulled her close in response. "There's nowhere I'd rather be," he said as he breathed into her hair.

R

Maggie had fibbed to John the night before when she told him she always got up that early. The truth was she hadn't been up at four fifteen in years. She sent him off to his house for a shower and shave with a cup of coffee in hand, fully intending to crawl back into bed. Sleep eluded her, however, and she finally threw in the towel and got up at five thirty.

She decided to get dressed and head to her office at Town Hall. She was on her way to retrieve her coat when her eye settled on the box from the attic that Susan had brought down but neglected to return to its place. What was it Susan had told her about the box? That it was full of household guest books, menus, and memorabilia? She had a few minutes before she needed to leave; surely it wouldn't take long to make a quick assessment of the contents.

An hour and forty-five minutes later, Maggie was happily ensconced in the middle of the living room, surrounded by stacks of invitations, menus, and ledger sheets detailing Rosemont's active social life at the turn of the century. What a treasure trove this was. Weddings, cotillions, card parties, and picnics on the lawn; Rosemont had hosted them all. There was even a dog-eared recipe for a Pink Lady cocktail. Judging by the stains on the card, this recipe had seen a lot of use.

Of particular interest to Maggie was an invitation to a Christmas tea. The hand-lettered calligraphy was a work of art; she'd frame it and display it on the sideboard in the dining room as a Christmas decoration. Maggie checked her watch and was shocked at the time. Instead of arriving at her office early, she was going to be late.

She carefully replaced the items, other than the invitation for tea, in the box that had housed them for over a century. As she rose to her feet an idea hit her—she'd host a Christmas high tea at Rosemont. The place was decorated to the nines, and it would be a shame not to let other people enjoy the manor's festive beauty. Her mind began spinning. She bent down and retrieved the cocktail recipe.

On the short drive to Town Hall, she mentally sketched out her to-do list. She'd invite Sam and Joan, Alex and Marc, of course, Pete and Laura and the baby, the Knudsens, Judy Young and Ellen, the Holmeses, and that nice elderly couple from Fairview Terraces who had just gotten married. She was warming to her subject. If she invited Tonya Holmes, would she need to invite the other town councilmembers and their families? She supposed she should. And what about the town clerk and the other Town Hall employees? This was getting complicated. One thing was certain; she wouldn't invite that obnoxious editor from the *Westbury Gazette* or anyone else who'd been openly critical of her.

Still, the guest list was swelling. Her eye caught the beautiful old invitation on the seat beside her. What in the world was the matter with her? So what if she invited a hundred people? She should be thankful that she knew a hundred people in Westbury to invite, and she had a house that would easily accommodate them. This was going to be tremendous fun.

Maggie stole another glance at the invitation. She would have someone carefully copy it, inserting the new date. There was nothing like a real invitation to set the tone for a party. She'd head over to Celebrations as soon as they opened to place her order.

Linens, china, and silver? Rosemont had more than enough. She had plenty of tables and chairs scattered around the house, too. She'd call Sam to help her arrange them.

She'd place a large order for pastries with Laura's Bakery and she would handle the tea sandwiches herself. She pulled into her parking spot at Town Hall and fished a sheet of paper out of her briefcase. She scribbled a few notes and, satisfied, made her way into Town Hall.

R

At nine forty-five, Maggie headed toward the town square at a brisk pace. It would be faster to drive, but the morning was clear and sunny and Maggie was eager to stretch her legs. By the time she placed her orders at Laura's Bakery and Celebrations, word was already out about the upcoming Christmas tea at Rosemont.

While she waited for the elevator to take her back upstairs to her office, the town clerk approached Maggie. "That's so nice of you, Ms. Martin. We're all so excited."

Good heavens, Maggie thought. *There's no such thing as a secret in this town. I don't know why anyone would pay for advertising around here; you just need to tell Judy Young at Celebrations. She's got the best news-delivery system in town.*

Maggie didn't mind. It was nice that people wanted to come. Wasn't that why she was throwing this party, anyway?

She managed to put the Christmas tea on the back burner until lunchtime when her cell phone rang. Her caller ID showed it was John. She answered as soon as she could grab her phone.

"Hi there," she said. "How are you doing? Did you make it through your surgeries okay?"

"Yes. Everything here's fine. Just another day. Except Judy Young and her Schnauzer just left here. She tells me that Mayor Martin is hosting a 'really grand, formal Christmas high tea at Rosemont.' That

177

she's doing the most amazing invitations, the decorations are stunning, and it'll be the social event of the season."

Maggie laughed. "She's something, isn't she? I'm having a few people over for tea two weeks from Sunday."

"You didn't mention it last night. Am I invited or is this just a woman thing?"

"Of course you're invited! I didn't mention it last night because I just thought of it this morning."

John was silent for a moment. "You're amazing. And crazy. You know that, don't you? But after the way you got the Easter carnival going last year in only a few weeks, I have no doubt that this tea will be a huge success. People'll be talking about it for decades to come."

"I don't think it's that big a deal," she replied.

"*Au contraire*, my dear. You've done it again. I'm here to help you. What can I do?"

"I don't have any idea. I haven't thought too much about this," she said. "I'd love your help. Why don't I take you to dinner tonight so we can put some plans together?"

"You're on."

"Come over after work and we'll go from there. In fact, how about I pick up takeout from Pete's on my way home and we stay in and make plans?"

"I'll never say no to staying in with you. Not sure how many plans we'll get made, but I'll do my best to fight you off."

Maggie laughed. "After last night, you're going to have to! See you later."

Chapter 41

Frank Haynes locked the door of Haynes Enterprises and watched as Loretta Nash got into her car and pulled out of the parking lot. He returned to his office and placed the call he'd been thinking about all day. Professor Upton picked up on the fourth ring.

"Don. Frank Haynes here."

"Frank, how's it going down there? Any more untimely deaths?"

"No. But that's one of the reasons I'm calling. I've been thinking. Maggie might be right about Wheeler. He may have been connected to the mob. God knows, he wasn't smart enough to think up that sophisticated embezzlement scheme on his own."

"So you want to call the feds in, too?"

"Not necessarily. Chief Thomas and Scanlon are more than capable of handling it. What I'm worried about is Maggie. As you said the other day, she's in over her head."

"I said that *she* feels she's in over her head."

"Come on, Don; you think so, too. If Westbury were the sleepy little town it's supposed to be, she'd be more than capable of handling the duties of mayor. But we're up to our eyeballs in trouble. We need someone with experience."

Haynes paused to let Upton comment. When Upton remained silent, he continued. "You agree with me, don't you? And she'd admit it, if she were honest with herself. She didn't choose to run for the position after all. And now she might be in real danger. We should encourage her to resign."

"She'd never do that; she's no quitter."

"I'm not so sure. We owe it to her to try, don't we? You care for her, and so do I."

"Who'd fill the gap, Frank? What's the process?"

"The council would select longterm Councilman Russell Isaac to serve until the next regular election."

"Wasn't he defeated in the special election?"

"He was, but that was because of a backlash against Wheeler. He's clean and capable. He filled in when Wheeler resigned, and he can handle the job again."

Both men remained silent.

"She's getting hate emails from constituents. You said it yourself, Don; she's doubting her capability. And now Chief Thomas and Alex

Scanlon are at odds with her. We'd be doing her a favor to encourage her to resign. Plus, we both feel that Westbury would be better off under different leadership. The town needs someone who can bring people together." *And it wouldn't hurt to have someone in office who wasn't determined to uncover every detail—every participant—in the fraud scheme,* he thought.

"You could be right." Upton sighed heavily. "And I might be able to help. I'm looking for someone to be an expert witness in a fraud case I'm working on in California. It'll require a tremendous number of hours for the next year and will involve frequent trips to Los Angeles. If she wasn't the mayor, Maggie would be perfect."

"And she'd love going to California because she could see her family. This could be the carrot we need to convince her to resign." Haynes sounded almost giddy.

"And the fee she could charge is very high; this would be an extremely lucrative engagement. Cases like this don't come along very often—"

"All the more reason to phone her," Haynes interjected.

"I was thinking of offering the opportunity to her, even before you called."

"Good. Then it's settled. Let me know if there's anything I can do to help convince her."

Chapter 42

Business was brisk at Haynes Enterprises during the weeks before Christmas. People weren't just buying gifts; they were going out to eat, too. Swamped with work for the first time since she had started, Loretta was finally feeling useful. The uptick in revenue had lightened her boss's mood, as well. When he wasn't barking orders at her, Frank Haynes was pleasant enough, she supposed.

Loretta was absorbed with this week's payroll when she heard Haynes' cell phone ring through his closed office door. Though muffled, the urgency of his tone in response to whomever had called brought her to full attention. She was leaning across her desk to eavesdrop when he tore out of his office, shrugging into his coat with his phone to his ear. He charged the door then turned back to her.

"I'm on my way," he stated firmly into the phone and hung up. "Store number eight's been robbed."

Loretta gasped. He held up his hand to stop any conversation.

"Nobody was hurt. The store was packed, and it's chaos over there. I'm going to talk to the police and shut the place down for the rest of the day. God, this hurts revenue," he spat. "Everybody gets nervous about going in the place. And all because some tweaker wanted a little cash. The idiot just got what was in the drawers; he didn't go after the safe. What a pain in the ass."

"I'm glad everyone is okay," she stated lamely. She reached for her purse and started to come around the side of her desk. She assumed he would send her home; he'd never left her there alone before.

"No. You stay here," he ordered. "I need you to answer the phone; the media will be calling. You're to tell them that Haynes Enterprises is grateful that everyone is safe and appreciates the careful actions of its employees in handling the situation. And the quick response of the police."

Loretta typed furiously while he spoke and nodded her understanding.

"Can you stay late tonight?" he asked. "I don't know how all this is going to play out."

"I think my kids can stay at their afterschool sitter's house." She picked up the phone. This might be her one and only opportunity to be at Haynes Enterprises without the watchful eye of Frank Haynes. "I'll call her now. I'm sure it'll be fine."

Haynes was halfway to his car before she finished her response.

R

As he had predicted, the media began calling before he had even left the parking lot. Loretta handled them all on the fly. She smiled in satisfaction when she hung up on one especially persistent reporter. She hadn't gotten flustered and didn't allow herself to be drawn off the message Haynes had given her. She was quite good at this.

She leaned back in her chair. It was almost six o'clock. The phone had been quiet for the last ten minutes. Her kids were cleared to stay at the babysitter as long as necessary; it was the holidays, and the woman needed the money. Loretta wondered, did she dare snoop around a bit?

She rose from her desk and crossed the room to look out the window at the parking lot. She needed to be sure that Haynes wouldn't walk in on her going through his office. He'd fire her for sure, or worse. She shivered involuntarily. Maybe it was the company he kept; that Delgado creep was a thug straight out of central casting. She had no reason to think that Haynes was anything other than an honest, successful businessman—a bit formal and unfeeling maybe, but not a criminal. Still, her gut told her to proceed very carefully.

Loretta threw the deadbolt on the entrance to Haynes Enterprises. It was after hours and Haynes wouldn't question this precaution. She closed all of the blinds and turned off her radio. She needed to be able to hear his car pull up. That should give her enough time to get back to her desk.

She entered his office. Papers were scattered across his desktop and his computer was still on. She had never been farther into this room than a few feet in front of his desk. She noted the orientation of his chair before she sat down; she'd have to make sure everything was exactly as he'd left it.

Loretta gingerly sifted through the paperwork on his desk, all of it related to franchise agreements. She turned to his computer screen and found the same reports. She'd toyed with the idea of snooping around in his computer, but didn't dare. She wasn't sure she could restore it to its current setting.

She leaned back in his chair and scanned the office. She carefully slid open his top desk drawer and was greeted with a neat array of pens and pencils. She was sliding it back into place when her knee brushed something sticky on the bottom of the drawer. Loretta slid the chair back and got down on her knees to look. On the underside of the drawer, she found a small metal key affixed to the underside of the drawer with an old strip of tape, curling at the edges. Loretta's heart leapt into her throat. This was it. She knew it.

Loretta checked her watch—almost seven o'clock. Haynes could be back at any time. She surveyed the papers on his desktop; they were as he had left them. She quickly went to the reception area window to make sure he wasn't driving into the parking lot. She had to find what that key opened.

Loretta slipped off her shoes and left them by her desk; she didn't want to be hampered by her heels if she needed to move quickly. She returned to his office and slowly circled the room, looking for anything that locked.

The filing cabinets opposite his desk were unlocked. She had been in all of them at one time or another. Another quick look confirmed that they contained only the employee files and leasing records she was familiar with.

She turned to his desk and credenza. They held nothing more than carefully labeled files on each of his stores and records detailing every penny he had donated to the community. All neat, clean, and orderly. There was no reason to keep any of this a secret, she thought. Unless he wanted to conceal his wealth, but that was belied by his constant grandstanding.

It didn't add up.

Frustrated at having come to a dead end, Loretta stood and meticulously returned his chair to its original position. She double-checked to make sure that every drawer was completely closed.

On her way out of the office, she noticed that the small painting hanging to the left of the door was askew. She absentmindedly straightened it, then stopped dead in her tracks. A bead of cold sweat ran down her back. Had it been crooked when he left, or had she jarred it by opening and closing the filing cabinets underneath it? Would he notice it?

She opened and closed several of the drawers and the picture didn't move. It must have been crooked when he left, she reasoned. She'd need to set it that way again. As she adjusted the frame, the back caught on something. She pulled the bottom of the frame forward and pressed her face against the wall to see what lay behind the picture. And there it was. The door to a small wall safe, no more than eight-by-ten inches, with an opening for a key.

Loretta gingerly lifted the picture from its hook. *I've hit pay dirt,* she thought. She had just succeeded in removing it from the wall when she heard the telltale sound of a car coming down the driveway, fast.

Loretta panicked as she realized that Haynes had pulled up. He'd be at the bolted door in moments. He must not find her in his office.

She replaced the picture on its hook, set it on an angle, and hoped it looked like it had when he'd left his office earlier in the afternoon. She hurried to his desk and replaced the key under the middle drawer, managing to get to the front door just as he was inserting his key into the lock.

Chapter 43

After rushing out of Haynes Enterprises the afternoon of the robbery, Loretta was surprised that Haynes didn't even enter his office when he returned later that evening. He looked exhausted, and his complexion had a gray cast to it.

"Are you feeling all right?" Loretta asked.

"I'm fine. Get your things," Haynes replied impatiently. He clearly wanted to lock up and leave.

She quickly complied. When she tried to ask how things were at the restaurant—to get the details of the robbery—he cut her off saying they'd go over all of it in the morning. She was almost to her car when he called out to her.

"Thank you for staying late tonight, Loretta. I appreciate it."

"No problem," she answered.

"I'll pay you overtime," he grumbled.

He reached into his wallet and pulled out a small stack of twenty-dollar bills. He motioned to her as she was unlocking her car, approached, and thrust the money into her hands.

"Here. This is for the babysitter. Thanks again."

Then he turned on his heel without waiting for her response.

R

Loretta arrived at Haynes Enterprises before seven the next morning. She was anxious to observe him in his office. She had wanted to arrive by six fifteen, since she knew Haynes was usually there by six thirty, but her kids had been sluggish after their late night the day before. She finally deposited them at the babysitter's at six twenty and headed straight for the office.

Relief that Haynes had not yet arrived turned to impatience as she waited for him in her cold car. He finally pulled up at seven fifteen. She met him at the door.

"Good morning, Mr. Haynes," she said in her most cheerful top-of-the-morning-to-you voice.

Since he didn't remark on her being there so early, she decided to blow her own horn.

"After what happened yesterday, I figured you might need me. I got here half an hour ago."

When he turned to her then, she saw that even that small movement took effort. He looked even worse than he had the night before.

"You're not feeling well, are you, Mr. Haynes?"

"I'm fine," he replied through gritted teeth. "And thank you for coming in early," he added as an afterthought.

He unlocked the door and held it open for Loretta to precede him. Without further conversation, he headed directly to his office.

Loretta settled herself behind her desk and resumed her work on the payroll. She was relieved to see that he had left his door ajar, so she could surreptitiously keep an eye on him. He spent the morning reviewing his product orders for the next month.

She knocked lightly on his door at eleven fifteen, letting him know she was going to the bank to make the daily deposit. He didn't turn around from his computer, contenting himself with a tiny wave to acknowledge that he had heard her.

Miffed at his dismissive attitude, she set off. Who did he think he was that he could ignore her like that? If he took such little notice of her, would he even know if she took some extra time and did a bit of Christmas shopping? She'd combine the bank run with an early lunch hour.

After she had completed her business at the bank, she headed to the superstore at the edge of town. It was busy on this weekday in early December, and her shopping took longer than expected. She kept glancing at her watch, telling herself she needed to get back. Then the memory of Frank Haynes' seeming indifference to her flooded back, and she continued to shop.

It was shortly after one thirty when she pulled into the lot at Haynes Enterprises. Had she lost her mind? She hadn't intended to be gone that long. If he took her to task, she would tell him that her son had gotten sick at school and she had needed to pick him up and take him to the babysitter. He'd never check her story.

She quietly opened the door to Haynes Enterprises and slipped behind her desk. No point in drawing attention to herself. She cautiously glanced toward his open door; he was not at his desk. He must be rummaging in his filing cabinets. She turned back to her computer and became absorbed in the accounts payable report. When she glanced at his office thirty minutes later, she was surprised to see that he still wasn't at his desk. She paused to listen but couldn't hear any sounds coming from his office.

Alarmed, she rose and approached his door. She raised her hand to knock when she saw, from this vantage point, what she hadn't seen from her desk. Frank Haynes was on his knees under his desk, slumped over, clutching his stomach and chest. His breathing was shallow and sweat trickled down the sides of his face.

"Oh, my God." She raced over to him and snatched the phone from his desk, dialing the emergency number. "You're going to be fine," she told him. "I'm calling 9-1-1."

"No," he gasped. "I'll be okay. Just help me up. Indigestion's all it is."

She eyed him closely as the emergency dispatcher answered. "9 1 1. What is your emergency?"

Loretta hesitated as Haynes attempted to pull himself back into his chair. Watching him double over in pain convinced her. "We need an ambulance at Haynes Enterprises." She gave the address. "Frank Haynes may be having a heart attack."

He tried to protest, but Loretta remained firm. "Mr. Haynes, something is terribly wrong. You need to go to the hospital."

He finally nodded his assent.

"The paramedics will be here soon," she reassured. "You'll be in good hands shortly."

Haynes fumbled in his pants pocket and extracted his keys, which he dropped on the floor. Loretta bent and retrieved them.

"These are your office keys, right?'

Haynes nodded imperceptibly.

"I'll make sure that everything's locked up tonight, and I'll open up tomorrow. I'll keep the office running while you're out," she said, feeling a twinge of excitement at the prospect of being in charge.

"Is there anyone I should call?" she asked, as the sound of a siren could be heard approaching.

With great effort, Haynes croaked out, "Delgado."

Loretta pretended not to hear; that was the last person she wanted to contact. "I'm going out front to meet the ambulance," she said as she skirted his desk. "Hang on. Help is here."

R

The events of the last two days had taken a toll on Loretta. She was exhausted. The ambulance crew told her that Haynes' vital signs were all strong; they didn't think he was having a heart attack. The son of a bitch had managed to grab his cell phone, and she heard him make the call to Delgado, asking him to keep an eye on his office. She knew what that meant for a creep like Delgado; he would use this as an excuse to drop by and harass her. She desperately wanted to take this opportunity to unlock that wall safe and examine its contents, but she didn't dare if Delgado might come charging in at any moment.

She didn't have long to wait. Delgado swaggered through the door of Haynes Enterprises shortly after four. He greeted her warmly, as if they were old friends bearing a common burden.

"My dear," he said, grasping her hand in both of his, rubbing her wrist in a way that made her flesh crawl. "I know this has been very frightening for you."

Loretta extricated her hand and stared at him, without speaking.

"I've just come from the hospital," he stated. "Frank asked me to make sure you're all right."

She knew this was a lie; Haynes wanted to make sure his business was all right. She continued to stare at him.

"Mr. Haynes is going to be just fine. I want to assure you of that." Loretta nodded.

"He hasn't had a heart attack, as you feared. They think he has a kidney stone."

She nodded again. "I wondered about that after they took him away. I guess the pain can mimic a heart attack."

"Exactly," he replied.

"So what are they doing for him? Are they keeping him in the hospital?"

"Yes. They're going to do some new procedure to break up the stone. They've got him on morphine, so he's not feeling any pain."

"That's good. He was miserable."

"He was lucky to have you by his side," Delgado said, his breathing quickening as he moved closer.

Repulsed, she involuntarily took a step back. "When will he get out of the hospital? When will he be back to work?"

"They don't know yet," he replied. "Couple of days; week at the most. But don't you worry about anything. Frankie's asked me to stop by every day. I'll be here whenever you need me; as much as you need me—for anything you need," he concluded suggestively.

Loretta ignored his innuendo. "That's very kind of you, but I can manage the office for a few days on my own. We just finished payroll and the accounts payable. It'll be slow the rest of the week. I'll be fine. But thank you for your kind offer," she added hastily.

"Just the same, Frankie asked me to keep an eye on things around here, and there's nothing in Westbury I'd rather keep my eye on than you," he stated pointedly.

Loretta was accustomed to brushing off randy old married men; she'd have to keep him at bay while making him think she was flattered by his advances. She swallowed her disgust. "Why, thank you. That's a great comfort. What's your number?" she asked coyly. "I'll call you if I have any questions."

Delgado gave her his phone number, which she made a big show of posting by her computer monitor. "So I know where it is at all times," she said. Delgado beamed.

"I've got to leave a bit early today to make the bank deposit," she lied in the hopes of disentangling herself. "With all the excitement around here, that didn't get done."

"You go do that and I'll lock up. Frank said you have his keys."

No way was Loretta giving up those keys. On the other hand, she didn't need to antagonize him. She regarded him thoughtfully, taking in his florid complexion and protruding belly. This guy got drunk every night—she was sure of it.

"Mr. Haynes likes to open the office early. In the restaurant business, everything happens before seven o'clock," she improvised. "I think we should open by six tomorrow morning. So I'll meet you here?"

She was secretly pleased to see that her words had the desired effect.

"Uh ..." he stammered. "I have a breakfast meeting in the morning. With constituents. I can't be here until about ten. Why don't we lock up now and you keep the keys. You can open up, and I'll come over as soon as I can. I'll be here by lunchtime, for sure. Will that be okay?"

Loretta smiled brightly. "Yes, of course. That'll be fine. I know that a busy man like you must have a schedule full of important meetings."

Her flattery was working.

"Frankie won't mind. And I'll be here in a heartbeat if you need me. Like I said, you just call."

They headed to the parking lot, Loretta barely listening to Delgado's boastful chatter. She knew what she had to do. She had to get back here as early the next morning as possible to get into the wall safe. With her luck, Haynes would recover in record time and Delgado would ensconce himself at Haynes Enterprises as soon as his hangover wore off. Tomorrow morning might be her only chance to uncover the secrets of Frank Haynes.

R

Loretta arrived at Haynes Enterprises shortly after six the next morning. She carefully removed the key from its hiding place under the desk. As she suspected, it unlocked the wall safe. In that safe she found a solitary item: a jump drive bearing no legend or markings.

Loretta held her breath as she inserted it into the external drive of her computer and waited to see if she could open the contents. All the data was accessible to her—real estate documents, bank account numbers, and spreadsheets. She scrolled through everything as fast as she could. From the legal descriptions on the documents, she knew the properties were in Westbury. The bank accounts were in foreign institutions, mostly located in the Caribbean. She didn't have time to figure out what the spreadsheets meant, but she knew they were related to the other data. Given that all of this had been kept hidden, she suspected she held evidence of something criminal. What was it she had heard about there being fraud or embezzlement from the town? Were these files related to that? She shuddered. She didn't know what she expected to find, but it hadn't been something of this magnitude.

She froze. What should her next step be? Should she simply replace the evidence carefully in the safe and forget she'd ever found it? But what if they (whoever *they* were—she had no idea) could detect that the files on the jump drive had been opened? She would be their first suspect. For her own protection, she needed to copy the data.

Loretta checked her watch. It was almost eight. She'd have to run down to the drugstore on the corner and buy a second jump drive on which to store the copied data. She had no other choice. She hesitated, and then decided to take the evidence with her. She closed the safe and replaced the painting and the key, just in case she found Delgado on her doorstep when she got back. Chances were good that he was involved in whatever this was.

She'd get the new drive, take it to her house, and download and copy it there. She didn't know how long that would take, and she couldn't risk being discovered in the middle of the task. If he were waiting for her when she got back, she'd say that she'd had car trouble and apologize for being late to work.

She logged off her computer and turned out the lights. Satisfied that the office looked like it had when they'd left last night, she cautiously checked the parking lot and made her way quickly to her car. By ten forty-five, Loretta had copies of everything she needed. She breathed a long sigh of relief once she'd returned the jump drive to its hiding place behind the painting in Frank Haynes' office and retaped the safe's key back under Haynes' desk.

R

Loretta spent the rest of the day unsuccessfully trying to focus on month-end revenue reports. She'd have to think carefully about what to do with the information she'd uncovered. It was like a little savings account, she decided; something to hold onto until the perfect moment. She smiled to herself—she was a clever girl. And with all of the commotion in his office from the paramedics, Frank Haynes would never notice that anything had been disturbed. She couldn't have planned it better herself.

She was deep in thought staring at her computer screen when the door to Haynes Enterprises opened behind her. She turned and suppressed a tremor as Chuck Delgado swaggered into the reception area. Hiding her repugnance, she settled a serious expression on her face.

"Good afternoon, Mr. Delgado," she said, adopting a formal tone.

"Hello, sweetheart," he replied, undressing her with his eyes.

"Mr. Haynes is still in the hospital. He's doing much better. If you need to talk to him, you can see him there," she supplied, hoping to get rid of him.

"I heard. I'm not after Frankie. I told him I'd look in on you while he was out. Like I said yesterday, keeping an eye on you is pure pleasure." Delgado moved around her desk to stand behind her chair. She tried to get up, but he had her blocked.

"That's not necessary," she replied, trying to keep the note of panic out of her voice. She would not give this creep the satisfaction of knowing he was scaring her. "Everything here is going fine. In fact, I was just getting ready to make the bank deposit."

Delgado pressed himself against the back of her chair and began to massage her shoulders.

"You're all tense here," he crooned. "You're letting this job get to you. That's not good for a pretty girl like you. Let me help you relax," he said. He slid his hands down her shoulders and onto the softness at the top of her breasts, simultaneously releasing the top three buttons of her blouse.

"Hey," Loretta cried, grabbing his hands and thrusting them aside. "That's not okay."

She shoved her chair back hard, knocking him off balance. Scrambling to her feet, she headed for the door. Delgado recovered himself and came after her.

"You little bitch," he began, but stopped abruptly as Frank Haynes strode into the office.

"What the hell's going on here?" Haynes asked, eyeing them both closely.

"Nothin', Frankie. I was just lookin' in on things, like you asked." Delgado said, shooting Loretta a warning glance. "You're outta the hospital," he added, stating the obvious. "How ya feelin'?"

"Just fine, thank you, Charles. Wanted to make sure everything was okay before I go home. If you'll excuse us, we need to get back to work."

"Sure. Glad you're doin' good."

Delgado reached for the door and turned to Loretta. "I'll see you later," he said pointedly.

Haynes turned his steely gaze toward Loretta, noting her rumpled blouse unbuttoned halfway down the front.

Loretta turned toward her desk and discretely attempted to repair her disheveled appearance.

"Looks like you and Mr. Delgado were having fun until I came in," Haynes stated coldly.

"No. It wasn't like that at all. He was forcing himself on me. I was trying to get away from him. I'm so glad you came in," she replied firmly. "I don't know what would have happened."

"Delgado fancies himself the playboy. If you hadn't been flirting with him, I'm sure nothing would have happened," her boss replied derisively.

Loretta stared, aghast. Was he taking that creep's side in this? She opened her mouth to protest further but Haynes raised his hand to stop her.

"I don't have time to listen to all this petty drama now," he stated dismissively. "Have you made today's bank deposit yet?" he asked, checking his watch.

"No. I was just about to do that."

"Then be on your way. And you can go on home after that," he said. "You've evidently had a hard afternoon. Just give me back my keys."

Loretta straightened and picked up her purse. "Okay," she said. "Will you be all right here by yourself? Did they tell you that you could leave the hospital and come to work? I can come back after I go to the bank."

Her concern with his welfare paled next to her worry about what he might uncover if left alone in the office. She wanted to be there to gauge his reactions now that he was back.

"Thank you," he said without looking at her as he entered his office. "Not necessary. I'm perfectly fine."

She came to stand in the doorway of his office. He pushed paperwork aside and sat in his chair. "The paramedics sure made a mess in here," he growled.

He looked up at her. "Well?"

"They were concerned about you," she answered. "And I didn't straighten things up because I know you don't want me in your office."

"Just give me my keys and get out of here."

Loretta crossed to his desk. She wanted to throw them at the arrogant bastard, but she didn't dare. She held them out to him, and when he gestured to leave them, she placed them on the corner of his desk. He barely noticed, already tearing into unopened mail. Apparently he hadn't detected anything out of order.

"See you tomorrow," she said, willing her voice not to reflect the relief she felt.

Haynes nodded distractedly and she was off.

Chapter 44

Maggie took one last look over Westbury's November financial statements and leaned back in her chair, encouraged by the results. The town wasn't exactly operating in the black, but it certainly wasn't hemorrhaging money like it had been for the past year. It'd be nice to share some good news for a change. She reached for her phone and dialed Professor Upton. He deserved a lot of the credit for the reversal; he should be the first to know.

"Don," Maggie burst out as soon as he picked up. "It's Maggie. Good news here. The November financials show the town is operating almost at break even."

"That's fabulous, Maggie. Are you sure?"

"As far as I can tell," Maggie assured him. "I've poured over the books."

"Good for you. But don't forget, November and December will show increased seasonal revenue. What about January and February?"

Maggie sighed heavily. "You're right. Westbury will run in the red both of those months. This is just a transitory blip. But it's a good sign."

"I don't disagree. I'm not trying to be a joy kill. But you've still got a tremendous task ahead of you, Maggie."

"I know that; it's on my mind every second of every day."

"Things getting any better for you down there? Has the press lightened up? Are you getting any support from anyone?"

Maggie laughed mirthlessly. "No, it's still a parade of horribles everywhere I turn."

"I'm sorry to hear that, Maggie. You didn't ask for this; maybe you shouldn't put up with it."

"What do you mean?"

"I've been debating whether to offer this to you or not. If you were still a consultant, I would have." He paused to take a swig of his coffee. "I've been working on a fraud investigation involving a large utility company in California. I'm going to testify as an expert witness and my client would like to hire an additional expert. They've asked me to find someone. You would be perfect."

"I can't do that while I'm serving as mayor," Maggie answered hastily.

"I know. That's why I hadn't asked you. I'm mentioning it now because I think you should consider resigning and taking this engagement."

"That's ridiculous, Don. I can't just up and quit."

"Hear me out, Maggie. This assignment would require a tremendous amount of time, but the client is paying top dollar. You'd make more on this in one year than you'd make in ten years as mayor of Westbury. Think of that, Maggie. You could retire when you were done."

He heard her sharp intake of breath. Encouraged, he continued. "These opportunities only come around once in a career. And you'd have to travel to California on a regular basis, so you could see your family. You've told me that you miss them and you've been too busy to keep your promise to visit. This could be the right job at the right time, Maggie. You know that being mayor isn't something you ever wanted. Surely there are others who can step in and do the job."

They remained silent while Maggie searched for words. What should she say? What did she want to say?

"Promise me you'll think it over carefully, Maggie. Don't turn this down out of some misguided loyalty to Westbury. The good citizens don't sound like they are being very loyal to you."

Maggie found her voice. "All right," she said slowly. "I'll consider it."

"Good. I'll send you some of the materials to review; you'll find this case fascinating."

"Sounds good. I'll take a look at them. And I'll really think about it. And Don, thank you. I appreciate your offer."

Chapter 45

Over the next two weeks, John and Maggie spent almost every free moment together. She and John talked about going skating again, but never found the time. When they weren't arranging furniture for the upcoming tea party, they were addressing invitations, running errands, and Christmas shopping. Maggie silently marveled at the joy of working on these projects with a partner; Paul had never lifted a finger to help her with any of the parties she had thrown for his benefit. Most of John and Maggie's nights ended with them drifting off to sleep in each other's arms.

At final count, Maggie had invited over one hundred twenty people to "High Tea at Rosemont," as the invitation called it. Of that number, only seven declined. Sunday would be a busy day.

"As I predicted, this is the hot ticket of the season," John remarked the evening before the event. Maggie sagged into his embrace as they stood at the bottom of the stairs, surveying the living room and library. Both rooms had been transformed into tearooms, with clusters of tables decked out in Maggie's collections of vintage linen and china. Centerpieces of ivy, white tulips, and red roses splashed color across the space. Expectation hung in the air. Illuminated by the towering Christmas tree, the scene resembled a festive watercolor.

"I don't know what I would have done without you," Maggie said looking up at him.

John shrugged.

"No, really. I bit off way more than I could chew. If you hadn't helped me, I'd still be ironing those blasted tablecloths." She laughed. "Where in the world did you learn to iron like that?"

"My mother thought it was a useful skill every man should master. I sew on a mean button, too."

"Wise woman, your mother. I would've liked her."

John regarded her seriously. "She would've adored you. You share a lot of the same fine qualities."

Maggie drew her arms tighter around him and snuggled in. "I believe we're all set. Not another thing to do until tomorrow. The night is still young—any idea how you'd like to spend it?" she asked with a twinkle in her eye.

R

Sunday arrived, cold and gray. Snow was predicted that night and clouds blocked the sun. The inclement weather only served to accent Rosemont's charm and coziness. The fireplaces and candles were lit, the Christmas tree sparkled.

Sam and Joan Torres arrived right after church, insisting that Maggie put them to work. Maggie sent Sam and John to tend the fires and whip up the first batch of Pink Lady cocktails—the only alcoholic beverage on the menu—while she and Joan set out the tea cakes, scones, and finger sandwiches, and brewed vast quantities of tea.

Although the invitation stated that this would be an open house with tea served from two until five o'clock, all but a few stragglers had arrived by two fifteen. High-spirited laughter filled the house as people visited the buffet and Maggie, Joan, and Nancy Knudsen restocked the trays and ferried hot tea into the dining room.

Maggie was on her way back into the kitchen when someone tapped her shoulder from behind. She turned to face a beaming Judy Young, flanked by Tonya Holmes.

"Turn right around and fix yourself a plate," Judy ordered. "If we don't force your hand, you won't get a bite to eat at your own party."

Maggie laughed and shook her head in protest.

Tonya stepped in. "Judy's right. We've got it from here. Get a cup of tea and go enjoy your guests. Besides," she added with a malevolent twinkle in her eye, "you need to check out Frank Haynes and Mr. and Mrs. Delgado. They're sitting in the far corner of the library."

"You're kidding. They RSVP'd, but I didn't think they'd actually show up."

"The Mrs. is loving it. I overheard Chuck ask John if there was any real booze around the place—not just that 'girlie drink.' And Frank's examining Rosemont as if he were an appraiser. It's Christmas; I shouldn't be so catty. But those two are definitely odd."

"You've got me there; that's a sight I want to see," Maggie said. "Everything you'll need is out on the counters. I won't be more than a few minutes."

"Take your time and enjoy yourself," Judy reiterated.

Maggie selected a buttermilk scone and lemon bar, filled a cup with fragrant white tea, and made her way into the party. She crossed the living room, greeting her guests and exchanging pleasantries as quickly as politeness would allow. Her destination was the library, more particularly the Delgado-Haynes table. Taking a deep breath, she approached, setting her cup on the table and drawing up a chair.

"May I join you? I don't believe we've met," she said, extending her hand to Bertha Delgado.

"Lovely place you got here, ma'am," Mrs. Delgado gushed, rocking the table and sending tea sloshing into saucers as she stood to take Maggie's hand. "So Christmas-y and all."

"Thank you," Maggie replied simply. "Please, sit."

"I can't get Chuck to hang so much as a single strand of lights from the eves," she continued, shooting her husband a reproachful look. Delgado turned aside and fixed his gaze on the swirling snow outside the window. "No. It's all on me." She sighed heavily. "How on earth did you get this done by yourself? I can't imagine."

"Oh, I had plenty of assistance." Maggie assured her.

"Who do you use? I'd like to have his name, since I get no cooperation from this one," she said, gesturing to her husband with her elbow.

"Actually, my friend John Allen pitched in."

"Ahhh," Bertha replied, intrigued. "That's not the usual service you get from a vet. How do you know Dr. Allen?"

"I met him when I adopted a dog—or, rather when she adopted me during my first week in Westbury. John's our vet."

Bertha raised one brow quizzically. Maggie took a breath and continued. "We started seeing each other, took a break, and got re-matched through an online dating service."

"Now *that* is very nice. He's quite the looker isn't he? Quite a catch. He's been the most eligible bachelor in town for years."

Bertha noticed Haynes' grimace out of the corner of her eye. "Right behind our Frank, here," she quickly added, tapping his knee. "Which online dating service? Maybe Frank should try it, unless he's a confirmed bachelor." She nodded at Frank. "Too successful to want to share any of it with someone else?"

Haynes turned away in disgust. "Give it a rest, Bertha. Nobody cares," Delgado said.

Maggie cleared her throat.

"So, which online dating service?" Bertha repeated.

"DogLovers.com," Maggie replied. "As a matter of fact, I was DogLover7717 and John was DogLover7718. We got a big kick out of that," she said to fill the awkward silence.

Haynes lost his grip on his empty plate and it clattered to the carpet. He rose quickly, picked it up, and fished his fork out from under Bertha's chair. "Nice spread, Maggie. I think I'll go back for seconds. Will you excuse me?" he asked before walking stiffly away.

"Now you've done it, Bertha," Delgado exclaimed. "You've pissed him off. That's the last thing I need."

Bertha smiled uneasily. Maggie could taste the tension at the table. She took a quick bite of her lemon bar and scanned the room for an out. At the far side of the fireplace she spotted Glenn and Gloria at a small table. Gloria glanced in her direction and waved. Seizing the opportunity, Maggie rose.

"I'd better go mingle with my guests. Don't get up," she said to Bertha. "Please help yourselves to more of everything," she added, gesturing toward the dining room. She turned to leave. "And have a very Merry Christmas."

Maggie made her way to Glenn and Gloria as quickly as possible while balancing a full cup of tea. She always felt vaguely sleazy during an encounter with Chuck Delgado, and his wife didn't do anything to minimize that effect. She needed the warmth and goodness of this older couple.

Glenn stood and pulled out her chair. Gloria took Maggie's hand in her own as she sat down. "My dear, Rosemont is a lovely home, but you've transformed it with your efforts. It's absolutely stunning. Everything's perfect."

Glenn nodded his agreement. "We've been combining our households since we got married," he said, shooting Gloria an adoring glance. "So we decided we wouldn't bother with a Christmas tree this year. Looking at all this, we've decided we're wrong on that score. We'll be stopping on the way home to pick one up."

"Just a small one," Gloria rushed to add, giving Glenn a stern look. "Tabletop size only."

Glenn rolled his eyes and Maggie laughed. "Sounds like a wonderful idea. You've got to have a tree for your first Christmas as husband and wife."

"That's what I've been saying," Glenn chimed in. "But until we came here and saw your tree, Gloria wasn't having it."

"You know, I didn't plan to put up a tree or any decorations this year, either," Maggie stated. They looked at her incredulously. "I was going to spend Christmas with my children and grandchildren in California. I didn't see the point of decorating this year."

"So what changed your mind? Who convinced you to do all this?" Glenn asked.

"My family was here for Thanksgiving and found boxes and boxes of vintage decorations in the attic; most of what you see here. My daughter was the ringleader; she decided that we should drag everything out of the attic, get a tree, and decorate Rosemont. There were lots of people to help, and one thing led to another. You know how that goes."

They both nodded in unison.

"By the time they went back to California, all of this was done."

"How wonderful!" Gloria exclaimed. Her gaze swept the room. "It'll be a big job taking it all down. We can't get up on ladders anymore, but we could help you wrap and pack things back up."

Maggie smiled and rubbed Gloria's hand. "What a nice offer. You're right; this will be a lot of work to take down. I considered that when we were decorating. My family was having such fun, I didn't have the heart to be a wet blanket. We moms get ourselves into hot water that way, don't we?" she asked, turning to Gloria with a smile.

"We most certainly do. For better or worse, if my family wanted something, I'd usually find a way."

"Exactly. But the most unexpected thing happened. My kids—even my granddaughters—decided that they'd rather come back to Rosemont for Christmas than have me go out to California. So I get to host them all again."

"How wonderful! I can see why they'd want to come back," Glenn said.

"Be sure they help you put all this away," Gloria admonished.

Glenn turned to Maggie. "Did I see Frank Haynes over by the French doors? I want to wish him a very happy holiday and invite him to join us for dinner some evening when he's available—to thank him."

Maggie smiled. "I'm sure he'd like that. He just went to get something from the buffet. He'll be back any minute," she replied. "Now, I should check on things in the kitchen. We'll talk before you leave. And do get yourself a Christmas tree. I'd be sorry if I hadn't."

R

Frank Haynes scanned the buffet table, but he'd apparently lost his appetite. So Maggie was the one woman online who had interested him? She was DogLover7717, the woman who had cancelled their coffee date? *Didn't that just figure,* he fumed. And now she was involved, again, with the good doctor.

He halted at the base of the staircase and thought of the night he'd rescued her from the attic. *What was it she'd called him? Her white knight?* He flushed as he remembered the feeling of her body stumbling into him; of his arms around her shoulders, steadying her. Then he cursed himself for thinking there'd ever be anything between them.

Suddenly another memory surfaced, the folder labeled *F.H./Rosemont,* and Frank Haynes smiled his Grinch Who Stole Christmas grin. He knew what he had to do. He glanced swiftly over his shoulder. When he was sure no one was paying any attention to him, he ascended the stairs.

R

By late afternoon, Maggie's guests had had their fill of teacakes and scones. Still, no one made a move for the door. Instead, people lingered and relaxed. Maggie was headed toward the kitchen when John intercepted her and pulled her through the back door onto the porch.

"What are you doing? It's freezing out here," she cried.

John wrapped his arms around her. "Better?" he asked. "I've watched you flit around all afternoon. I wanted a moment with you by myself," he smiled down at her.

"Since you put it like that, fine." She placed her arms around his neck and they kissed, gently swaying like teenagers at a school dance.

When they finished, Maggie rested her head on his shoulder. "This has been nice. I think everyone's had a good time."

"Are you kidding? It'll be the talk of the town for the next year. Judy's been snapping photos like mad. She's probably already posted them to Facebook."

"Really? That'll be good. I didn't even think of taking pictures. I'll send them to Susan and Amy. And the twins. They'll think this is pretty neat."

Maggie shivered.

"This will have to hold me for a while," John said. "Let's get you back inside."

As they entered through the kitchen door, they heard the first strains of "We Wish You a Merry Christmas" coming from the grand piano in the conservatory.

"Music!" Maggie cried, slapping her forehead with her palm. "I completely forgot about music!"

"Looks like someone else thought of it," John observed. "I'll bet that's Marc playing."

The melody, skillfully played, filled the air. "Must be," Maggie agreed. "I don't know anyone else who plays like he does."

As they made their way to the conservatory, they heard the first, tentative voices take up the chorus. By the time they entered the room, a large group surrounded Marc at the piano. Clearly delighted, he stood at the end of the tune and waved his arm for silence.

"Let's have an old-fashioned Christmas carol sing-along. What do you say?" he asked.

The crowd whistled and clapped.

Maggie leaned close to John. "Never in a million years did I think this would happen. I'll tell you what; this house is magic. It has such an effect on people."

"It's not the house, darling. It's you who're magic," he replied, but his words were drowned out by a rousing chorus of "Hark the Herald Angels Sing."

Maggie squeezed his arm and joined in the singing.

R

Frank Haynes could hear the strains of Christmas carols up in the attic. *Perfect,* he thought. If everyone were in the conservatory singing, no one would notice his absence. He continued to weed through boxes, but he couldn't find the file he sought. In fact, it looked like someone had been working in the attic, rearranging and tidying things. *Damn it,* he thought. *Did Maggie discover the file and destroy it?* Or was it still here, lurking somewhere out of his reach?

Haynes cursed again when he noticed that the singing had stopped. He'd better get back downstairs before anyone missed him. One thing was certain, he thought as he headed down the steps, he would return to the attic somehow, and he would find that file.

R

Afternoon tea was still going strong at five thirty. Maggie was thrilled that everyone was having such a good time, but anxious to start cleaning up. She had a full schedule at Town Hall the following day. Sam Torres had been watching her carefully and now drew her aside.

"I think it's time we broke this party up, don't you?"

Maggie sighed. "I can't just yell 'Time's up! Get out!'"

"Leave it to me," he stated confidently. He circled behind Marc at the piano and whispered something in his ear. Marc concluded "O Come, All Ye Faithful" with a flourish and lowered the lid on the keyboard. He ignored the cries of protest from the crowd and turned to acknowledge a smattering of applause.

Sam Torres clapped his hands above his head. "Everybody, grab your coats and follow me. The outside lights are set to come on shortly. You won't want to miss them."

An excited murmur rippled through the crowd as people hurried to retrieve their coats and congregate outside. The wind bore an icy bite. A few drifted away to their cars, but most remained, stamping their feet and rubbing their hands to stay warm. Maggie and John stood at the bottom of the steps and waited.

At precisely five forty-five, Rosemont's façade jumped into brilliant relief against the night sky. The crowd gasped and John and Sam exchanged proud nods.

Before Maggie could utter a word of thanks to the crowd, Sam jumped in front of her, tugging Joan along with him. He took Maggie's hand and pumped it, saying in a voice too loud for the distance that was between them, "Thank you so much for having us, Mayor. We had a wonderful time, but we must be going now."

"So that's your game, is it?" Maggie uttered softly, gazing over his shoulder. "Get everybody out of the house and then start the procession to their cars? Brilliant. And it looks like it's working. Thank you."

"I hate to leave you with all the cleanup," Joan said. "Maybe we should come back in half an hour."

Maggie laughed. "Don't be ridiculous. You helped me set up. You go on home now," she ordered, giving Joan a hug.

"Come on now, honey," Sam said, pulling Joan aside. "Other people want to say their goodbyes."

By six fifteen, Maggie and John had waved goodbye to the final guest. Arm-in-arm, they climbed the stone steps and crossed the threshold to the sight every hostess hates—the aftermath of a party.

Maggie slumped into the nearest chair. "Right now, I want to slap myself silly. Why did I do this?"

John grinned. "Buck up; it's not that bad. And you've got me to help. You just need to get your second wind."

Maggie nodded unenthusiastically.

"Tell you what. Why don't I go pick up Eve and Roman, plus a pizza, and bring them back here? Go soak in the tub while I'm gone, and we'll make short work of this after we eat."

Maggie opened her mouth to protest, but John was already pulling her to her feet and turning her toward the stairs. "Don't waste time arguing with me. Just do it," he said with a familiar smile.

R

Maggie was still relaxing in the tub an hour later when Eve bounded up the stairs and into the bathroom in search of her master. Maggie quickly snatched her towel and stepped out of the tub, fearing that Eve would launch herself into it at any moment.

"You silly girl," she cooed, rubbing her ears. "You were only gone for one afternoon. And you love your friend Roman."

She turned as she heard John's tread on the stairs.

"You decent?" he called.

"Not yet," she replied

"Good. Then I'm right on time."

"I don't think so, Mr.," she hollered through the door. "Take yourself back downstairs, and I'll be there shortly. I barely ate at my own party, and I'm starved."

Maggie and Eve bounded down the stairs ten minutes later, Maggie snug in her favorite flannel pajamas.

John burst out laughing.

"Don't start with me," Maggie warned. "I love these pj's. I live in these pj's from November through May. Just accept it."

John nodded. "As long as I can get you out of them from time to time."

Maggie shot him a sideways glance. "Let's eat," she said, flipping open the lid to the pizza box. "We've got a lot of work to do."

John had been right—the bath and the food restored her energy. By ten o'clock, all the dishes had been stacked in the kitchen, waiting to be run through the dishwasher; the dirty linens were in the washer; and John had moved most of the furniture back to its original position.

Maggie threw her arms around John's back and hugged him. "Let's call it quits for tonight. I can finish up during the evenings this week."

"You sure?" John replied, stifling a yawn.

"Positive. Let's take these two outside to do their business and head upstairs to bed."

It was just beginning to snow as they headed to the back lawn of Rosemont. Fat, wet flakes floated lazily from the sky. They watched the snow drift and catch the light from the back porch until the dogs returned, eager to dash back into the warm house.

"I'm really tired," John sighed as they climbed the stairs. "If I snore, elbow me."

"I was just about to say the same to you," Maggie replied.

Chapter 46

For the second time since she'd moved to Westbury, Maggie was snowed in at Rosemont. She just didn't know it. The storm had shifted direction after midnight and the full brunt of it settled on Westbury. John had set his alarm for his usual Monday morning wake-up time of four thirty. Maggie had intended to get up and make coffee; instead she looked up only briefly before rolling over. She was back to sleep before her head hit the pillow.

John padded downstairs to let the dogs out and give them their breakfast. A drift by the kitchen door made it almost impossible to open and the snow was falling at an alarming rate. He crossed to the front of the house and looked out at his car, dimly illuminated by the entryway light. The snow was almost to the top of his tires. John returned to the kitchen and found the TV remote. He flipped to the weather channel and waited for the local weather segment to hear what he already suspected: schools and government offices were closed. Citizens were instructed to stay off the roads.

The morning's surgery would have to be cancelled. Thank goodness, they weren't currently boarding any dogs. He'd call his office manager in a few hours about adding something to their voicemail recording about the closure and ask her to contact today's appointments.

He smiled broadly and stood in the kitchen, savoring the delicious freedom and possibilities that only a snow day could bring. The first order of business was to slip back into bed with Maggie Martin.

R

Maggie stirred and stretched, then snuggled back into the warmth of John's arms. It took a moment for the oddness of this to register. She sat straight up in bed and threw off the covers.

"John!" she cried in alarm. "Good grief, it's light out. You should have been out of here hours ago. We've overslept."

She hurled herself into her bathrobe as John turned over in bed.

"Slow down there, princess. Nobody overslept. We're snowed in."

Maggie stopped dead in her tracks. "Really?" she replied, a note of schoolgirl hopefulness in her voice.

"Yep. The storm changed course overnight and they're saying Westbury is at the center of the blizzard."

"No kidding."

"I got up as usual and had a devil of a time getting the kitchen door open to let the dogs out. I turned on the TV, and found out they've closed down the town. I'm surprised nobody called you, being mayor and all."

"I am too, now that you mention it." Maggie turned toward her nightstand. "I didn't bring my phone upstairs last night. It must still be in the kitchen."

"That would explain it."

"I'd better go get it," Maggie replied, heading to the door. "You can stay in bed. How often do you get to sleep in?"

"Nope, I'm coming. Knowing you, you'll get started on the rest of the cleanup, and you'll work until you drop. I can't be the lazy boyfriend lounging in bed while you lift that barge and tote that bale."

"You're the best. You know that, don't you?" Maggie called over her shoulder as she headed downstairs.

R

John had been correct in his prediction. Maggie pulled out the leftover pizza pronouncing it the "best day-after-the-party food ever" and tackled the remaining cleanup with gusto. They worked companionably together and managed to completely restore order by noon.

Maggie poked through her pantry and refrigerator, and decided that the best she could offer for lunch was omelets. John started a fire in the library, and they ate their lunch nestled on the rug in front of the hearth.

"You're a million miles away," John observed. "Worried about the mess that is Westbury? Can't you put it aside for one afternoon?"

Maggie tore her gaze from the fire. "It's always with me; like a black cloud that follows me around. I wake up in the middle of the night thinking about it. But that's not what's on my mind just now."

John cocked an eyebrow. "The floor's all yours."

Maggie sighed. "I got a call from Don Upton. He's my professor friend that's consulting with us on the town's finances."

John nodded. "I remember you mentioning him. You said he's been very helpful."

"He has. He has also offered me a new job—one that would require me to resign my post as mayor."

John let out a low whistle. "Tell me about it."

Maggie settled against the back of a chair. "It's an expert witness consultation in a big fraud case involving a California utility."

"Would you need to move back to California?"

"No," Maggie answered hastily. "But I'd have to make frequent trips out there."

John breathed a sigh of relief. "You'd get to see your kids and the girls? You'd like that."

Maggie nodded. "It would be extremely lucrative; I'd make enough to be able to retire comfortably. And it's work I'm experienced in and good at. I'd love doing it."

"You can't take this on and continue as mayor?"

"No way. The demands of both jobs would be way too much. I'd put in long hours on the expert witness job, but I'd largely be able to control the timing. So I could work around your job. We'd have more time together."

"I'd love that," John said, holding her gaze. "What's the downside of taking this job?"

"Resigning. Being a quitter. Letting people down," Maggie replied in a rush. "But with all the critical press and hate mail I'm getting, I'm not sure that anyone would really care."

"Honey, that's a small percentage of the people. I'm sure the vast majority support and appreciate you. Don't let the few malcontents influence your decision."

Maggie smiled and reached over to rub his hand. "You're always on my side, aren't you?"

John raised her hand and kissed it.

Maggie sighed. "Still, I'd like to be done with all of this. I feel like a fish out of water all the time. Nothing comes easily at Town Hall. With Don's job, I'd be back in my element—in my zone of genius, as they say."

"Sounds like there are a lot of compelling reasons to take him up on this offer. I won't hide the fact that I'd love to see more of you, but I'm behind you, no matter what you decide."

Maggie nodded.

"Thank you, John. I know that. But enough about me. What's on your mind today?"

John took Maggie's hand and pulled her down onto the thick rug. "I've been thinking about ways to get you out of these ridiculous pajamas all morning. I think it's time to put theory to the test, don't you?"

Maggie smiled. "Anything for science," she replied.

Chapter 47

Frank Haynes was restless and ill-tempered when he finally made his way into his office at Haynes Enterprises on Tuesday morning. Snow days meant lost revenue to him, nothing more. The day at home had given him plenty of time to stew over Maggie Martin and her seemingly perfect life. At Rosemont—the property that in his mind had been destined to be his.

The schools were closed and Loretta wouldn't be in until ten, but at least she'd be there. What an enigma she was. The lady was certainly tight-lipped about her past. From what Haynes knew about it, she had reason to be secretive. The conservative folks around Westbury wouldn't take to a kept woman with a sugar daddy.

What was Loretta's game? he wondered. *Did she actually want a fresh start in Westbury? Was she turning over a new leaf?* Haynes snorted in disgust. *If she were after redemption, it wouldn't last long. What was the saying—leopards don't change their spots?* He'd just have to find a way to make that work in his favor. Soon.

He turned in his chair to look out at the snow-covered parking lot. Loretta would have been jealous of Maggie if she'd been at that ridiculous tea party of hers. Maybe he should have brought her along. Too late now. An idea flashed through his brain. Maybe he could work that angle after all.

R

Loretta pushed through the door of Haynes Enterprises at ten minutes before eleven. She dropped her purse on her desk and rushed directly to Haynes' office, an apology on her lips. Their two cars were the only ones in the lot, but Loretta knew that he wouldn't find the fact that none of the other tenants had opened their offices to be a good excuse for her tardiness.

She drew in a breath and prepared to deliver the speech she had rehearsed in the car when he cut her off.

"No need to apologize, my dear. The roads are horrible. Just glad you made it here safely. Do you have snow tires yet? No? Then you need to get them. They'll make a world of difference."

Another one of his startling mood changes. Loretta eyed him guardedly.

"Before you get started, I've got a couple of things I'd like your help with," he said smoothly. Loretta nodded. "First, I'd like you to order a large flower arrangement to be delivered to Mayor Martin."

Loretta raised one eyebrow. "What do you want the card to say?"

He paused and tried to appear thoughtful and solicitous: "Thank you for your spectacular hospitality on Sunday afternoon. Merry Christmas.

"What do you think?"

Loretta shrugged. "That sounds fine. What did she do on Sunday afternoon? If I may ask."

"Didn't you hear about it? She had a party at Rosemont. I believe they call it a high tea. For more than a hundred people. Very fancy and grand. The place was all decked out for Christmas." He watched her expression carefully and could see that he'd piqued her interest.

"How nice," she replied tersely.

"You would have loved it," he continued. "All the women did. In fact, are you on Facebook?"

Loretta nodded. "Why?"

"One of the women there—Judy Young from that gift shop on the square—was snapping photos right and left to post on her page. I'd like to see them. Will you log in so we can take a look?"

Haynes didn't have the slightest interest in those photos. Once around had been plenty. On the other hand, seeing Loretta consumed with jealousy could be most entertaining and useful. This day was starting to look up.

"Sure," Loretta replied. "You could set up your own Facebook account if you wanted; I could show you how."

"Absolutely not." He had to stop himself from adding, "I don't have time for that sort of idiocy."

He leaned over her shoulder as she brought her Facebook page onto her computer screen.

"Celebration's page," he reminded her.

Within seconds, Loretta was scrolling through Judy's album of photos from Sunday afternoon. Haynes could see that they were having the desired effect; Loretta twitched with envy. He'd been right; part of her felt as if all that could have been hers. He decided to press his advantage.

"Didn't you say that Paul Martin talked about Rosemont?" he asked innocently.

"Not much," Loretta muttered absentmindedly, scrolling through the photos a second time. "He never told me it was anything like this."

Keep her talking, Haynes thought. "What did he tell you?"

"That it was old and run down. That it would cost a fortune to restore." She was indignant. "This sure doesn't look like a fixer-upper to me. He said that she could have it."

Haynes nodded. Now they were getting somewhere.

Loretta glanced up at him and abruptly stopped. She hadn't intended to talk about any of this, and she certainly wasn't going to confide in her boss.

He nodded at her in encouragement. "Meaning Mrs. Martin could have it?"

"I don't know what he meant. I really didn't know him very well."

She closed out of the Facebook page. "Where shall I send the flowers? Rosemont or Town Hall?"

Haynes swallowed his frustration. "Town Hall will do," he said as he retreated to his office.

Chapter 48

Maggie entered the parking garage half an hour before the scheduled arrival of the plane carrying the returning California contingent. John pulled in right after her. She didn't have enough room in her car to transport all five of them, plus the extra luggage they were bringing for the holiday. John had offered his services.

Mike expected her to pick them up at the curb, but John suggested they meet them inside. "They'll have too much to wrangle on their own," he insisted. They checked the flight's status on the large screen and decided they had time for a cup of coffee while they waited. They gathered their paper cups and settled into chairs facing the checkpoint.

"Excited?" John asked.

Maggie nodded. "Absolutely. I love having them here. The girls are so excited about Santa. They've written him every day to make sure he knows they'll be at Rosemont this year." She smiled. "Nothing is more magical than Christmas through the eyes of a child."

John turned to her. "I haven't experienced that as an adult," he said with an air of sadness.

"You will now," Maggie assured him. "In fact, I'll bet the twins would love to go see Santa tomorrow. Deliver their forwarding address in person. Why don't we take them?"

"The mall will be a madhouse. The line for Santa will be a mile long," John said, but he couldn't keep the excitement out of his voice.

"That's part of the fun of it. Perfect plan!"

"What else is on the agenda?"

"We'll go to the family service on Christmas Eve. And I'd like to take the girls skating at The Mill. You're welcome to join us for everything. Whatever you can fit in."

John nodded. "I've got a light schedule this week; nobody brings their animal in for surgery during the holidays unless it's an emergency. But you'll need time alone with your children; I don't want to interfere."

"Nonsense," Maggie replied. "They love you. They'll want you there. And I want you there."

They sipped their coffee. Maggie checked her watch. "They should be on the ground by now. They'll be here any minute." She turned to John and took a deep breath. "One more thing. I hope this doesn't upset you, but—"

John put his arm around her shoulder and drew her close. "I know, sweetheart. As much as I've loved sleeping with you these last few weeks, you're not ready to have me there with your kids and grandkids in the house. I'll take myself back to my lonely bachelor pad every night. We'll be the soul of discretion."

Maggie sighed. "You are the most understanding man on the planet." She looked up at him. "And you know what else? I'm still pooped from the tea party, and we haven't even started this visit yet."

"Oh yes, we have," John cried, standing and pulling her to her feet. He pointed to the walkway. "Here they come!"

R

After a day of collecting everyone from the airport and getting them settled into their rooms, Maggie longed for her bed. She was glad she'd had the wherewithal to make dinner in advance and that the slow-cooker pot roast had been a big hit. The twins, wired after their long confinement on the flight, had spent the evening racing through the house, chasing a willing Eve from room to room. They, like the rest of the recent arrivals, were on California time and probably wouldn't wind down for another three hours.

She had finally slipped her feet under the covers when she heard the soft knock on her door. She briefly considered ignoring it, but a corresponding sense of guilt prompted her to call, "Come in."

Susan slipped gracefully through the door and plopped down on the bed next to her. Maggie knew her daughter; she glowed with excitement and clearly wanted to talk. How many of these opportunities would Maggie have? She hoisted herself to a sitting position, propped herself up on some pillows, and willed herself to remain alert.

"I haven't told you much about this because I didn't want to jinx it," she began breathlessly. "You know how I told you I'd had a text from Aaron? Alex's brother?"

Maggie nodded. "Of course I remember. And I think he's going to be in Westbury with Alex for Christmas."

"He is, for sure," Susan replied. "And we're going to spend as much time together as we can." She burrowed under the covers. "We've been emailing and texting every day. We've talked on the phone for hours. There's something there, Mom. I know it."

Maggie looked at her daughter and nodded encouragingly.

"We love each other. We really do. I've never felt so comfortable and in tune with anybody. Do you think we're crazy? Please don't throw cold water on this," she pleaded.

"Honey," Maggie chose her words carefully. "I certainly don't think either of you is crazy. I had an idea about this, because I ran into Alex last week and he said his brother is nuts about you. He also told me he's the real deal—kind and dependable, honest and loving. You just need to make sure that you really know each other."

"That's the thing, Mom. I always thought long-distance relationships were doomed to failure because you couldn't spend time together. There may be some truth to that, but the distance has forced us to learn to communicate. We can't get distracted by physical chemistry."

Maggie smiled. "Good point. He's welcome here anytime. And Alex and Marc, too, since he's supposed to be here to see them."

"Plus John, right?" Susan asked.

"Absolutely. We'll have a full house again."

Susan rose and smoothed the blanket. "You know what, Mom? Westbury has been wonderful for both of our love lives. Maybe you should work up some sort of Chamber of Commerce-type advertising— Westbury: Supplying Fine Men to Womankind."

Maggie laughed. "You might have something there. Now go get a good night's sleep. We've got a full day tomorrow."

R

The mall was pandemonium the next afternoon. Alex, Marc, and Aaron caught up with them as they waited in line for Santa Claus. After the bare minimum of pleasantries, Susan grabbed Aaron's arm and announced, "We're outta here. Where shall we meet you?"

"We'll be here a while," Mike said with a sigh. "What're we doing after this?"

"It's a surprise," Maggie replied. She turned to Susan and Aaron. "I'll call you half an hour before you're supposed to be there."

"For Pete's sake, Mom, just tell us," Susan scoffed, but Maggie could tell she liked the intrigue. Just as she always had. No matter how grown up, Susan loved a secret.

Maggie ignored her and motioned to Alex. She leaned in and whispered briefly in his ear. Alex nodded and a smile spread across his lips.

"Perfect. We'll be there. I can handle those two," he said, gesturing toward his brother and Susan.

The wait for Santa Claus dragged on interminably. The girls grew fussy and impatient and their parents increasingly short-tempered. John finally dispatched Mike and Amy to get a snack. He turned his attention to the twins. "Have I ever told you about the time Roman had to help Santa Claus?"

"No," they replied in wide-eyed unison. John winked at Maggie and launched into the tall tale.

By the time Mike and Amy returned, Sophie and Sarah were next in line. They opted to go up together. Santa listened to both intently and assured them he would know where to find them on Christmas Eve. Satisfied, the girls bounded off his lap, shouting they were ready to "go to the surprise."

Maggie placed the call to Alex. "Time to launch," she said into the phone as they made the long walk to their cars.

R

The twins bombarded Maggie with questions on the way to The Mill while Amy napped in the passenger seat. John and Mike brought up the rear. The skies were partly cloudy, but the air was still. *A lovely afternoon to learn to skate,* Maggie thought.

Alex, Marc, Aaron, and Susan were waiting by Alex's car when they pulled into the lot. There were other skaters on the rink, but it was far from full. Maggie gathered her brood and announced that she and John would be giving them skating lessons.

"You're kidding, right?" Mike asked. "I was never any good at inline skating as a kid. Getting on ice can only be worse."

"Don't be such an old stick-in-the-mud," his sister scolded. Mike turned to his wife. "I'm with Susan," Amy replied.

The girls, delighted at the prospect, raced up the stairs to the rental kiosk. Their parents followed.

"Aaron and I used to skate on a small pond near our house as kids," Alex told Maggie. "I was never any good, but Aaron got the hang of it."

Aaron quickly added his disclaimer. "I haven't been on skates in years."

"I hadn't been on skates in *decades*," Maggie said. "Until John brought me here last year on our first date. So I can assure you from personal experience, it comes back to you. Like riding a bike."

Aaron gave her a tentative smile.

"I'm counting you as one of the instructors," she declared. "Along with John and me."

Resigned to their participation, the adults donned skates and the group proceeded to the rink. Only Amy hung back, insisting she had a headache, and would enjoy watching them from a comfortable chair inside. The twins promptly lined up beside John, declaring that they wanted to be in his class. He beamed, pleased to be their first choice. *The afternoon is unfolding perfectly,* Maggie thought with delight.

"Let's mix things up, shall we? Alex and Mike, come with me. Marc and Susan, go with Aaron," she called to the assembled group. "To make this interesting, keep track of the number of times you fall down. I've got a prize for the beginner who stays on his or her feet the most."

She looked at her competitive children.

"It's on," Mike called to Susan.

"You won't even be a challenge," Susan replied tauntingly as she took Aaron's arm and tentatively stepped onto the rink.

R

For the rest of the Christmas visit, long after the skating had ended, Sophie and Sarah stuck like glue to John. He didn't mind in the least. He even allowed them to be junior helpers at the animal hospital one slow afternoon. Mike was skeptical, but John reported that they had been patient and helpful, and that he'd offer them jobs if they lived in town. The girls beamed with pride.

Maggie kept short hours at Town Hall, attending to the few essential matters that presented themselves during the holidays. She was surprised to find an enormous arrangement of pine boughs, white orchids, and red roses, festooned with glittery ribbon and candles on her desk, and stunned to read the accompanying card from Frank Haynes. From the look on his face, she would have assumed that he had hated her Christmas tea. Either he had good breeding or she had misjudged him. She took out a sheet of her official "Mayor of Westbury" stationery and penned a thank-you note to slide under his door.

Aaron slipped in and out of Rosemont with Susan. They volunteered to do all the grocery shopping and any other errands that needed running; anything to get some time alone together. Mike reassured Maggie that Amy was fine; she was just taking advantage of the opportunity to sleep in every morning. By Christmas Eve, life at Rosemont had settled into a companionable rhythm.

Maggie stopped by Town Hall on Christmas Eve morning to drop off plates of Laura's Christmas cookies for each department, and to officially close Town Hall at noon. She had just returned home and settled into her favorite chair by the French doors in the library when the doorbell rang. When she opened the door, Sam and Joan wished her a very Merry Christmas and presented a dog collar for Eve.

"It's adorable! Look at this fabric, and the pretty bow," Maggie said, bending down to show it to Eve. "Won't you be the best-dressed doggie in town?" she crooned.

Joan beamed. "I thought that fabric looked like Rosemont, elegant and vintage-y."

"You made this?" Maggie asked as she secured the collar around Eve's neck.

"I did. Glad you like it," Joan smiled.

"It's perfect. You could sell these."

"I don't know about that," Joan laughed. "I've made another one out of the same fabric, with a bow tie, for Roman. Our next stop is Westbury Animal Clinic."

"Won't they just be the perfect pair," Maggie said as she walked them to their car.

She had barely reclaimed her seat when the doorbell rang again; this time, it was the Knudsens bearing two bottles of champagne. "You've got a lot to celebrate this year," Tim Knudsen observed.

When the bell rang a third time, Maggie abandoned all hope of putting her feet up. By the time Judy Young appeared at her door in the late afternoon, Maggie remarked that she hadn't expected so many visitors.

"It's Westbury's Christmas Eve tradition," Judy proudly informed her. "We visit our neighbors to wish them Merry Christmas and bring them something we think they'll enjoy. Used to be everything was homemade, but people have gotten away from that. I'd have been here earlier, but I just closed the shop. You were my first stop."

"Now I'm really embarrassed," Maggie said. "I don't have anything to give anybody. I had no idea. We don't do this where I'm from."

"Don't worry about it, honey," Judy stated firmly. "You've probably had everybody over to your house at one time or another, even if they didn't attend the high tea. You've done your share all year long. People want you to know they appreciate your kindness."

Maggie blushed. "Take a look at this collar that Joan Torres made for Eve."

"You've got to be kidding me. It's too cute."

"She made a boy version for Roman, too."

"I should carry these in Celebrations. They'd sell like hotcakes. I'm calling Joan as soon as I get home."

The steady stream of visitors finally stopped as the late afternoon sunshine slanted low through the trees. Church was at seven o'clock. She checked the large pot of chicken tortilla soup that she'd started as soon as she got home from Town Hall, then called her family to the table for a simple kitchen supper of soup and salad.

"Mexican for Christmas Eve?" John asked.

"Absolutely. Like all true immigrants to a foreign land, we're bringing some of our traditions with us," Maggie said with a wink. "Okay everybody, go get changed for church. We leave in fifteen minutes."

"Can't we stay here?" Sophia whined.

"With Eve and John?" Sarah added.

"I'm going to church with your Gramma," John interjected. "And I don't think Santa likes children who whine about going to church on Christmas Eve, do you?" he asked, turning to Maggie.

Sophie exchanged a look with Sarah. "We're going," she shouted as they raced upstairs to get ready.

"Well played, sir," Maggie said, planting a kiss on his cheek.

"I'll finish cleaning up the kitchen. You go powder your nose or whatever you women do," he replied, taking the dishtowel from her.

R

The joyful family church service featured a living nativity scene and enthusiastic singing of the familiar carols. Snow had begun to fall when they exited the sanctuary. Light from the enormous stained-glass windows painted a mosaic on the white canvas accumulating outside.

"Time to get ready for bed," Amy told the twins as the car turned onto the long, winding driveway to Rosemont. "The sooner you get to sleep, the sooner Santa will come."

Maggie caught Sarah's eye in the rearview mirror. "Tell you what. You two get your bath done and pajamas on without any fussing, and I'll fix some hot cocoa. We'll light the fire and turn out all the lights except for the Christmas tree, and we'll sip it in the dark. How would that be?"

They both nodded and raced into the house.

"Good work, Mom," Mike said as he and Amy trailed after their children.

Maggie turned to John. "Did you see Susan and Aaron? Weren't they right behind us?" she asked, looking for their car on the driveway.

"Aaron told me he had somewhere he wanted to take her after church."

Maggie raised her brows. "Don't worry, they'll be fine," John said reassuringly. "He's a terrific young man, and he's crazy about her, if you haven't noticed."

"With all the commotion, I haven't had much of a chance to talk to Aaron. Susan is nuts about him, too, I'm afraid," she replied. "I hope she doesn't get her heart broken. Especially at Christmas."

John drew her into his arms. "I wouldn't worry too much about that." He kissed the sides of her face, working his way to her mouth.

"He said they might be late and not to wait up," he whispered against her lips.

"On Christmas Eve, for heaven's sake? Where in the world can they be going? Nothing's open. This is ridiculous," she sputtered.

"Don't go getting yourself all worked up. They're adults and it'll be fine. Now kiss me," he insisted, "like you mean it."

R

As they exited the church, Aaron had taken Susan's hand. "Can I steal you away for a few hours? I've got something I want to show you."

Susan turned to him in the dark and nodded. "Sure. Let me go tell Mom."

"I've already told John that we won't be back until late. I hope that was all right."

Susan smiled and glanced at her retreating family. "Let's get out of here before anyone discovers we're missing," she whispered conspiratorially.

Aaron led her to his car, and they set off into the countryside. The pavement was wet but still warm enough that the snow wasn't sticking. Susan tuned the car radio to a station playing sacred music of the holiday; they allowed the rhythms to wash over them as they traversed the back roads surrounding Westbury.

Some forty minutes outside of town, Aaron turned off the highway onto an unmarked farm road. They bumped along the narrow track through a tunnel of trees until they broke through to a large field dominated by a lone pine tree. Majestic and tall, the tree was washed in moonlight and adorned at the top with a single silver star.

Susan inhaled deeply. "It's extraordinary. Simple and pure and absolutely beautiful."

Aaron nodded in satisfaction; he'd hoped she'd react this way.

"Who did this?" Susan asked. "The farmer who owns this field, I suppose."

Aaron shook his head.

"Then who?"

"I did," he replied. "I've put that star up for the last several years, for as long as I've been spending the holidays here with Alex. I don't know how many people see it, but I do it in memory of my uncle."

Susan turned to face him in the dark car. She waited.

"My uncle made the star in his workshop but he died before he ever got to put it up. Nobody else wanted it, so I took it. He was a very simple man, a farmer all his life. I knew that his star wouldn't be comfortable displayed in town. I found this spot and like the light. It's

218

very peaceful. I've been putting the star up here on Christmas Eve ever since."

"What a lovely tribute to your uncle," Susan replied, a catch in her throat. "I'm sure he can see it; I'm sure he's so proud of you."

She turned and locked eyes with him. "Thank you for sharing this with me. You are the most wonderful man," she murmured as he pulled her to him.

After what seemed like an eternity, he drew back and took her face in both of his hands. "I know this has been fast, but I feel like you're part of me. I can't imagine a future without you. I love you totally and completely."

Susan drew a ragged breath. "I'm in love with you, too. I'm just not sure where this can go, since I practice law in California and you're going to set up your medical practice here."

"That's why I'm bringing this up so soon. Before you may be ready," he said looking intently into her eyes. "I'm committed to you; I want to spend the rest of my life with you." He pressed a finger to her lips to quell her response.

"I don't want to disrupt your career. You've worked hard to launch it, and you're happy where you are. I can start mine anywhere. I was looking at Westbury because Alex is the only family I have. But I'm picking you over Alex. I've accepted a position with an orthopedic surgical practice about an hour away from you. We can make that work."

He brushed back a strand of hair that had fallen over her eye.

"My decision in no way binds you to me. I made it for me, without consulting you. You don't need to feel guilty if you don't feel the same way. I don't want to put any pressure on you. I just want to tell Alex what I've decided, and you needed to be the first to know. In private."

Susan struggled to hold back her tears.

"That'll give you time to decide if you really want to be the wife of a busy doctor," Aaron added. "It isn't for everyone. You're so independent. I think you'll be fine, but you need to decide that for yourself."

Her tears broke free. He fumbled in the glove box for tissues.

"Aaron—I love you, too. I'm head over heels for you. But if you think this counts as a proposal, you're wrong," she managed to choke out between sobs. "If you want me, you're going to have to kick this off old-school—on your knees and everything."

Aaron grinned. "Duly noted, counselor," he replied as he restarted the car. "And now I'd better get you back to Rosemont before the mayor sends the sheriff after us."

Chapter 49

Christmas Eve had taken its toll, and Sophie and Sarah had finally fallen asleep. Their parents turned in shortly thereafter. The house was quiet and peaceful for the first time in days. Maggie settled into a chair by the hearth to wait for Susan to come home. *Just like when she was a teenager,* Maggie thought; *I could never go to bed while the kids were out.* She sighed and dozed lightly in the glow from the Christmas tree.

Eve was the first to hear the car approaching on the driveway. Maggie managed to silence her after the first tentative woof; she didn't want the twins to wake up. She was about to throw the door open, but stopped herself. Didn't her daughter deserve a leisurely goodnight kiss on Christmas Eve?

Susan eventually inserted her key in the lock and crept quietly into the dimly lit foyer. She didn't see Maggie and Eve standing in the corner and nearly jumped out of her skin when Maggie softly spoke her name.

"Mom," she said, beginning to laugh. "You scared me to death. What're you doing down here? Waiting up for me?"

Maggie smiled. "Of course. And there's still something so satisfying about scaring the life out of a child who's sneaking into the house past curfew."

"I wasn't sneaking. And curfew? Honestly, Mom," Susan laughed. "But I am glad you're up. I was going to wake you if you weren't." She grabbed her mother's hand and pulled her into the living room. "He's proposed!" she cried.

Maggie gasped.

"Sort of. He's taken a job in a practice close to me. So we can be together."

Maggie squeezed her hands. "Oh, honey, that's wonderful. Though I half-hoped you'd come here to be with him, and then I'd have you near me," Maggie confessed. "If it got serious between you two."

"Oh, Mom." Susan sighed. "I'm all set in my job, and he hasn't started his career yet. That's why he decided to move to me. He said it would give me a chance to see what it was like to be a doctor's *wife*." She squeezed her mother's hands back. "He said I was the one for him, but he wasn't asking me to commit just yet. And I told him I loved him, Mom." She paused, and then smiled. "And that he'd still have to propose properly; down on one knee and the whole bit."

Maggie laughed. "You've always been an incredible romantic."

She held her daughter's radiant face between her hands and looked into her eyes. "Honey, I'm delighted for you. Aaron is a good man, and it's clear to me that he adores you."

"You don't think it's too soon?"

"I don't. Not at your ages. You should be able to know quickly. When it takes a long time, you're trying to talk yourself into something. The fact that he's setting up his practice to accommodate you tells me that he's thinking of you first. That's a good thing."

"Thanks, Mom. This has felt right since the moment I met him. I know that sounds cheesy, but I knew he was the one." Maggie drew her daughter close, and they hugged each other hard. "Now let's go to bed and enjoy happy dreams," Maggie murmured. "The girls will have us up before you know it."

R

Christmas Day and the rest of the week flew by in a flurry of activity. Mike and the girls made a towering snowman in the front yard, Eve was taken for more walks than she knew what to do with, and the kitchen at Rosemont was always in service. By their scheduled departure on the thirtieth, Maggie was exhausted and ready to have Rosemont to herself again. With the baggage loaded in the cars and the twins saying a long goodbye to Eve, Maggie took Amy's arm and summoned John and her kids.

"Quickly," she said. "I have an important announcement to make before we head out."

All eyes turned to her. "I've been offered a very lucrative expert witness engagement, and I've decided to accept it." She noted the smile that spread across John's face and the puzzled expressions of the others. "That means that I'll be resigning my position as mayor."

"Oh, Mom," Susan began, but Maggie held up a hand to silence her.

"I've talked this over with John and thought this through carefully. It's the right decision. And I'll be traveling to California regularly, so I'll be able to keep my promise to come see you."

"That'll be lovely, especially now," Amy replied. She glanced at Mike.

"We were going to wait," he said. "But since we're making family announcements, Amy and I are expecting."

Maggie swept them both into a hug. "Congratulations! I had my suspicions," she said, smiling. "This trip has been full of wonderful news," she said, her eyes cutting to Susan.

"When will you make your news official?" Mike asked.

"I plan to turn in my resignation to the town clerk tomorrow, effective January 31. I'll start my new engagement mid-February."

Maggie turned to John. "If the good doctor here can spare the time, I'd like us to take a vacation during the first week of February; maybe go somewhere warm?"

John's smile stretched so wide his cheeks hurt. "You can count on it. Now, these folks have a plane to catch. Let's get going."

Chapter 50

Loretta stared out the window of Haynes Enterprises at the swirling snow. By midafternoon, it was coming down hard. The office was quiet; the phone hadn't rung for hours. She didn't have any plans for the evening, other than staying home with her kids. Eyeing the accumulation in the parking lot, she was anxious to get out of the office and off the roads before the weather got worse.

She sighed and glanced at her boss's office. He worked behind closed doors now more than ever. Summoning her courage, she knocked softly on his door. At the gruff "come in," she opened it a crack and stood in the doorway, one hand remaining on the knob. He didn't bother to look up.

"In light of the snow, I was wondering if I could go to the bank early and then head home."

He paused and his gaze narrowed. "Got big plans tonight, have you?"

"No," she answered defensively.

What business was it of his if she had, anyway?

"I'm not going anywhere. Just staying home with my kids. These roads are going to be bad, and I'm still not used to driving in snow. I just want to get them home safely."

Haynes sighed. "Okay, sure. You can go."

He was turning back to his computer when he swung around quickly. "Loretta, since you're driving right by on the way to the bank, would you drop something off at Chuck Delgado's for me?"

He sensed her unmistakable trepidation. "It'll be fine. He probably won't even be there. You can leave it with the clerk in the liquor store downstairs; his office is upstairs."

"I'm really not comfortable with this. Can't we mail it?"

"I'd like him to have it today."

"What about a messenger service?" she suggested.

"You're going right by. I don't see the point in wasting money on a messenger." He was getting annoyed. "You're the one who asked to leave early. If you want to go to the bank now, you need to drop this off."

Loretta nodded slowly.

Haynes grabbed a stack of papers from his desk and sealed them in a large envelope. He held it out to her and said, "If you run into him,

224

don't come on to him. I'd think a pretty girl like you would know how to handle men by now."

His patronizing remark stung her, but she dared not reply. She snatched the envelope from his hand and turned on her heel.

R

As she had expected, Loretta found the roads treacherous; she was thoroughly unnerved by the time she pulled into the tiny parking lot of Delgado's liquor store. The next day was New Year's Eve and the store was busy. She was waiting in line to hand her package to the clerk when a familiar voice made her prickle with fear.

"Hello, little lady. Look who's here in my humble establishment. I knew you couldn't stay away," Delgado said with a smirk.

"I'm just here to deliver this to you from Mr. Haynes," she said, thrusting the package into his outstretched arms. She turned to leave.

"Hold on a minute," he stated, grabbing her arm. "We've got some unfinished business from the other day."

"I don't think so," she said, trying to extricate herself. Other patrons were beginning to stare.

Delgado loosed his grip and leaned in. "I think something funny's been going on at Haynes Enterprises," he whispered.

His breath was stale with alcohol and whatever greasy sandwich he had eaten for lunch. She took a step back. Whatever did he mean? Had he learned about the evidence of fraud and embezzlement she had uncovered? Was he part of it? Or did he know that she had copies of the documents? Loretta hesitated. She had to know what he was referring to.

Delgado realized he had her. He stepped back and released her arm. "Let's go upstairs to my office; we can talk privately there," he stated softly.

Loretta nodded and followed him out the rear door and up the stairs.

When they reached his office, Delgado pulled out his desk drawer and removed a half-empty bottle of Jameson and two Styrofoam cups. He poured a generous portion in each and handed one to Loretta. When she shook her head, he pressed it on her.

"It's almost New Year's Eve. Lighten up." He raised his cup to her. "Cheers," he said, and drained it in one gulp.

He grabbed the bottle and steered her to the decrepit sofa, motioning her to sit. She obliged.

"So. What did you want to tell me about Haynes Enterprises?" she asked.

"All business, aren't you?" He poured himself another generous portion of whiskey and sat down, close to her. She pressed herself into the arm at the end of the sofa.

"I like to get to know people before I talk business, don't you?" he said, running a finger up her neck, tracing her jaw line.

"I didn't come here for this," she said angrily as she heaved herself out of the sofa.

Delgado downed his drink and tossed the cup to the floor. With surprising agility, he leapt up and caught her hair in his fist, yanking her around to face him. "Limiting yourself to Frankie, are you?"

He saw the surprise in her eyes. "We all know what's going on. He don't need no financial analyst or whatever trumped up title he gave you. Everyone knows you're just his whore. Frankie and me, we's partners; he won't mind sharing. And you might find that you need what I got for you," he added with a leer, pressing his body against hers.

Loretta wedged her right hand against his chest while she tugged with her left to release his hold on her hair. Delgado shoved her against the wall, trapping her there. He let go of her hair and clamped his hand over her mouth as she screamed and squirmed wildly. His free hand reached under her skirt and ripped her underwear down her legs. She felt the bile rise in her throat and knew she would be violently sick.

Delgado was fumbling with his zipper when Frank Haynes flung the office door open. Delgado staggered backward, stumbling over the edge of the sofa. Loretta bent over and wretched violently on the carpet. Sobbing, she wiped her mouth with the back of her hand and reached for the underwear in tatters at her ankles.

"Well, what have we got here?" he asked sarcastically. "Sorry to interrupt."

Loretta stared at Haynes. What did he think was going on?

"What the hell you doin' here, Frankie?" Delgado asked shakily. "Don't you know to knock?"

"I left something out of your package," Haynes said, waving a stack of papers in his hand. He tossed them on the desk. "The guy at the register said that you'd come up here. So I thought I'd join you."

Delgado quickly tried to regain his composure. "Wanna drink? Toast the new year with me and Loretta?"

"No. It's a bit early for me, Charles. And Loretta can't stay; she's got to make the bank deposit. We need to be going."

Ignoring her discomfiture, Haynes steered Loretta to the top of the stairs. She pulled her coat around her shoulders and tried to smooth her skirt. He followed her down the stairs and to her car in the parking lot.

She fumbled for her key and unlocked her car. She turned to Haynes. "He was going to rape me. You stopped him. If you hadn't come in, he'd have succeeded. You know that, don't you?"

"I know nothing of the kind," he stated matter-of-factly, avoiding her gaze. "I saw two adults getting friendly. Too friendly. I don't want you to get involved with him."

Loretta's gaze hardened. "I've never wanted to get involved with that creep! How can you say that? That was assault. I should call the police right now."

Haynes trained his piercing gaze on her. "I wouldn't do that if I were you. I'll be a witness, and the only thing I'll be able to say is that it looked consensual to me."

Loretta shot him a look of pure hatred.

"Quit coming on to him and you won't have any problems. You should have known better than to go up to his office with him. This was your own fault."

With those words, Frank Haynes sealed his fate.

R

Loretta clamped down on her raging emotions as she drove to the bank and made the final deposit of the year for Haynes Enterprises. By the time she picked up her children from the sitter and pulled into the parking lot of her apartment complex, her head was pounding. This move to Westbury was supposed to be a fresh start for her, not a further descent into hell.

"Mommy, are you okay?" Marissa asked.

"I'm not feeling well, honey."

"When's dinner? I'm starved," Sean asked from the backseat.

Loretta opened her mouth to deliver a short retort and stopped herself. She looked in the rearview mirror at her children. She loved these little guys, and she had made her mind up that things were going to be different for them here. She was in possession of the means to make that happen. Delgado and Haynes weren't going to get away with abusing her and turning a blind eye or, worse, making Delgado's attempted rape her fault. She'd show them.

"Let's order pizza," she replied. "It's almost a new year. We need to celebrate."

"Really?" the older two chimed in unison. They hadn't had any pizza other than Loretta's homemade version with sauce from a jar and crust from a can since they had moved to Westbury.

"I know just the place," Loretta said. "And we can play board games and you can stay up an hour past your bedtime." She was suddenly feeling much better.

In the wee hours, long after the kids had gone to bed, Loretta settled on her plan. She would put the evidence in the hands of someone she could trust. She was new to Westbury and didn't know many people. She'd seen enough from Haynes' secret spreadsheets to know that the former mayor had been involved in fraud and embezzlement. Delgado and another person named Isaac probably were too. It was impossible to know how widespread the corruption was. If she put the evidence into the wrong hands, she was finished. She shivered involuntarily.

The one person who couldn't have been involved was Mayor Maggie Martin. She hadn't been in Westbury long enough. Paul had said many derogatory things about his wife—she wondered now how true they had been—but he always spoke of her scrupulous honesty and integrity. He even mocked her sense of fairness and justice. What was it he called her? A goody two shoes? When she put this evidence in the hands of the authorities, she would be putting her safety and that of her children in their hands as well. If she were going to trust anyone, it was going to be Maggie Martin.

Chapter 51

Maggie paced in front of the library fireplace, clutching the sheet of paper and re-reading her resignation letter for the hundredth time. She'd spent the best part of two hours drafting it. In the end, she'd decided that the less said, the better. Maggie returned to her laptop, pressed print, and sealed the letter in an envelope addressed to the town clerk. She sent an email to Don Upton accepting the expert witness assignment and logged off her computer.

She checked the time; it was almost noon. John was picking her up at three for a movie and an early New Year's Eve dinner. Their plan was to be home by eight, in bed by nine, and asleep by ten. Maggie wanted to get this letter out of her hands. Then she could relax. Besides, the early-morning snow had continued unabated and the roads were getting worse all the time. She'd nip down to Town Hall, give the letter to the town clerk, and come home to get ready for her date.

R

Between the slippery roads and endlessly second-guessing herself, Maggie was in a state of jittery exhaustion by the time she reached Town Hall. Her stomach churned as she pulled into her assigned parking spot with the placard "Reserved for the Hon. Margaret Martin." She sighed and heaved herself out of her car.

The sidewalk was getting icy; she proceeded gingerly up the steps and into the lobby, which was deserted on this final day of the year. She was greeted unenthusiastically by the receptionist, an elderly woman with a head cold. "I'm the only one here today," she answered when Maggie asked for the town clerk. "We've all been sick. You don't want to get near any of us."

"I'll just leave this on her desk then."

"I can take it back for you," replied the woman.

"No. You stay put. I don't mind," Maggie said as she made her way to the town clerk's office. She hesitated, then quickly propped the envelope against the phone, pivoted, and walked resolutely toward the lobby.

"I hope you feel better," she said over her shoulder to the receptionist on her way out. Feeling slightly shaky now that she'd actually delivered the letter, Maggie pushed against the heavy door to the building. The wind was against her so she had to throw all of her weight against it. The door finally opened and Maggie burst through, slipping on the ice over the threshold, sending her purse and its contents scattering. Frank Haynes, ascending the top step, dodged the contents and grabbed Maggie's elbow, preventing her from sprawling on the concrete.

"Thank you, Frank," Maggie said shakily. "You do have the habit of rescuing me, don't you?"

Haynes eyed her warily. "Are you all right? You don't look so good."

"I'm fine. Good, actually. I was just here delivering something to the clerk."

Haynes looked at her quizzically. "Anything I should know about?"

"Not now. You will." Maggie got down on one knee and began to retrieve the contents of her purse.

"Let me help you with this," he said, setting his phone down while he collected her wallet and keys from the bottom step. Neither of them noticed when she scooped up his phone, and placed it in her purse.

"Let me help you to your car," Haynes insisted. "It's getting treacherous out here. The roads are bad; drive carefully getting home."

"Thank you, Frank. I will. And Happy New Year."

Haynes smiled warmly, in spite of the inclement weather, as he watched her car pull away. He'd have to let Upton know that their plan had been successful. If she hadn't turned in her resignation, he'd eat his hat.

R

John picked Maggie up shortly before three. She pasted a bright smile on her lips as she showed him a copy of her resignation letter and told him that she'd delivered it to the town clerk.

"You're sure about this?" he asked, trying to sound neutral.

"Absolutely," she assured him. "And I've printed off a stack of stuff from the Internet for us to plow through together about cruises and luxury vacation spots. By this time tomorrow, we'll have reservations for the most romantic trip anyone's ever taken."

John swept her into his arms and held her tight. "I can't believe I almost let you go," he whispered into her hair. "I can hardly wait to get you away from here and have you all to myself."

Maggie leaned back. "We don't have to go out, you know."

"Renege on a promise to my girl?" he scoffed. "On New Year's Eve, of all nights? No way. When was the last time you relaxed and watched a movie? Let's get going."

R

They settled into the movie—a predictable but pleasant romantic comedy that he knew she wanted to see—with their oversized movie theater sodas and big buckets of popcorn. New Year's Eve was no time to count calories.

The movie was well underway when a phone cheeped noisily. Maggie started digging frantically in her purse. John turned to her and whispered, "I saw you put your phone on silent."

"I did," she replied, "but it definitely came from here." She pulled out Frank's phone and looked at the text message as she flipped the switch to vibrate mode. She shielded the screen with her hand and read the message, then read it again:

We did it! M accepted job. Thnx for your help. M and town better off.

She passed the phone to John, who did the same. He turned to her, grabbed her arm and led her into the lobby, telling her to leave the soda and popcorn behind.

R

They sat on a bench along the wall of the movie theater. "This is Frank Haynes' phone," Maggie said quietly, turning to John. "I ran into him—literally—on the steps to Town Hall when I was leaving today. I dropped my purse and scattered my stuff everywhere. He helped me retrieve it. I must have picked up his phone by mistake."

She handed the cell phone to John. "Do you recognize the phone number that sent the text?" he asked.

Maggie slowly shook her head, then stopped abruptly. "It's a Chicago area code. And the only person I've told was Don Upton. I sent him an email accepting the job."

"Do you have his number in your contacts?"

Maggie was already digging her phone out of her purse. She scrolled through her contacts and held her phone next to Haynes'. The numbers on the screens matched.

"What in the world?" Maggie exclaimed.

"This means that Upton and Haynes were in on this together. To get you to resign."

"But the expert witness job is legitimate," Maggie said, shaking her head.

"Maybe Upton's participation in this is innocent," John said.

Maggie considered his statement. "I don't think so," she said slowly. "They never let on that they were friendly. I thought they'd only met once, briefly, at a finance committee meeting."

Maggie turned to John. "Come on. Upton has Frank's cell phone number? Something's fishy. They've been covering up their relationship, whatever it may be."

"It looks that way."

"I trusted Don. I'm the one who brought him in to assist us. And he's given the town wonderful advice on our finances. I just don't understand this," she cried, raking her fingers through her hair.

She dropped her head into her hands while John silently stroked her back.

"God," she spat, looking up at John abruptly. "I'm an idiot. I can't believe I didn't see this coming. I've played right into their hands."

"Don't berate yourself, honey. Nobody would have suspected Upton of conspiring with Haynes. And you're not sure that's what's going on. Those text messages aren't enough to prove anything."

"What should I do, John?"

John looked at her steadily and held her gaze. "I suspect you know what you want to do."

"Part of me wants to say, '*Hell no, you don't!* You're *not* getting rid of me that easily.' But another part of me wants to just take this consulting job, so I can keep my promises to you and my kids. So we can take that trip we were going to plan tomorrow. I'm tired of disappointing everyone."

"We can take a trip another time. And I'm not going anywhere. I told you I'd support you when you took this job, but the minute I had my knee surgery and you weren't there at my beck and call, I got pouty and selfish. I went back on my promise. Our breakup wasn't all your fault, and I'm sorry I let you think so." John took both her hands in his. "Sweetheart, whatever this is, it's not right. We can't let them get away with it. I won't stand by and let that happen."

"It's done," Maggie cried. "No going back now."

"You didn't really want to resign, and you know it," John said. "I've been selfish, wanting more time with you. But," he stood and pulled her to her feet, checking his watch, "we've got twenty minutes before Town Hall closes. Let's go get that resignation letter."

"Yes," she said with a nod after consideration. "We'll burn it in the fireplace at midnight. I'm not going to let those bastards win."

R

Later that night, John slipped out of bed, carefully extricating his arm from under Maggie's neck, and crept downstairs. He started a fire, opened a bottle of champagne and set two flutes on the mantel. He roused Eve and Roman; after all, they needed to be part of this historic moment. When the fire was blazing, he ascended the stairs.

"Sweetheart," he whispered as he gently shook her shoulders.

Maggie rolled over and brushed the hair off her face. "Sorry; I fell asleep. Is it past midnight?"

"Not yet. You've got fifteen minutes to get downstairs and ring in the New Year with me."

"Good," she said, getting out of bed and putting on the robe he held for her. "I want to burn that damned resignation letter."

"It's waiting by the fireplace, right where you left it."

Maggie took John's hand and together they slowly descended the stairs. At the fireplace, she glanced at John and he nodded. Maggie tossed the letter over the hearth, and they watched as the flames touched—and then consumed—the paper that would have spelled a different future for them both.

Maggie inhaled. "It's done. Thank you for building the fire."

"One more thing." John stepped to the mantel and poured them each a glass of champagne. "To the most courageous woman I know, with the biggest heart and most generous spirit."

"I don't know about that," Maggie began.

"I do," John insisted. "Now drink."

Maggie took a sip as John guided her into a wingback chair by the hearth.

"What in the world are you doing?" she asked as John gingerly placed one knee on the floor. "You're not supposed to be on your knees after your surgery."

"There's one exception to that bit of medical advice."

He took both of her hands in his. "Maggie. You are the light of my life; the woman I've been searching for, always. You are my first thought in the morning and the last at night. I am never going to let you go. No matter what is ahead for us, I want us to meet it together. Will you do me the honor of marrying me?"

Maggie slipped out of the chair to her knees, flinging her arms around his neck. "Yes. For God's sake, yes!"

The End

Thank you for reading!

If you enjoyed **Weaving the Strands**, I'd be grateful if you wrote a review.

Just a few lines would be great. Reviews are the best gift an author can receive. They encourage us when they're good, help us improve our next book when they're not, and help other readers make informed choices when purchasing books. Reviews keep the Amazon algorithms humming and are the most helpful aide in selling books! Thank you.

To post a review on Amazon or for Kindle:
1. Go to the product detail page for **Weaving the Strands** on Amazon.com.
2. Click "Write a customer review" in the Customer Reviews section.
3. Write your review and click Submit.

In gratitude,
Barbara Hinske

Just for You!

Wonder what Maggie was thinking when the book ended? Exclusively for readers who finished **Weaving the Strands,** take a look at Maggie's Diary Entry for that day at https://barbarahinske.com/maggies-diary.

Acknowledgements

I am deeply grateful to my incomparable husband, Brian Willis, my wise and creative editor, Linden Gross, my irrepressible coach Mat Boggs, the remarkable design team at MonkeyCMedia, and my friends Jeffrie, Donna, Georgia, Mark, and Norma, for their unfailing support, confidence, and enthusiasm. With you in my corner, how could I fail?

Book Club Questions

**(If your club talks about anything other than
family, jobs, and household projects!)**

1. We've all met someone like Frank Haynes, who refuses to be
    the better person that he shows us—on rare occasion—he can
    be. Have you ever convinced someone to be his or her best self?
    How did you do it?
2. Do you enjoy entertaining, as Maggie does?
3. Do you know your neighbors and is your neighborhood a
    friendly place? Would you welcome more interaction with your
    neighbors?
4. Did the book engage you right away or did it take a while to get
    into?
5. Have you ever ended a relationship because the other person
    didn't make you a priority? Should Maggie have handled her
    relationship with John differently?
6. Have you ever been assigned to work on a big project with
    someone you didn't like? In the course of working with them,
    have you learned to like them better?
7. Did any of the passages or dialogue strike you as insightful or
    ring particularly true? Have you said or felt any of those things?
8. Have you ever spent a major holiday away from home? How did
    you handle it? Would you do it again?
9. What would you like to ask the author?
10. What would you like to see happen in the third
    installment of the Rosemont series?

About the Author

BARBARA HINSKE is an attorney by day, bestselling novelist by night. She inherited the writing gene from her father who wrote mysteries when he retired and told her a story every night of her childhood. She and her husband share their own Rosemont with two adorable and spoiled dogs. The old house keeps her husband busy with repair projects and her happily decorating, entertaining, cooking, and gardening. Together they have four grown children, and live in Phoenix, Arizona.

Please enjoy this excerpt from **Uncovering Secrets**, the third installment in the **Rosemont** series:

Chapter 1

Maggie Martin snapped her laptop shut and set it on the coffee table. She'd been reviewing spreadsheets for hours. The formidable financial problems facing Westbury would still be there tomorrow. It was New Year's Day after all, and Westbury's hard-working mayor deserved some time off. She'd worked every day since she'd taken office last spring. She stretched and slid over on the sofa to snuggle her fiancé of almost twenty-four hours, John Allen.

John put his arm around her and hugged her, his eyes glued to the college bowl game on television. "Only two minutes left," he mumbled. "Then we can …"

Maggie interrupted him. "And there's another game right after this one. Enjoy. I know you're reliving your glory days on the gridiron. I'm going to let the dogs out and call Susan and Mike. I have big news, you know."

John smiled and patted her arm.

Maggie summoned Eve and Roman, tucked her chestnut bob into the collar of her down jacket, and wound a scarf around her neck. She picked up her cell phone and headed to the back garden. The dogs raced ahead of her as she sought protection from the icy wind under a pine tree on the lawn and tightened the scarf around her neck. She'd lived in Southern California most of her adult life, and these Midwestern winters were not easy to get used to.

She turned to study the edifice of Rosemont. The warm tones of its stone walls and the symmetry of the mullioned windows elicited the same visceral response in her as the first time she saw it. Rosemont embodied stability, order, and security—exactly what she was looking for when she moved here to restart her life after her husband Paul's sudden death. And not at all what she'd found. Never in a million years would she have imagined she'd be elected to public office as a write-in candidate.

Just yesterday, she'd been prepared to hand in her resignation as mayor. The constant criticism of the local press and a vocal segment of the community were demoralizing, and a lucrative assignment offered by her once trusted colleague, Professor Lyndon Upton, seemed too good to turn down. Uncovering collusion between Upton and local town councilman Frank Haynes had changed everything. They weren't going to get rid of her that easily. She would stand her ground and do everything in her power to restore the town's financial footing. She'd make sure those responsible for the fraud and embezzlement that left the general fund and the town workers' pension plan on the brink of bankruptcy were brought to justice. So much had changed in the last day. She pulled her phone out of her jacket pocket and dialed Susan's number.

"Hey, Mom, Happy New Year!" Susan sounded cheery, as she almost always did these days now that Aaron Scanlon had come into her life.

"Same to you. How did you two ring in the New Year?"

"We went to dinner at this swanky hotel that had a ten-piece orchestra, and dancing afterward, like out of an old movie—so glamorous."

Maggie smiled. "What did you wear?"

"That long, slinky midnight-blue dress with the slit. Remember? We found it on clearance, and you insisted I buy it. You promised I'd have a chance to wear it. You were right, Mom."

"What was that again? You're breaking up—I can't quite hear you."

"You heard me, Mom. But if you want to hear it again—you were *so* right."

Maggie laughed. "The words every mother loves to hear."

"How about you? Did you and John do anything special?"

"It was quite a day."

"Did you turn in your resignation?"

"Turned it in and went back and tore it up."

Maggie heard Susan take a sharp breath.

"So you're not going to take the expert witness gig that Professor Upton offered you? You won't be traveling to California all the time and coming to visit us?" Maggie could hear the disappointment in her daughter's voice.

"No, honey, I'm sorry. It's a long story. I suspect Frank Haynes and Don Upton have been working together to convince me to resign."

"Why do you think that?"

"I saw a text message from Don on Frank's phone—congratulating him on my resignation."

"How?"

"I ran into Frank—literally—on the steps of Town Hall after I turned in my resignation yesterday. I slipped on the ice, and my purse went flying down the steps. When Frank helped me pick everything up, I grabbed his phone by mistake."

"When did you see the text?"

"Later that afternoon—when John and I were sitting in a movie. The phone started beeping. I scrambled through my purse to find it, and that's when I saw the message."

"Why would Councilman Haynes and Professor Upton conspire against you? It doesn't make sense."

"I agree. I don't know, but there's something more between the two of them."

"So what did you do?"

"John and I sat in the lobby of the movie theater and talked it out. The more we talked, the madder I got. One thing is certain: I am not going to let them orchestrate my resignation."

"What does John think about all this?"

"He's in total agreement. He drove me to Town Hall, so I could take back my resignation letter. We burned it in the fireplace at Rosemont."

Susan was silent.

"What are you thinking, honey?"

"You did the only thing you could do, Mom. It all sounds very fishy. I'm disappointed you won't be here on a regular basis, but I'm behind you one hundred percent, and Mike will be as well."

"Thank you, honey. I'm really sorry I won't be seeing you guys more often. Plus the money would have been nice."

"You've got enough money, Mom. Sounds like your New Year's Eve sucked. I'm sorry."

"It wasn't all bad …" Maggie paused, unsure how her daughter would take the news of her engagement. Both of her children got along famously with John, but changing status from boyfriend to husband might be another matter entirely. "John proposed. And I accepted."

Susan squealed. "Mom! That's fantastic news! Mike and I were both hoping the two of you would get married. I was devastated when you broke up last year. You belong together."

"Thank you, honey. Your blessing means the world to us."

"Mike will be thrilled." Susan drew a deep breath. "We need to get going on the wedding."

"We haven't made any firm plans yet. It'll be a small affair, here at Rosemont. I'd like to get married in the garden," Maggie said, looking over the now empty flowerbeds. "Maybe June? We wanted to check with you and Mike to see when it would be convenient for you."

"I've got a trial that ends in April, so June is fine with me. The whole town will want to be there, with you being mayor and John a hometown boy and the local vet."

"That's why we're going to keep this really quiet. We don't want a massive affair."

"It would be lovely …"

"You can have a big wedding at Rosemont or anywhere you choose. John and I don't want that."

"Come on, Mom. You love to throw a party. You and Dad got married at the courthouse, and you didn't even have a new dress. This has to be a grand affair. The back garden would be lovely, but outdoor weddings can be tricky. Why not get married inside Rosemont? The place looks like a movie set from an English period drama. A gorgeous stone manor home—it's a perfect wedding venue. You could be in front of the fireplace in the library, or in the living room. We could all sweep down that staircase." Susan sighed. "And you have to wear a wedding gown."

"Honey, I'm too old for a wedding gown, don't you think? Won't I look ridiculous? I was thinking of getting a really nice evening suit. Then I could wear it again."

Susan snorted. "Get yourself an evening suit if you want one, but you're not getting married in it.

"I'm logging into Pinterest right now. I'll create boards for your dress, the food, and the flowers. What does your ring look like?"

"He didn't give me a ring."

"What? You've got to have a ring, Mom. You love jewelry. I'm starting a board for your ring, too."

Maggie laughed. "Slow down, princess. All in good time."

"Check my Pinterest page tonight—I'll have gobs of pins by then."

"I will. And I'm grateful for your enthusiasm. You get busy with Pinterest. I'm standing outside and am frozen stiff. I need to round up the dogs and head inside."

"Give John a big hug from me. Love you both."

Maggie opened the back door, and Eve darted inside to her warm basket in the corner of the kitchen.

"Where's Roman?" Maggie asked as her beloved terrier mix nestled into her blanket. Maggie leaned out the back door and whistled, pausing to listen for the familiar sound of Roman's tags jingling on his collar as he ran up the hill. The only sound was the wind rustling through the branches.

Roman must have found a dead bird or some other treasure at the bottom of the vast lawn; she'd have to go back into the blustery afternoon and bring him inside. She trudged down the hill, alternatively whistling and calling Roman's name, becoming more concerned with each step. She'd never known John's Golden Retriever to disobey a command. By the time she reached the thin strip of woods at the bottom of the hill, Maggie knew he was gone. She raced up the hill and burst into the library of Rosemont.

She bent over, thoroughly winded, and gulped air. "Roman got out. He's not in the garden."

John leapt to his feet. "It's not like him to run away," he said, rushing past her to the back door, not stopping for his coat. Maggie followed in his wake.

Available at Amazon in Print and for Kindle

Novels in the **Rosemont** series

Coming to Rosemont

Weaving the Strands

Uncovering Secrets

Drawing Close

Bringing Them Home

Shelving Doubts

Also by **BARBARA HINSKE**

The Night Train

And Now Available on The Hallmark Channel …

The Christmas Club

Upcoming in 2020

Guiding Emily, the first novel in a new series by Barbara Hinske

The seventh novel in the Rosemont series

I'd love to hear from you! Connect with me online:

Visit **BarbaraHinske.com** to sign up for my newsletter to receive your Free Gift, plus Inside Scoops, Amazing Offers, Bedtime Stories & Inspirations from Home.

Facebook.com/BHinske
Twitter.com/BarbaraHinske
Instagram/barbarahinskeauthor
Email me at **bhinske@gmail.com**

Search for **Barbara Hinske on YouTube** for tours inside my own historic home plus tips and tricks for busy women!

Find photos of fictional Rosemont, Westbury, and things related to the Rosemont series at **Pinterest.com/BarbaraHinske**.